'There's a marvellously mons
Catherine Menon's first novel . . . a book saturated with the sensations
of Southeast Asia, where, in Menon's pungent turn of phrase, you feel
as though you could "grab the air in two hands and wring it out"'

The Times

'Always here for a cross-generational family story, especially one that
involves moral ambivalence'

Marian Keyes

'Lyrically beautiful writing'

i

'An intriguing, fast-paced, imaginative novel'

Bad Form

'A cleverly crafted family saga that explores themes of truth, belonging
and shame across multiple generations'

Asian Review of Books

'Believe the plaudits from Hilary Mantel and Colm Tóibín . . . There is
so much to love in this novel: it is deeply felt but never sentimental,
multifaceted and a page-turner to boot'

Canberra Times

'A novel as strange and as beautiful as the fireworks she has
Durga release for Diwali . . . Menon burns into the imagination
with this spectacular debut'

The Monthly

'Spellbinding'

Tatler Malaysia

'Beautiful, lyrical writing'

Scotsman

Fragile Monsters

CATHERINE MENON

PENGUIN BOOKS

PENGUIN BOOKS

UK | USA | Canada | Ireland | Australia
India | New Zealand | South Africa

Penguin Books is part of the Penguin Random House group of companies
whose addresses can be found at global.penguinrandomhouse.com.

First published by Viking 2021
Published in Penguin Books 2022
001

Typeset by Jouve (UK), Milton Keynes
Printed and bound in Great Britain by Clays Ltd, Elcograf S.p.A.

The authorized representative in the EEA is Penguin Random House Ireland,
Morrison Chambers, 32 Nassau Street, Dublin D02 YH68

A CIP catalogue record for this book is available from the British Library

ISBN: 978-0-241-98897-8

www.greenpenguin.co.uk

Penguin Random House is committed to a
sustainable future for our business, our readers
and our planet. This book is made from Forest
Stewardship Council® certified paper.

To my grandmothers, Kitty and Goury Amma

Prologue

A slap. A cry. Distress, which seems a poor enough start to things. Or perhaps it's only temper. Mary, who will one day be my grandmother, is a little too young to distinguish yet.

In a year or so Mary will begin to talk. She'll master words quickly, unlike her brother, but she'll never enjoy his flights of fancy. She'll want to keep her feet on the ground – unwise here in Malaya, where you never know if a dredging pit will give way or a swamp will open its jaws. Still, for the next seventy years Mary will travel cautiously, keeping a tight hold of what she knows.

To deal with Mary – to pin her stories down and get at the bones beneath – I'll need something definite. Some rules that explain her, some axioms that strip away all those half-truths and quarter-lies and never-happened-at-alls. I'll need something mathematical, incontrovertible as a proof from first principles. And if it goes wrong, I've only got myself to blame.

1.   Thursday, 7 p.m.: 1985

'Aiyoh, Durga, you went to Letchumani for fireworks?'

Ammuma glares at the bright red bag I'm lifting out of my car. The trip's only taken me an hour, but she's already moved her rattan chair to the verandah's edge to watch for me driving back into the compound yard. Her white widow's sari is immaculate and clean-starched, and her skinny thighs make a shallow, mounded lap. She spends nearly all her time on the verandah now, rocking back and forwards in the sleepy heat. That was the first shock about returning to Malaysia: somewhere in the last decade my grandmother's become old.

'Kill us all,' she adds, 'these crazy ideas of yours, getting fireworks from the washer-man.'

Or perhaps not that old. She likes proper fireworks, I remember. All noise and glare, with a spice of danger if you stick your nose in too far.

It's raining, and my sandals slip on the limestone steps as I carry the bag up to her. Sweat trickles down under my nylon shirt; I've been back two months but still can't remember to dress for the climate here.

'I was going to drive to Kuala Lipis, Ammuma,' I say, 'but Letchumani had a sign advertising fireworks and I thought . . .'

'Thought, hanh! Covered market in Lipis for good fireworks only, you should know that, Durga.'

'This mathematics rubbish you study,' she mutters not quite under her breath, 'all thinking and never common-sense.'

She's fetched a plate of pandan cakes while I've been out and she pushes them across the table towards me with a not-to-be-argued frown. I left home a decade ago and Ammuma's convinced I haven't eaten since. Granddaughters, she thinks, ought to stay where they've been put.

'Too late to change fireworks now also.' She looks up at the evening sky. 'Have to manage.' She's relishing this, like she does all small crises; running out of onions can last her all day.

'Diwali puja will do now,' she tells me briskly. 'Prayer first, then play fireworks, ah?'

'What, light the fireworks *now*? Ammuma, it's pelting down.'

I sit next to her, on a small wooden bench that she ordered Karthika to move from the front room. I drove up from Kuala Lumpur four days ago, and the house still feels familiar and strange at once. My childhood home, but I can't quite manage to be sentimental about it. It's the wrong sort of home, or perhaps I was the wrong sort of child.

Just like on the day I left, the compound yard's flooding. There are puddles under the stone walls and a few dry patches near the biggest trees. The angsanas have lost most of their blossom in the rain, and the scatter of yellow petals makes me catch my breath. Another memory, one I hadn't even realized I'd forgotten: crouching behind those trees playing five-stones with Peony after school. Her laugh, her tangled hair, her ballpoint tattoos. In Canada I pushed her out of my head, but back here in Pahang she's everywhere I look. *Friends for ever, Durga*, she whispers, and for a second I'm fifteen again and everything is about to go wrong.

I take a deep breath, clenching my fists. Of all people, I should know Peony's gone. Dead and gone; drowned in the banyan swamp fifteen years ago and nothing to be done about it. She's a null object. She's a zero module. She's the limit of an empty diagram.

I unclench my hands and look deliberately over to the angsanas again. They've grown since those days, and there's nothing behind their trunks except a sodden crate of banana leaves for the dining table tonight. I'd forgotten this about Pahang, the way the rain gets under your clothes and under your skin.

'Durga? Are you listening?' Ammuma prods. 'Of course light

the fireworks now. It's Diwali, when else is it we'll light them? Christmas? Birthdays-graduations? Next you'll be asking for eating non-veg tonight.'

'But there's only us here to see them.' I'm on edge, arguing when I know I shouldn't. 'Why bother just for us, and when it's raining, too? I never did in Canada.'

Ammuma sucks in her breath, then lets it out again in a shower of scolding words. It's a festival, she tells me, punctuating her sentences by slapping the broken wicker of her chair, how dare I suggest we ignore it? It's far more important than rain, she says, far more important than grandmothers, even, and ungrateful granddaughters who've forgotten how they were raised.

'But you don't even believe in Lakshmi, Ammuma. You never did.'

Diwali's for Lakshmi, a goddess who's supposed to visit the brightest and cleanest houses every year. Ammuma doesn't hold with her and never has: some goddess, she says, to go poking her nose into other people's housekeeping.

'Story is important only,' she insists. 'Doesn't matter if it's true.'

'But you –'

'And fireworks are important too, for driving away evil spirits. Cannot tell, Durga, when a spirit is walking –'

She stops. There's a loud clang from the compound gate, then another. Someone's knocking. I can just make out a figure through the ironwork, then an arm snakes down to open the catch.

'Who's visiting today?' Ammuma mutters to herself, and then the gate opens. A white man walks through, carrying a striped bag. He has a cap of combed brown hair that looks oddly familiar and he's wearing a neatly tailored suit.

'Mary-Auntie!'

He ignores the mud and walks jauntily towards us, then sees me sitting next to Ammuma. He stops, squinting against the evening light. His smile falters and loses its way.

'Durga?'

I start to shake. I know who he is, this man with his John

Lennon hair. Peony's voice is in my head again – *friends for ever* – and this man is bad news, he's worst news. He's fifteen years old news, fresh as yesterday's eggs.

*

'Durga,' Tom says for the third time. 'I can't believe you're back in Pahang.'

We've rearranged the verandah table for him, an extra chair and all of us tight-tucked as chickens. His well-stitched leather shoes are paired neatly on the steps, edging mine off into a puddle. Ammuma's made him a cup of tea in a mug I've never seen before. It has 'Tom' written on it in curly green letters and she must have bought it at the tourist market in Lipis. She always refused to let me spend my pocket money at the stalls there when I was small, or to buy me anything either. Too expensive, she said; too dirty. I wonder which of those doesn't matter when it comes to Tom.

I can't take my eyes off him. I haven't seen him since the inquest fifteen years ago, when both of us were sitting on a polished wooden bench at the Kuala Lipis government house. I remember the smell of his sweat as they pronounced the verdict: an accident. Nobody's fault. And I remember how Ammuma gave me a single fierce hug and how that evening she threw out everything I'd worn that day, from underwear to shoes. Love was one thing, but forgiveness was a whole new bag of thorns. Accidents have causes, she told me. Cause and effect, I think, theorem and proof; Durga and Peony. We always were inseparable.

'I'm not back in Pahang,' I say, too loudly. 'I live in KL now; I'm just visiting for Diwali. When did *you* come back?'

Ammuma clicks her tongue. That's a Canadian question, too straightforward for her tastes. I've lost the rhythm of how I'm supposed to speak in Malaysia, how I'm supposed to imply and hint and keep my meaning for the spaces between words.

'Five years ago.'

Tom's voice is exactly how I remember: far too good for the rest of him. Like sugar-syrup, I once told Peony, and I didn't even care that she laughed. I sit there and look at him and my face feels scholarly and short-sighted. It's a good face, usually, good enough for proofs and theorems, but not the right face for meeting Tom again. Too old, or perhaps too young. Too lived-in, as though I could have helped it. A sudden gust of wind whistles through the bow-legged palms in the compound yard.

'Tom trained in Liverpool and now he's top doctor in Lipis hospital,' Ammuma says.

'But very good job Durga also has,' she adds with a greedy rush. 'Ten years in Canada, but two months ago she gets this lecturing job in KL. Maths professor, wah, so good.'

Tom and I look at each other awkwardly over the litter of cups and plates. I wonder what he'd think if he knew about Deepak, Deepak and his fourth-generation Ontario wife with her shoulder-pads and terrifying vulnerability. What would he – and Ammuma – say if I blurted out I only took this job because Deepak went back to her? Perhaps nothing at all; perhaps it's what they'd have expected from me all along – second best, second helpings, second hand.

'Well done, Durga,' Tom says, stiff as his own shirt collar. It makes me unreasonably cross, how he's shrugged Pahang back on like an old coat. He's strolled into the space I left and he's managed it all much better – top doctor and still apparently finding time to chat with his dear old Mary-Auntie every week. It would be delightful, if only it weren't.

'Too Canadian, she is, though, now,' Ammuma grumbles to nobody in particular. 'Like some tourist playing at Malaysia only. Ammuma, let's help the servant-girl wash up, she's saying. Ammuma, here's some Diwali fireworks from Letchumani. Tchee, fireworks from the washer-man! Whoever heard of this thing?'

'Oh, fireworks! That reminds me,' Tom interrupts her, leaning down to where his striped carrier bag nestles against the table. 'I picked up a few for you, Mary-Auntie, just some Diwali gifts. They're from the covered markets.'

Of course they are. Good-quality best-quality, and a permit too, no doubt. I'd forgotten I'd need one and Letchumani – used to foreigners and tourists – hadn't bothered to tell me. Tom's competent parcels make me feel even more out of place than Ammuma's complaints. It used to be Tom who was foreign, once.

Ammuma beams. He's good, she says, to remember an old woman like herself – Ammuma is only ever old when it suits her – and would he believe her own granddaughter's refusing, actually refusing, to play fireworks for Diwali because of the rain. 'What's a little bit of rain?' she says. 'You children used to run out in it every day.'

Tom gives me a sympathetic look. He's about to say something but a sudden beeping chimes out, silencing us. It's a pager clipped to his smart leather belt.

'It's the hospital,' he says. 'They'll be busy down there, with Diwali tonight.'

Ammuma gives me a triumphant look. 'See, Durga? So dangerous, these rockets Letchumani makes. Better instead to use Tom's fireworks.'

Better to use Tom's fireworks. Better to work in Tom's job and wear clothes like Tom's and be as patient as Tom. Easy enough for him; she's not his grandmother.

He glances down at the pager, pushing his chair back.

'Will you come and help me put the fireworks in the kitchen?' I say quickly. 'It'll only take a minute.'

'Of course.' Tom starts to rise politely, but Ammuma's already glaring at me.

'Wanting to wander off alone in the corridors with a boy? Aiyoh, Durga,' she says, sucking disapproval through her teeth. 'This is your home, this is a respectable house. Not so-so like these student accommodations in Canada.'

She leans over to confide in Tom, her voice loud enough for me to hear. 'Boys and girls all together. Mixed up like slum-puppies.'

I sink back into my chair. I'd forgotten how fragile girls are in Pahang, how easily soiled. A fingerprint is enough to put anyone off.

'Sorry, Mary-Auntie. I'm sure she didn't mean it. And – I hate to go so soon – but I can't stay anyway. I need to drop in on the wards.'

He takes his time putting his shoes on and tying his shoelaces, looking up at me with queer little ducking movements of his head. Any moment now, I think, he'll slip me a letter, a flower – a peony – that'll mean nothing except to the two of us. He wouldn't just walk away, not after coming halfway across the world.

But he does. He tugs his smart suit jacket straight and waves as he crosses the compound yard. There's a backward glance as he reaches the gate, but that's all. He mouths something to me – or perhaps he doesn't – and then the gate closes. He's gone, and there's nothing here but the rain and a half-eaten pandan cake.

'So, Durga.' Ammuma's brisk. 'You light these.'

She pushes his bag over to me. 'I'll go upstairs, wash hands, then come back for Diwali puja.'

She tips herself upright, scraping her rattan chair over the concrete. 'Use Tom's fireworks,' she calls back as she hobbles out of the room. 'Not this Letchumani nonsense.'

I sit there in the fading light and stare at a line of ants nudging across the floor. *How dare he?* I think. How dare he saunter in here with top-class fireworks and without having changed in the slightest? He should have had some wrinkles, or an apologetic thirty-something paunch. He should have had capped teeth and a worried smile. He should have been ashamed of himself.

I shove his bag away. He doesn't know better than me, despite all his meaningful glances and his market shopping and his so-important pager. I grab Letchumani's bright red bag instead, and tuck it under my arm.

The front room's dark, with no lamps lit and a dusty bare rectangle where the wooden bench used to be. And the hallway's even darker, with a single yellowing bulb doing nothing but splash shadows around. The kitchen and dining room are at one end; great stone-flagged rooms that Karthika rules as the only servant in the house. The hall floor's slippery with the paraffin wax she uses to polish wood, and I can smell the burn of Jeyes Fluid from the kitchen sink.

I push the back door open and the wet air hits me with a slap. My bare feet press water up through the grass as I walk slowly down to the far end of the compound. There's a strip of grass running the full length of it, nearly twenty metres straight from the house to the crumbling rear wall. The Jelai river roars from behind its banks, and the wind flecks my hair with spray as I turn to look at the house.

From here, it's ramshackle. It's three storeys high, casting a deep shadow over the side of the compound yard where the wells are. Half of the house was torn down during the war, but it is still a sprawling mass compared with Canadian condos. And it's far too close to the Jelai. Ammuma's father Stephen didn't know or care about floods, and over time the ground's been submerged so often it's taken on a slippery, aquatic tinge.

A light goes on in Ammuma's bedroom. She's watching, then, her eyes on me like always. I set my teeth and pull the first firework out of the bag. It's a night for locked doors in Pahang tonight, with all those ghosts and goddesses creeping about – and men like Tom, too, come to that. Let them in and you'll never get any of them out again.

The firework's a rocket, and for a moment I think Ammuma was right. The damp cardboard sticks to my fingers and the whole thing's lumpy and misshapen, like a tube stuffed with paper towels. There's a sulphurous whiff as I hold a match to it. I daresay the gunpowder's home-grown in Letchumani's spare washing vat: magnesium and cuttlefish bile and God knows what else. And then, just when I'm about to give up, the rocket flares into life.

It soars up and up in a glowing scatter of green and red. Sparks tumble down and the whole garden jumps into relief. All the shadows are scalpel-sharp, frozen in their places by that brief, beautiful glare. The rocket arcs over the back wall, and even after it lands in the Jelai, the compound's still lit by the last glowing pinpoints that it left behind. I turn around and see Ammuma silhouetted at her upstairs window. Her face is in shadow, and I wave at her. At this distance, I wonder if she can see me smile.

She lifts a hand in response and I turn back to pull out the next firework. I feel lighter now, with the kind of excitement I always used to have at Diwali. I choose the biggest firework in the bag to light next, something that looks a bit like a Catherine wheel. A couple of rockets have been tied together, and nailed loosely to a small wooden post. I set the end of the post into the dirt and hold a match to the rockets, but just like before they don't burn immediately. The wooden post's swollen in the damp air and the nail holding everything together feels hot to touch. I try with another match but the rockets just hang there in a sulk of reddened smoke.

A movement at the window catches my eye. It's Ammuma, putting her hands on her hips. *Get on with it, Durga*, she's saying, *those evil spirits don't have all day*. I scrape my damp hair back and light another match. This time I shove it deep into the body of one of the rockets, and there's a little spurt of flame. The rocket moves – once, twice, and it's spinning in a shower of golden sparks. They rise this time, in a blown breath of honey-coloured light. I can hear a ripping sound, and then I see that the end of one rocket's come loose, flinging gunpowder into the air as it spins. A second later the whole rocket rips open, flaring up in a bright naphtha glare. It tumbles high as the palm trees, head over tail in a fizzle of sparks.

I take a step back, my eyes fixed on it. And then it comes apart in the air, one chunk soaring towards the house and another flying back near the Jelai. I take a few steps to the back wall, pulling myself up to lean on the chest-high stones. I can see the fragment of firework that's heading for the Jelai. It plunges down, high over my head but still spitting brave sparks. It looks like it's going to land in the jungle and I hold my breath, but instead it plummets straight into the water. As soon as it's extinguished, I can't see anything. My eyes are dazzled from the flare, and the lights from the house seem fitful and dim. Not a success, they tell me quietly.

I prop myself up on the compound wall. The light in Ammuma's room has gone out – she's not going to watch, not after that performance – and I turn back to the compound wall. The scrubland belukar stretches for fifty metres or so on the other side, and then the jungle takes over. Peony and Tom and I used to play a game out here, I remember, after dark. We'd climb over the compound wall into that scrubland and creep slowly towards the looming darkness. The winner was the first to reach the point – the infinitesimal, knife-edge point – where the jungle suddenly became grey and green and brown instead of featureless black. Where it stopped being terror and turned back into trees.

I look back at the house, but Ammuma's light's still defiantly out. I sigh, dropping the bag. I'll take a few breaths of air before going back, I think, before swallowing my pride and sparking up Tom's fireworks. I trail my hand along the rough top of the stones, walking carefully until I reach the corner of the yard. The wall's crumbling here, and there's a pile of bricks that have worked their way loose. There could be scorpions in there, I think, there could be spiders and centipedes and who knows what else. It's a Canadian thought, well scrubbed and careful.

I look back at the house once, then step onto the tumbled bricks. They give way underneath my feet, sliding and shifting until I'm grabbing at the gritty wall. It takes the skin off my palms. As I pull myself up to sit sideways on the top I feel my nails tear, and then I'm over and in the wide spaces of Pahang.

It's the first time I've been out at night here since I came back. I never used to be scared. I'd been good at our game, sometimes making out the shapes of jungle trees while I was still in arm's reach of the compound wall. Then a second later Peony would sing out in triumph – *I see them!* – and finally Tom with his pale, poor eyes. But I'm walking steadily forward now, and I must be nearly at the end of the scrubland but I still can't see a thing. The house is round a bend and downhill, and even the lights from it are cut off. The river seethes behind its mudbanks on my left and there's a rattle of wings as a guinea fowl takes off from somewhere.

I can hear the trees – I can even feel them in the slap of cool air as the wind forces their leaves up and out. I just can't see where I'm going.

I turn and my foot slips on the mud. I stumble forward, catching myself on my hands, and a squeeze of panic grips me. It's wetter than I'd thought out here. I can feel leaf stems and rocks under my fingers, but I've lost all sense of direction. I don't know whether I'm in the jungle or still in the scrub. Worse, I don't know how close I am to the river any more. It might be metres away, or it might be tonguing at my feet with little wet laps. I feel as though I'm slipping downward, as if I'm clinging to the banks like a spider scuttled under a rock. I can't move. There's a blind terror waiting for me out here: something about the wet scent of trees and the way my skirt clings to my legs.

And then I see something. A glimmer, a sheen and lick of light all the way through the trees that I can suddenly make out, too. My eyes have adjusted, and the river's a hundred metres away and safe behind its banks. I get to my feet, pushing hair out of my eyes and patting myself down. I'm on a sloping hill that leads from the house to where the convent used to be. It reassures me, recognizing this hill. For the first time since I came back I feel *exact*, sharp and clear and fitted into a single place and time. I turn and start slowly walking back down the slope. I can't see the house from here, just a strange dullish red glow. Ammuma must have turned the hurricane lamps up and lit all the candles. She's doing her work there, keeping the spirits away while I thrash through the night.

I look over to my right, feeling my skinned palms with the tips of my fingers. I'm closer to the river now, and I can see it's risen a metre since this afternoon. It's black and muscular, littered with driftwood from upstream and matted with vines. Out here, I remember, floods happen fast as an ambush.

As I stare at it the water glints and brightens. It looks as though there's a tiny light underneath. Phosphorescence, I think, luminous fungi, but it isn't any of these. It's a hot, burning glow, getting bigger and bigger, just round the bend where the house is. It's a reflection.

I spin round. That dull red glow over the treetops is brighter now, and I can hear a hiss. Another sound, which I recognize slowly, stupidly, from public safety videos: the crackle of flames beginning to lick their way through wood. I stare at the glow in horror, but my legs won't move. *That rocket*, notes some tiny, ice-cold part of my brain, it went towards the house. I start to run. I trip when I'm near the compound, but I'm up again with my hands bleeding and my throat thick with spit. I can see the house now. Flames are coming from one of the windows, inside a wing that Ammuma keeps sealed up. I scramble back over the wall, and now I can hear her voice over the snap and surge of the fire.

'Durga! Get away!'

She's above me at her bedroom window, fumbling at the shutters. A piece of wood drops on my shoulder, flaming, and flies off in a burst of pain. I hesitate at the kitchen door – Is it hot? Is there anything left inside except Ammuma, unbelievably in the heart of the fire? – but the door's cool and solid. The kitchen and dining room are clear, without even any smoke, and I run through into the hall. Out here I can smell burning paraffin wax, as the fire gallops along Karthika's polished, deadly floors. There's a crash and scream from Ammuma's room and smoke blurs my eyes as I race upstairs.

I tug the door to Ammuma's room open. There's a screen of smoke in here, with a red, snarling core at the side where the wall's been broken through. My eyes are stinging and my throat's raw and I'm pushing through the blackness, just like out in the jungle. I'm blundering forward, with my breath screaming and my eyes wide open, trying frantically to reach somewhere – some infinitesimal, knife-edge *somewhere* – where I'll finally find Ammuma behind the smoke.

2.   Once Upon a Time: 1922

'Mary-Miss! You have to be *nice*.'

Mary looks up from the full stretch of her six-year-old height to consider this. She's not so different even now from the grandmother she'll grow up to be. She's snappish, small, with fierce knees and uncompromising elbows; a little bit more trouble than anyone wants to take on.

'No,' she says, having given her amah's plea all the consideration she thinks it deserves. Her hair is in two satiny plaits, her fists are on her hips and she's standing over her new baby brother.

'It's *my* house,' she tells Anil, stamping a tiny foot. 'You don't even live here. You don't even have a bedroom. It's just the old rattan-patch.'

'Mary-Miss!' Ah Sim, her amah, gasps. Technically Mary's right. Her father, Stephen, flung some floorboards on the termite nests when he found his wife was pregnant again, nailed up a wall or two, slapped a roof on the whole thing and called it a day and a nursery. But it's the way Mary says it that sticks in Ah Sim's throat. Ah Sim's a black-and-white amah – white blouse, black trousers, that's all she ever wears – from mainland China. She's left her own baby brothers behind and she misses her family dreadfully. She's used to sons being treated like little gods, and Mary's cavalier attitude shocks her.

'The jungle spirits brought him, Mary-Miss,' she says. Fairy tales like this are supposed to be appropriate for girls of Mary's age. Truth without the bones in, as the bomohs say.

'Well, I don't want him. And if he doesn't stop crying, I'll – I'll drown him in the banyan swamp.' Mary glares at baby Anil, who screws his face up in a terrified howl.

'Mary-Miss!' Ah Sim's hand flies to her mouth and she glances around, worried that Mary will bring vengeful spirits flying in through the windows. Stephen's built this house like an Indian bungalow to make his wife feel at home, and all the doors and windows lie in straight lines. Once a spirit gets into a house like this, Ah Sim knows it's going to be hard to get it out.

'The jungle spirits won't like that,' Ah Sim tries to reason with Mary. 'They'll cry too.'

'Well then, I'll drown the bloody spirits,' Mary snaps, and her mother, Radhika, walks in just in time to hear her.

If Radhika had taken more time to reflect, she probably wouldn't have boxed Ah Sim's ears for encouraging that sort of language. And if she hadn't slapped Ah Sim then the amah might have stayed and taught young Mary a thing or two. She might even have spotted what was wrong with Anil before it was all too late. But Radhika's not a woman who thinks ahead, and so she slaps Ah Sim – and Mary, for good measure – packs one off to the servant's room and the other off to bed, then sits down to cry. The sound of his mother's sobs gives baby Anil the fright of his life. Shock fills his gummy mouth and he gasps. Gulps. Swallows his own howl once and for all. For good, as it turns out.

*

When Radhika unlocks the door an hour later, Mary hurtles out with her mouth set to quarrel. She's bursting to tell her mother what's what, to insist it's all *her* fault. It's always Radhika's fault, according to Mary.

'You scared Anil! Look at his little face! Ah Sim-amah doesn't teach me bad language, I just *know* it. All by myself.'

'Mary. Go back into your room.'

Mary stares her down, three feet of defiance. An hour ago she'd have slapped Anil herself, but she won't stand for her mother feeling the same way.

'You don't like either of us! You hate us!'

It's a lucky guess, and Mary doesn't realize how right she is. Radhika's life hasn't turned out quite as she imagined. She met

Stephen in her hometown in Kerala, married him and sailed out to Malaya with hopes so high she can barely remember them. Like any good Kerala girl she'd have liked a fine, manly boy-child to light her funeral pyre; she'd have liked a sweet, pretty girl-child to carry on the family name. Come to that, she'd have liked love, too, a comfortable house in town, a husband who didn't mumble as though he were speaking a foreign language. Radhika – who *is* speaking a foreign language, who will eventually lose her mother tongue and die out here with a hundred forgotten words in her mouth – can't quite bring herself to comfort Mary. She does her best though, holds out her hands and lifts her daughter to perch on the windowsill.

'I daresay it'll all get better,' Radhika says doubtfully, some-where over Mary's head. She takes a package of betel nut from her pocket and starts to wad it against her gums.

Mary wriggles down and stands on one leg, irresolute. The crickets are screeching outside, Ah Sim's sobbing in the servant's room and a tok-tok bird is sounding its mechanical call. There's something ominous in all this din, some note that's missing. She looks at her baby brother, lying here in the nursery and pawing at his mouth. Amongst all this noise, this chewing and birdsong and sobbing, she realizes – he hasn't made another sound.

*

'Cook's excelled himself tonight. Soup looks almost good enough to eat.'

Mary's father, Stephen, makes this joke nearly every evening. They're gathered in the dining room, under a buckling roof held together with nails and spit. The family still dress for dinner: Radhika in her saris of glittering thread, Stephen in his rapidly rotting dinner jacket and Mary buttoned into smocked gingham and good behaviour. Candles are set out on the table and the soup is tinned mulligatawny, with a dash of evaporated milk from another tin. Stephen's determined not to go native – bad show, he mutters over his solitary evening whisky – just because he's alone in a Malayan swamp with a couple of civet-cats fighting somewhere in the roof. It's seven miles to the next kampong, and half of Pahang lies between him and the nearest Englishman. It's all right for his wife and daughter, he thinks. Radhika's Indian; she's used to privation. And as for Mary – well, Mary's a little hooligan.

Stephen keeps his spirits up, though. He likes to take stock at dinner; he likes to make little jokes and tease his wife over laxities in the housekeeping. He's earned it, after all. He's extricated Radhika from the jungle and established her at the head of a table glittering with silverware. She can stand a little teasing.

'But Daddy, we *are* eating the soup.' Mary isn't usually this demure. On bad days she refuses to speak English, insisting on using bazaar Malay and overturning her water glass. Not today though. Today she's nervous. Anil still hasn't uttered a single cry since the afternoon. He looks puzzled and miserable, doubling his fists and smacking the side of his head. Mary can hear trouble in the air, like a finger sliding over wet glass.

'Hush, Mary. Children should be seen and not heard.'

Mary scowls, pushes her hands into her lap and kicks at the leg of her chair. She isn't hungry, having already gorged herself on ais kacang and kueh lapis in the kitchen with Maniam-cook. Maniam-cook is Mary's best friend. She sneaks him cigarettes from Stephen's private stash, gobbles palm-sugar lumps from his cupboard and brings him whatever gossip she's heard behind the door at Radhika's coffee mornings.

'Mary!' Her father snaps. 'Stop kicking your chair and eat. If you can't behave yourself, I'll have you sent to school.'

It's Stephen's favourite threat. His own school was a chilly Manchester institution, full of vicious masters and thuggish boys. He believes it was the making of him. It probably was, one way or another.

'I *won't* go to school,' she insists. 'I won't! You can't make me.'

Radhika nods vaguely, reaching out to stroke her daughter's

agitated head. At dinner Radhika ignores her family and their arguments. She smiles as though she's looking through glass, as though the glittering silver and the civet-cats in the roof are all one and the same to her. In a sense they are; Radhika's taken to chewing too many packages of betel nut, to smoking opium from a delicate long-handled pipe. She sits down with the gin earlier and earlier each day, and by dinner she's in a comfortable, softened world.

'Yes, of course you stay here, dear,' she says.

Stephen grunts and shoves his chair back. His soup was cold, there wasn't enough palm sugar in his coffee and even the nuts tasted strangely of his own cigarette ash. He's hungry and unsatisfied, and to make it worse, his authority's being challenged right here in the dining room he built himself. Stephen was once besotted with his chubby baby daughter, even insisted on naming her after his own mother. But Mary's baby stage was brief, and now at six years old she's all angles and elbows and arguments. No wonder Stephen's aggrieved.

'You're going, young lady, and no backchat. Whatever your mother thinks' – and he casts a contemptuous glance at Radhika – 'it's high time you had some discipline.'

Mary scowls as he stalks out of the room and Radhika sighs. *I'll poison him*, thinks Mary, who has far too much imagination. *I'll grow old and shrivelled and unloved*, thinks Radhika, who hasn't.

Anil, who isn't expected to think anything at all, slaps at the side of his crib. He coughs and splutters with a throatful of angry little whines. Mary escapes from the room to carry all her worries to the sympathies of Maniam-cook and Stephen sips whisky in the drawing room by himself. Radhika, left alone, pinches out the candles. Sighing, she slips her sari blouse up and flumps out a breast for Anil with her ashy fingers. She's quite a force, my great-grandmother, sitting there in the darkness with her milky nipples, her silent son tucked under her arm and her paan-stained teeth grinning out across the silverware. A survivor, like her daughter. They'll both stand it longer than anyone would have thought.

3.   Thursday, 9 p.m.

'Durga? Durga Panikkar? I'm Dr Rao.'

I'm sitting next to Ammuma's bed in a hospital emergency bay. The ambulance arrived quickly and two quiet Malay paramedics tucked Ammuma under a foil burns blanket. It wrinkled easily as milk-skin and I spent the whole journey squeezing the edge of it into a tiny, pleated ball. *It's only for shock*, they explained, *it doesn't mean she's burnt*, and one of them gently took my hand away.

The emergency department's busy, with full beds in every bay and even some in the corridor. We've been waiting an hour, watching people be wheeled in with burns, with wounds, with heart attacks. Each one of them feels like it's all my fault, because if Ammuma weren't here then we'd never have seen them at all. I tuck the end of Ammuma's dupatta in to the stretcher rail and she pats my fingers with a warning tap. *Enough with all the fuss, Durga*, that tap says. *Not so special one, is it?* She's no time for hysteria; any moment now she'll be informing me testily that plenty of people burn their grandmothers.

'Ms Panikkar, I understand there's a problem with your ICs.'

Dr Rao looks tired, as though he has better things to do than ask about people's identity cards. His eyes are red-rimmed like a toddy drinker's and there are dark patches under his arms. There's a nurse beside him who's young and pretty in a taut sort of way. She'll look good when she's Ammuma's age, I think. She'll have a sensible pension and some satisfying grandchildren and a few dependable packs of fireworks for Diwali and lunar new year. I swallow past a raw lump in my throat.

'I forgot the cards,' I say. 'I didn't . . . I've been living in Canada. We don't have ICs there.'

He frowns. 'Do you have any other identification? Any proof?'

I have proofs coming out of my ears. I have theorems and lemmas and elegant little corollaries and none of them any use at all.

'But she does live here,' I say. There has to be a solution but I don't know the words to ask for it any more. 'Can't I sign something, or make a statement or, or . . . ?'

'We need to check she isn't an illegal,' he says gently. 'We'll treat her, but we could admit her faster with her IC. Or even with someone to vouch –'

'Dr Harcourt!' I interrupt. 'Tom Harcourt, he's one of the doctors here. We were at school together, he knows her. Can you page him?'

Dr Rao turns away to confer with the nurse. They bend their heads like herons, then she scurries away to the phone by the door. Dr Rao holds one finger up: wait. He pulls the curtains around the bed with an old-fashioned gesture that belongs in black-and-white movies and everything's suddenly cut off. Even the noise of the Emergency Room seems fainter. From behind the curtains the glare from the rest of the department looks bright as a Dynamo advertisement.

Ammuma's still on her wheeled stretcher from the ambulance. Above her bed I can see the end of a sign directing people to other departments, to Neurosurgery and Spinal Care, to Cardiovascular and Chiropody and Podiatry. All those bunions and ingrown toenails. Serious enough, I daresay, if they're all you've got.

It feels like hours before Dr Rao comes back. He parts the blue curtains like a magician and gives me a tiny nod. He's brought two porters, silent men who move slowly and carefully as they wheel Ammuma out.

'They'll take you to the wards, Mrs Panikkar,' Dr Rao says loudly to Ammuma, then adds to me, 'They'll take her to the wards.'

'Yes,' I snap. 'You told her already.'

I hadn't expected her to go to a ward; I'd thought there'd be a dedicated department like the others we saw. Burns, perhaps, or Smoke Inhalation or Careless Granddaughters. I wonder what

Ammuma's going to tell them, when her words come back. I wonder what she won't.

'Ms Panikkar.' Dr Rao sits down on the other chair, across from the empty space where Ammuma's trolley was. That space feels like a no-fire zone, a glassy reminder of where Ammuma isn't. 'I'm going to need some details from you.'

He ticks them off. Home address, Ms Panikkar, your home address in KL please. And you're here in Pahang for a week? Diwali visit, eh? Employment: university lecturer, since two months only. In Canada for ten years before that, I see, I see. Marital status?

A maiden lady; that's how Ammuma once said she was described at her marriage ceremony. A different sort of grandmother might have cackled at that – a different sort of grandmother might have had nothing to cackle about – but Ammuma always kept a straight face. She used to tell me a lot of stories; folklore and memories all knotted up in a glorious tangle. *Is it true, Ammuma?* I'd ask, and she'd snort, and say it was the telling that mattered.

'Your marital status, Ms Panikkar?'

'Doctor.'

He glances at me, puzzled.

'It's Doctor Panikkar. Not Ms. Doctor. Doctor of mathematics.'

'Oh, yes?' His eyebrows say it all. 'Single?'

It's barely a question, this time. A husband, those eyebrows imply, would have sorted things out. Would have fixed the Catherine wheel. Would have bought quality market fireworks to begin with.

My eyes are tired and I rub at them. Outside these closed curtains there are desperate things going on, there are tiny quickenings and emergencies. Inside, though, everything feels muted. Stored medical kits look back at me with a helpless air, as though none of it's their fault.

'Cause of accident.' Dr Rao stops, clicks his pen with a deliberate twitch. 'Domestic fire. Cookery.'

'I . . .'

'We're busy tonight,' he says, without looking at me. 'Lots of burns from people playing Diwali fireworks and we're reporting most of them to the police. No permits, see? If it weren't for Dr Harcourt . . .'

He signs the form, then jams his hands into his pockets. His legs stretch out into Ammuma's empty space as he gets up.

'One of the nurses will take you through to the waiting room. Your grandmother won't be long.'

He opens the curtains, then looks back at me and smiles. It's a cheerful smile, it makes him look ten years younger, and it's as out of place in a hospital as a pink cocktail umbrella in the medicine glass. 'Welcome home, Dr Panikkar,' he says. 'Selamat datang.'

*

'Welcome!'

It was the first thing anyone said to me in Ontario. I was in the arrivals hall, with my brown trunk-case strapped and labelled, and clearly wrong compared with everyone else's wheeled cases. And there was an Indian girl near the doors, holding a big hand-lettered sign reading 'International Students' above her head and waving at everyone who came through.

'You must be Durga, right? I'm Sangeeta. I'm the international students rep.'

She stuck out a hand to shake, then pulled me into a hug. Sangeeta hugged everybody, I would find out later.

'Sangeeta Nair? They told me to look for you,' I said, and she grinned.

'I don't take much finding.'

She was right. For the next ten years, Sangeeta flitted about the maths department, bright, untidy and fierce as a quarrel. She turned up to topology lectures in bell-bottom jeans and peasant shirts. She gave set theory tutorials wearing tight emerald trousers and shady hats. She was daring and rude, the type to attend protests and scrawl graffiti on the walls of an underpass. The type to get away with it too; she had the legs of a racehorse.

After we graduated we shared an office, both of us crammed into a tiny grad-student room with lecture notes piled up on the floor. She would proofread my papers, scrawling a final, triumphant QED at the end in purple pen. I would cover her lectures, trotting to the department with snow banks high on both sides. I'd push my hands deep into my coat pockets and look up at the grey sky, canteen grease clinging to my tongue. They served hamburger loaf at the canteen, and Chinese chop suey that had nothing to do with China at all. It was at meal times I missed Malaysia the most.

But in the lecture theatres, I felt as though I'd finally come home. I'd stand at the front, a sheaf of notes in one hand and a piece of chalk in the other. *Co-limits*, I'd write on the board, and a hundred scratchy pens would copy it down. Categories, functors, equivalences: everything in its place and blackboard proofs that would always come out right. Sangeeta used to disapprove of those; she thought theorems were teacherly. *Tidy little facts for tidy little minds*, she said once and dismissed them just like that. Her words, like her trousers, tended to be undeniable.

She persuaded me to give a department seminar one day. There weren't many people there – it was a day full of rain and spiteful little gusts of wind – but the other post-docs had come. And right in the middle of the first row was one who'd enrolled only the week before. Deepak.

'I liked your talk,' he told me afterwards. He was older than the other post-docs, with two fine wrinkles that creased between his eyebrows. His hair was still black, though, and he had a sparse moustache like very fine pen-strokes. I watched that moustache move as he laughed, as he walked me to the staff common room, and offered to make tea. He brewed the tea with condensed milk and spices, the way I liked and nobody had heard of in Canada. That afternoon we sat on the common room's tattered green sofas for two hours and after that, on the metal chairs in my apartment's tiny kitchenette.

The night we first slept together, I thought about Tom. Deepak was propped on his elbows above me, the glow from my lava-lamp turning his mouth a reddish pink. He kissed me, and suddenly all I was thinking about was how Tom's lips used to dry out in the Pahang summer wind. How he'd rub Vaseline on them, and how Peony thought it was disgusting and dolloped Tiger Balm into his Vaseline pot. How he used to lie on the riverbank and talk about the snow he'd seen in England in the hope that she'd be impressed. How his dry lips felt on my own, too, and that sneaking sunrise joy that Peony would never know it wasn't disgusting at all, but tender and bare and more grown-up than we could have possibly imagined.

★

'Durga Panikkar? Your grandmother's ready for you now.'

It's Dr Rao. He leads me out of the waiting room and through to a ward with ordered beds. Ammuma's in the closest one, and she's far more alert now. She's been brushed and combed, she's been propped up against starched white pillows and her words tear out the instant she sees me.

'Can we go home now?'

She doesn't look happy; all this fluorescent light and soap doesn't suit her. She likes things dark and cramped; she likes yesterday's sweat on her sheets. She reaches for her false teeth, in a glass of water by the bed.

'Of course, Mary, we just need to keep you under observation for a day or two.'

Dr Rao straightens his collar as he approaches her and pulls his cuffs straight. He's trying to be respectful, but Ammuma just rolls her eyes.

'In hospital and this boy thinks his clothes is the problem one.'

Dr Rao coughs, resettles his glasses. 'How are you feeling? Do you have any pain?'

She shakes her head, folds her wrinkled lips over those too-bright teeth. They look like fangs, I think, not teeth; surely they're far too big for teeth. My head's spinning. Ammuma looks very small and far away on those pillows. She could be anybody at that distance. Someone from one of her own stories: a drowned woman in a well or a tiger-prince behind a mask. She could be dangerous.

Dr Rao bends over her bed. He pushes back the loose sleeve of her hospital gown and examines a weeping patch of pink skin. A bruise, on her wrist. He pauses at an old scar she's had as long as I can remember, puckering the skin of her forearm.

'She's had it for years,' I say, and he nods.

'A burn, I think. She would have got it from kerosene, hot oil, something like that?'

'She's here, ar,' Ammuma snaps. 'Can ask yourself.'

Dr Rao steps back, lowers his voice a little. 'Dr Panikkar? Durga?'

We move a few steps from the bed. Ammuma loses her focus, peers a little and then falls back. Her eyes droop and she tosses her head, frustrated. She's blinking, picking up her blanket and turning it over and over with a look of intense concentration. It seems to be brand new to her every time.

'It's the sedative,' Dr Rao explains, seeing my frown. 'It takes them like that sometimes.'

He draws me closer, drops his voice. 'Her lungs are a little damaged, Durga. There's smoke damage, but this is something more. She's never had TB, has she?'

'No . . . no. She's never mentioned anything like that.'

He nods, then looks at Ammuma again. He raises his eyebrows, gives her a reassuring smile. She glares right back at him.

'Mary, have you ever had TB? Consumption, in your lungs?'

'No,' she snaps instantly. 'No TB. So much questions, lah. Who are you to ask?'

'I'm a doctor here,' he answers patiently. 'Dr Rao.'

She looks away fretfully, then wipes at her mouth. 'Francesca, ah,' she mumbles. 'Francesca wants the doctor, isn't it, not me? Go see my daughter.'

Dr Rao looks at me. He steps back from the bed, telescopes his neck into his shoulders like an animal sniffing something it doesn't quite like.

'A daughter?' he asks quietly.

'She's dead. My mother's dead.' I consider this, turn it around for him with care, like a child stacking wooden blocks. I'm tired, and my tongue feels clumsy in my mouth. 'She was Francesca.'

Ammuma hears this and starts to mutter, beating softly on the bed with both hands. 'Francesca, in the black areas. You find her. In Kampung Ulu.'

My mouth dries. Kampung Ulu. It was where Peony died. Peony, laughing by the banyan swamp. Peony, one limp hand fathoms below the surface. Dr Rao gives me a questioning glance and I pull myself together.

'Kampung Ulu, Ammuma?' I ask her. My voice sounds very level, very normal.

'The San,' she mutters, and I frown. I haven't heard anyone talk about the San in years. It burnt down just before I was born, and in the playground we'd sometimes pretend we were lunatic patients escaped from its locked wards. *Locks on the gates*, I remember Peony singing, *I'm coming to find you, ready or not!*

'In the black areas,' insists Ammuma. 'The Emergency.'

'Of course, yes, the Emergency.' Dr Rao soothes her. I start to dislike him, with the kind of irritation that innocent objects provoke when they get themselves in the way. Tables in the dark. Chair-legs. Good intentions.

'Dr Panikkar,' Dr Rao murmurs in my ear. 'Can I have a word?'

He ushers me a few steps away. 'Does she often have confusion over time like this? Over dates?'

'I don't know.' She hardly ever talks about the Emergency, which lasted from just after the war until just after I was born. Our house was nearly in the middle of the black areas: a hundred metres further away and we'd have been thrown into a barbed-wire-fenced resettlement area by the British. But Ammuma doesn't talk about it. That's all in the past, she used to say dismissively, it's

27

all *water under the blood*. It used to annoy me, how she meddled with proverbs. And now I look at her in her bed, and wonder if she'll ever get another one wrong.

'I don't know,' I say again, uselessly. 'My mother's dead, though. She's been dead for thirty years, since 1955. She died having me.'

His spectacles catch the fluorescent light, blank and glittering. I wonder what he's thinking. *This one is thirty already*, perhaps. *Past her best. Missed her chance.* Ammuma watches us out of the corner of one slitted eye. She might agree but she's not going to put up with any insinuations from a toddy-eyed young doctor.

'We'll have to keep her in for a few days,' he says, pursing his lips. 'This confusion, and the shadow on her lungs . . . are you sure she hasn't had TB?'

'She told you she hadn't,' I snap. Ammuma and I tighten our lips, stare past him to where the morning's a glaring oily square behind the window blinds. I move back to the bed and feel for her hand under the blanket. She grips my fingers. We're on each other's side for once, even if we don't quite know it.

Dr Rao finishes his examination and tells me she can go home on Sunday. Two days in hospital, he says, will see her right. Ammuma, who's never considered she could be anything other than right, snorts at this.

'Do you want to stay with her tonight?' he asks. 'We can put a chair by her bed and give you a blanket.'

I nod. Ammuma's always been one for dwelling on the past, having so much more of it than future. She's always been inclined to ghosts and folklore, to mixing fairy tales with my bedroom stories and swearing the whole lot was true. Not easy to sleep after hearing some of those things: women drowned in wells, the tiger-prince and the frog-monster, demons and rakshasas and more devils than you can shake a happy ending at.

We'll pack them off together, I promise her silently. Tonight is Diwali and everyone and their god is out on the prowl, and those evil spirits will have to look sharp if they think they can get past us.

4.   A Prince and Two Princesses: 1924

By 1924, Mary's at school. It's a mission school, run by the Sisters of the Holy Infant, and once Mary arrived the Holy Infant never stood a chance. Mary spends her time flicking pencil shavings down other girls' necks, she coaxes fighting spiders into matchboxes and cheats her way through breathless games of marbles. She has things on her own terms these days, and she's even made a best friend. Cecelia. Cecelia is Chinese, she sits two desks away, she's the daughter of a cookhouse worker, and she's a thoroughly bad example.

'We'll take him to the bomohs,' Cecelia says. The girls are in the nursery at Mary's house, hands on hips and legs apart under identical ruffled skirts. Cecelia's watching Anil and Mary, to her surprise, finds herself watching Cecelia. She doesn't trust those guileless eyes.

'Why?' she asks. Mary and Cecelia have seen a bomoh in action only once, when Mohamed-the-butcher's teenage son went missing. The butcher called in a pear-shaped bomoh from Kedah, his face plastered with white mud and flowers strung through his hair. He paced, he flung coconut husks and he sat dirty-legged on a valuable carpet he'd demanded Mohamed drag out to the offal-strewn yard. Despite all that, the boy never appeared. Taken by a crocodile, was the verdict, and Mary and Cecelia shivered with a delicious, squirming horror whenever they slipped down the banks of the Jelai to look for fighting fish.

'He's been chomped,' Cecelia would sigh, opening her legs to the lapping waves and the suggestion of teeth, and Mary squealed and splashed and moaned in terror. When Mohamed's son turned up two months afterwards with the dumpy woman he'd run off to marry, Mary felt flat disappointment. She would have told it better, if only it had been up to her.

29

'We'll take him to the bomohs,' Cecelia insists again. 'They'll fix him.'

'What if they hurt him?' Mary objects.

Ever since Cecelia sat next to her during that first howling day at school, Mary's taken her best friend's advice. Cecelia has a sly twist to her mind, she comes up with the best games and the most exciting adventures, and lately Mary's felt like she's never going to catch up. It's Anil's fault, in a way. Ever since he was born there's been a cloud of bad feeling over the house. Everyone's felt it; Maniam-cook's handed in his notice, the knife-sharpener bicycles passed without a word and the kitchen cats have given up hunting mice and taken to scowling in corners. Mary's father, Stephen, his pale English skin sunburnt as he nails yet another verandah onto yet another annexe, can't understand it. Damn place has a mind of its own, he mutters.

Mary's mother, Radhika, too, knows something's wrong. She's started to talk to herself in Malayalam, the mother tongue of Kerala, which nobody here understands. She uses it to plead with her son, to whisper apologies into his unheeding ears. Radhika blames herself for Anil, which is handy for all concerned.

'Look, Mary, he isn't right.' Cecelia points an accusing finger at Anil. It's true that he never makes a sound, that he's slow to smile or open his eyes or grasp what's going on. But that's not always a bad thing, thinks Mary.

'The bomohs will fix him,' Cecelia insists. 'And everyone will be happy again.'

Mary sighs and gives in, gathering Anil up from the cot in all his knitted swaddling. Despite her reluctance, she's known all along that she'd do as Cecelia said. The two girls have never disagreed, at least not openly. When one arrives late to school, she finds the other waiting outside to scurry in and share her punishment. They divide their lunches, copy each other's spelling tests and have cross-my-heart promised to dress exactly the same. On good days, they're friends for ever.

Today, though, has started out badly. By nine o'clock Mary and

Cecelia have both bitten their mothers in a fight over bread and milk at breakfast, stamped out of their back doors, and attempted to drop their kitchen cats into the froggy depths of the well.

Neither girl has quite wanted to do all this. Mary loves her kittens and Cecelia, for her part, likes bread and milk. But Cecelia and Mary share a strange, unwanted bond, one that developed as soon as they met. When Mary claps her hands, Cecelia's own palms begin to sting, and when Cecelia outgrows her shoes, Mary's feet develop blisters. So neither girl is surprised that Mary's breakfast of bread and milk caused Cecelia to retch three doors away, or that Cecelia's scream of rage as her cat clawed her arm convinced Mary, with helpless sobs, to try and drown her own docile pets.

So now, having left two quarrelsome houses and a couple of dripping cats, the girls thrust Anil head-first through the nursery window and climb out after him. It's a hot day, right in the middle of the dry season, and as she carries him down the driveway Mary's arms begin to itch from the wool in Anil's blanket. Stephen insists on that blanket – no son of his is going to grow up like a half-naked savage – and without an amah to replace Ah Sim, nobody's thought to question the rash that's spread over Anil's delicate skin.

According to playground rumours, the bomohs live in a secret hut deep in the jungle that can't be reached without a map. Neither girl is quite sure she believes this – Mary wonders who drew the first map, Cecelia wonders what the bomohs eat – but at nine years old they're far too brave to suggest calling the adventure off. Mary navigates a flooded section of the river with Anil tucked under one arm while Cecelia scratches her elbows raw, and then Cecelia follows while grazes blossom on the skin of Mary's wrists. Anil, blissfully single-minded and with only one body to worry about, sucks on his thumb and watches the rustling leaves. If he were able to talk, he'd point out that the girls are going in circles. They've jumped this rocky outcrop twice already, and he's seen the thicket of hibiscus behind it at least three times. But he rather likes the look of those petal-soft flowers against the waxy green leaves, so he lies back placidly on Mary's shoulder and waits for them to appear again.

'Stop! You there, stop.'

Mary, in the lead, stops short and peers up into the leaves. Ten feet above her she sees a dark-skinned Indian boy – who will one day be my grandfather Rajan – astride the lowest branch and half-obscured by flame-tree blossom. Mary doesn't know this is a momentous occasion, and so her heart doesn't skip a beat, her stomach doesn't drop and her hand doesn't fly to cover a smile. Rajan looks put out. He hasn't climbed a ten-foot tree to be disregarded.

'Stop. I told you.' And then, when this doesn't have any effect, he adds, 'If you come any closer, I'll chop the branch off.'

Mary peers up at him and shrugs. She's only known him a few minutes, so she's clear-eyed enough to think he wouldn't really chop off the branch he's sitting on just to spite her. After a few years, she'll have learnt better.

'No, you won't,' she tells him.

She pats forward, Anil under one arm and the other hand on her hip. Her patent-leather shoes tap under ruffled socks, she's small and sweet and for the last time in her life she's on her best behaviour. The worst thing that can happen, she knows, is that in a few minutes the boy will make good on his threat. He'll tumble down onto her amid a mass of burnt-bright flowers and knock her to the ground where they'll live happily ever after, she thinks. She's read her fairy tales; she knows how the stories go.

'Stop! Mary, he'll do it!'

Cecelia comes panting up the hill, plump with baby-fat and good intentions. Seen from Rajan's perspective, through a screen of flowers and ten foot below – in other words, at a safe enough distance – she's even sweeter than Mary. Down on the ground the two girls glare at each other for a second like tomcats in a cage.

'He'll fall! You'll kill him!' Cecelia insists.

'Leave her alone.' Rajan veers round to Mary's defence. He's twelve years old and his family only arrived in the district a week ago, after his father was appointed as a government doctor in Pahang. The entire Balakrishnan family have been whirled up from Singapore on the very first passenger train ever to cross the Straits causeway and young Rajan considers that sets him ten feet above everyone else without any need for tree trunks.

But Cecelia knows how to get her own way. She ignores Mary and turns her lovely eyes up to the tree, pleading for him to hold on just one more minute.

'I'll come up,' she tells him and Mary, taken aback, stares with her mouth open.

'We're supposed to be taking Anil to the bomohs,' she says. 'You promised!'

Cecelia shrugs, and gives Mary an impish, provocative smile. 'Move over,' she calls to Rajan. 'I'm coming up.'

He frowns. This is all moving slightly too fast for him. Like he'll do so many times in future, he gives in to the snarling undercurrents between Mary and Cecelia.

'Both of you? Come on then,' he demands. 'I can't wait for you all day.'

'Oh.' Cecelia jerks a thumb towards Mary and Anil, all red and rashy in his heavy wool blanket. 'She can't come,' Cecelia says, all bare-faced lies and lower lip caught between her teeth. 'She's brought her brother.'

'No, wait. I can . . .' Mary looks around. There's a cleft in the path up ahead, just the right size to put Anil down in. But it's razor-sharp and rocky, and might hold anything at all. Scorpions, spiders, the odd jungle viper or two; she's heard you never see them until they strike. 'I can't leave Anil here,' she finishes miserably.

Nobody's listening, though. Rajan's watching Cecelia, who's already started to climb. Her monkey limbs are flung wide around the wrinkled bark and she doesn't look down.

'It doesn't matter,' Mary hears her say. 'It's only Mary. She won't mind waiting for us.'

Mary scoops Anil a little higher on her hip and kicks at a puddle of wilted blossom. She's not angry – not yet, not quite – but then she sees Rajan smile. He reaches down so Cecelia can grab his hand and Mary's stomach swells and drops. She feels a jolt as Cecelia reaches up to his fingers, feels the warmth of his palm on her own skin, and doesn't like it one bit.

'My name's Rajan,' she hears him say, and then a gust of wind tosses the branches aside. Cecelia's skirt flips up in that breeze to show a glimpse of her knickers. They're trimmed with lace, they're dirty and half a size too small, and Mary's wearing an identical pair herself. She's dragged them out of the soiled laundry on purpose, just so Cecelia would have to wear *her* pair. Mary herself has no compunction about wearing the same underthings for three days running, and Cecelia – cross-my-heart-promised to be Mary's mirror image right down to the skin – will just have to lump it.

But as that breeze sneaks under the frayed edge of Cecelia's ruffled skirt, Mary's stomach squirms. All of a sudden she can't feel the bark under Cecelia's knees, or even the squeeze of Rajan's fingers on Cecelia's hand. Instead, there's a stir of interest at the base of her belly, a muscling sort of swell that takes her by surprise.

'Come down right now,' Mary shouts up at the tree, and adds for good measure that Cecelia's a bloodless little mouse in dirty knickers.

But it doesn't help in the slightest, because this feeling isn't Cecelia's. It's Mary's own; it's to do with the way Rajan's eyes glint with half-hidden interest and his mouth's stained red with betel nut. Mary spits – she hates the taste, reminding her of Radhika and failure – and feels a ghostly, warning pressure on her lips. One day, she knows, Rajan and Cecelia will be kissing, will be doing a sight more than holding hands up in a tree. Mary, down amongst all those wilted flowers with only Anil for company, bursts into tears for the second time that day.

'I'll tell on you,' she whispers, and wonders if she might have learnt to like betel nut, if she'd only been given the chance.

5.   Friday, 5 a.m.

'Oh my God, a fire? Are you OK?'

It's a warm morning, still sticky with rain and with a pale glow where the sun's going to rise. I've calculated that it should be six o'clock in the evening in Canada, and Sangeeta will still be in our office. Her office, now. I grip the phone receiver and breathe out. It helps, to have told someone.

'I'm fine,' I say. 'A sore throat from the smoke and a few bruises, but that's all.'

'Maybe you're in shock,' she suggests, rather hopefully.

'Just some smoke,' I repeat. 'And a bruise.'

I'm in one of the phone booths outside the hospital. It's busy, with muttered conversations or one-sided anguish going on in alternate booths. There's an etiquette to grief, and we've all left as much space between each other as possible. Or perhaps it's a sense of self-preservation. Bad luck might be catching.

'It's my grandmother, though. She wasn't badly burnt, but –'

I take a deep breath, press my face against the side of the orange cubicle. It smells of metal, and the sweat from people's fingers.

'She was asking for my mother.'

'Your mother . . .' Sangeeta sucks in her breath. 'So she doesn't . . . she thinks . . . she's forgotten she died?'

'Yes,' I say. It's a little, tight word. It oughtn't to be big enough for a sob.

'Oh, Durga.' Sangeeta's voice is warm, hardly more than a whisper. I scrub at my forehead, push my hair back where it's sticking against my mouth.

'Anyway,' I pull myself together, take a few sensible breaths. 'My grandmother kept saying my mother was in the black areas.'

'The where?'

'The black areas. It's what they called the villages that were evacuated during the Emergency, right after World War Two.'

'Maybe she was evacuated in this emergency thing.' Sangeeta sounds pleased, like she's solved the puzzle. 'Your grandmother might be remembering it.'

'No,' I say. 'She lived with Ammuma. They weren't evacuated, I know they weren't.'

There's a pause, and I add, 'It wasn't really evacuation anyway. The British locked all the villagers up in resettlement camps in case they were giving food to the Malaysian independence fighters.'

'That's *horrible*.' Sangeeta, on her wipe-clean couch in Ontario, passes judgement. 'I think I'd have preferred the war.'

'Well, the Emergency *was* a war, really. We . . . they – Malaysia, I mean . . . was fighting the British for independence.' We. They. She doesn't notice the hesitation.

'So why would she think your mother was in these black areas now?'

'I don't know! I mean – Amma's dead. She isn't *anywhere*.'

'I know.' Sangeeta's voice is gentle. 'Maybe you can ask your grandmother a bit more, when she wakes up?'

'It isn't that easy,' I say slowly. 'She doesn't like talking about my mother, not usually. She just sort of . . . tells stories. All made up and exaggerated, like folk tales or something.'

I'm finding it hard to explain. In Canada, all that matters is facts: the who-what-why-when of everyday life. In Pahang, in Malaysia, what matters is how you tell it.

'And I'm supposed to be back in KL on Monday,' I say. Despite everything, I can feel myself calming down. This is familiar ground, at least. 'I've got lectures. They'll have to find a substitute for me. One of the post-docs or something, and God knows how he'll teach the proofs.'

Sangeeta laughs. 'That's the important thing, is it, Durga? How he teaches the proofs?' She sounds twice her age, coarse with the cigarette she's just lit. Sympathetic, too. 'If only I were there, I'd have taken your classes.'

'You never did at Ontario.'

Sangeeta laughs. She's not one of nature's substitutes. She'd fill the lectures with love-smitten teenage boys, I tell her, and Malay government officials who'd want to check on her credentials. I can picture her, handing out lumps of plasticine and Moebius strips made with bright yellow sticky tape. Those methods don't work here, not like they did in Ontario. I remember my first lecture in KL two months ago, tearing off a triumphant lump of clay to prove a cube and a sphere were the same thing under the skin. The students – Malay, Indian, Chinese – looked doubtful and made tiny, cautious notes. The skin, after all, has some significance in Malaysia.

'The post-doc's just like you,' I say. 'He'd end up teaching Yoneda's lemma using paper planes or something like that.'

She laughs dutifully, and then there's a silence.

'Durga?' she says finally. 'It's five o'clock there, isn't it? You didn't ring me at crack of dawn to talk about maths. You're not OK, are you?'

For a moment I don't say anything, watching a well-dressed Sikh man walk out of the hospital. His polished shoes clip smartly on the tarmac, his turban's neatly tied, and he's dapper right down to the waistcoat under his jacket. Except that jacket's buttoned on the wrong holes – as though he's put it on in a hurry – and it doesn't match the suit. Perhaps he's been wearing it for a week without noticing, sitting by someone's bed. Perhaps he thought bad news couldn't happen in his best clothes.

'Two months ago,' I say quietly, 'I'd have called Deepak.'

Sangeeta snorts. She thinks I should still call him. Get into a blazing, gorgeous quarrel with his family for urging him back to that shoulder-padded wife. Make a plan – apologies (for them), divorce and a trans-Pacific flight (for him), a wedding and babies (for me). She approves of all that, being a girl for drama.

'But don't do it *now*,' she adds quickly. 'Not at five a.m. I mean, it's evening here, he might even still be in his office . . . but you weren't really going to, were you, Durga?'

I shake my head, forgetting that she can't see. I've had a lot of practice at not calling Deepak during the small hours. For the last two months I've been lying awake in my tiny apartment in KL instead, eyes closed and imagining my Ontario apartment. That empty can of his pineapple cologne that nestled in the bin, a single sports sock, that jar of chutney he spooned out at every meal. The KL apartments are flimsier than Canadian ones and all night I listen out for thuds from someone upstairs breaking a glass, a vase, a heart. By dawn, I'm usually calculating the exact thickness of these thin walls between neighbours. A single blow would be enough to knock them down, I've worked out. To leave us all in our singlets and sarongs, squatting a careful arm's-length apart and staring into each other's faces. Imagining all our nose-hair and unpicked spots suddenly exposed to view.

'Haven't even thought about him,' I say, and Sangeeta laughs.

*

The beds in Ammuma's ward have filled up overnight, and a trolley full of breakfasts sits outside. I can hear her complaining from down the corridor. If I'd been away ten minutes longer I daresay she'd have discharged herself and stamped her way back home over the rattan patches. A real pioneer, Mother Agnes used to call Ammuma when she walked down the jungle paths to pick me up from school. Pioneer; it was a word I associated with covered wagons, with circling horses. With trouble, which was Ammuma through and through.

When I push the door open I see each bed has an old woman in it, identical grey cobwebs who barely make a dent in the pillow. Not Ammuma, though, who's jerking her head from side to side and cross as a traffic policeman.

'No good, this one. You bring from home, Durga.' Ammuma pokes a disparaging finger at the omelette she's been given. If she

38

were at home she'd be gobbling belacan, filling the house with its unapologetic smell. She's kept her taste for that kind of thing: bitter-tannin tea, rendang curries. Rural life. Take out the bones, Dr Tok Pek from the clinic in Lipis advised her ten years ago when Ammuma and I both went in for check-ups. From her food, he meant, but Ammuma got up from her plastic chair and walked straight out. She spat complaints from behind her seatbelt all the way home. 'Bloody Malay, ah,' she muttered. 'Village boy only, go back to the kampong.' Tok Pek lives in town and drives a Mercedes, but Ammuma's wrath is glorious and doesn't care for details.

'Mary, good morning.' Dr Rao comes up on noiseless feet behind us. I jump. Ammuma glares.

'Are you still having some difficulty with breathing?' he asks.

'Breathing fine, lah. No problems, no need for fuss.'

He looks dubious. Ammuma's voice is hoarse, her throat puffing out with each sip of air, but she won't admit it. She's not like the other women in the ward, hooked up to oxygen tubes and ventilators. They haven't managed breakfast; they're breathing by machine and digesting via tubes and Ammuma wouldn't lower herself to anything of the kind.

'We can try some more sedative.' He's frowning, creases netting his forehead from a sleepless night. 'We have to soothe those lungs of yours.'

'You mean you want to drug her?' I interrupt. 'Send her to sleep?'

'No, no. Not to sleep. Just to relax her. Slow her breath down.'

Ammuma gulps down the tiny white tablets he gives her and rejects the glass of water he brings over.

'Too chilling, eh, to take cold water in the morning. Need heating only, you didn't learn this?'

I sit back down by her bed, feeling that beige chair mould itself to my thighs again. Her hand's dry when I reach for it, and I can feel her muscles twitching in long streaks over the bones. The burn on her forearm looks redder and rawer than it usually does. She stares at it for a minute, as though she's never seen it before.

Dr Rao moves on to the other patients, recording medications and checking their charts. Ammuma and I drop into a deep silence, then she suddenly jerks upright.

'Francesca?' she asks. She grabs the blanket, then lets it go. 'Where's Francesca?'

Dr Rao doesn't turn. He doesn't want to be bothered with her, I think angrily. He only wants to know about her body, about the machinery of her blood and breath. He's not interested in anything else; not Francesca or the Emergency, or the fact that Ammuma's *never* eaten eggs for breakfast, or that she keeps her water-glass on the other side of the bed, not where this officious nurse has put it, or –

'Durga?' I look up. Everything's vivid, clear and glassy in the light from the window. A nurse has come in, and she's twisting the blinds open. Sunlight bounces off Dr Rao's gleaming hair and into my eyes.

'Durga,' he says again. 'You need to go home. Have some sleep, change your clothes. She'll be discharged on Sunday at 1 p.m. Please don't worry,' he adds. 'She'll be just fine here.'

I know I should stay, but I'm more tired than I thought possible. My head's starting to ache and my eyes feel raw, loose-boiled in my skull. I stand up and give Ammuma a kiss, but she doesn't move. Her forehead's warm and she smells of soap and smoke. She looks at me, though, whispers something that I can't quite make out as her eyelids droop and finally close. Perhaps she does see Francesca, I think, from under those swags of skin. Perhaps my mother's been here all along, waiting for me in Pahang. She's an imaginary number, a limit, an infinite sum. She's here all right, we just can't get our hands on her.

*

Half an hour later I'm waiting at the hospital bus stop. A few stray dogs hang around begging for food. A decade ago they wouldn't have bothered me, but now I eye them nervously. They're mangy things with anxious eyes and teeth on show, and I know how they feel. When the bus arrives some people settle for the long haul, bringing food and hot drinks out of carrier bags. Somebody pulls out a gold-dusted packet of laddoo and for a second I'm taken aback. I'd almost forgotten it was Diwali.

It's a half-hour drive back home. When I step out at the top of our road the smell hits me again, a wet stink of rot and ripped vegetation. It's the banyan swamp, which stretches out for miles all the way from Kampung Ulu. Four days here and I'm still not used to it. When the wind's in the right direction, everything smells like the day Peony died.

I push the gate open and see the churned-up mud left by the ambulance last night. The sides of the yard are filled with glittering puddles of rain, and under the raised verandah there's a slop of water as wide as the house. When we were small Peony swore she'd seen a catfish living under the school verandah, a monster that had been stranded there years before in a flood. 'Fooled you!' she'd told me after I'd crawled under to find it.

As I walk up the steps the banyan swamp smell fades, to be replaced by the stink of smoke. I shiver. I'm lucky the fire didn't spread; I'm lucky there's even a house to come back to. But that doesn't stop Ammuma's rattan chair with its worn-out seat from staring accusingly at me.

I turn away from that chair and start to pace the verandah. I'm exhausted, but far too much on edge to sleep. I need to reorient myself, like the pendulum equations I used to teach to first years. Back and forth I go, without ever finding home.

Every time I pass in front of the low verandah table, I catch sight of Tom's bag of fireworks underneath. On the third time I stoop down to pick it up, looping the string handles around my wrist. I don't want to see it, not right now when my mind's full of should-have-known-better. I walk quickly through the front room and the hall, still dim and tight-shuttered from last night, and drop the bag on the dining table. Karthika hasn't arrived to clean yet, and everything's still gritty with ash. The smell of smoke is so strong it feels like I could grab the air in two hands and wring it out. I go back out into the hall, tracing my finger along the grimy wall. At the bottom of the stairs I take a deep breath. *It won't be as bad as you think*, I tell myself.

And I'm right, it isn't. The smoke settles in my nose and on my skin, and I stop noticing it so much. The stairs creak just like they always did and for a second it almost feels normal. I pass the door that leads into one of those winding, looping wings that Ammuma closed off years ago. Karthika's paraffin-polished floors would have smouldered and caught in there, and who knows what sort of state it's in. But out here the bathroom's untouched, and so is my bedroom and the roofless little box room next to the attic ladder. The only real damage in this wing turns out to be one wall of Ammuma's room, where the fire broke through from one of the closed-off corridors. The wall panels are charred and her wedding photographs have crumpled from the heat. I wonder how much she'll mind. She deliberately hung those photographs facing away from her bed. She'd had enough mornings with my grandfather to last a lifetime, she said, and at his age he was hardly going to sneak up when her back was turned.

I close the door behind me. Even if Ammuma doesn't mind, those ruined pictures tap the guilt inside me. I wonder if she has any copies, perhaps in the prayer room. The prayer room's a small, dark alcove just off the verandah downstairs, with her shrines inside. She keeps things she doesn't need in there: spare green mosquito netting, my old picture books and even her wedding sari tangled up in an ice-cream tub full of Flit sprays. She doesn't go in for sentiment either, doesn't mind a few spots of grease on the past.

When I push the prayer-room door open it looks smaller than I remember. Shabbier, too. In Canada I got used to measuring the importance of things by how new they were, how outsize and shiny. Not here in Pahang. I'd never noticed before just how tarnished the shrines are.

Ammuma never used the prayer room much when I was young, but these days she spends so many hours in front of the shrines it seems like even the floorboards hold a memory of her knees. There are three shrines: one for her husband, Rajan, one for Anil and one for Francesca. No shrines for her own parents, who were killed in the war. She's never found out how they died and she won't put up a shrine, she says, until she knows for sure. She misses them more than I can understand in some complicated, angry way, like grief sewn together out of little patches.

My grandfather's photograph is the biggest. It's a pre-war portrait, Rajan looking clean-cut in sepia. Ammuma dutifully lays marigolds before it every morning. Rajan is, after all, a respectable memory – he was a government doctor, whatever unsavoury things he might have got up to off duty – and Ammuma always spent their wedding anniversary fasting for him. She used to love anniversaries and auspicious days, and she wasn't fussy about which religion they belonged to. Diwali, Christmas, lunar new year; she'd dip into the calendar and pull out a plum stuffed full of prayers and complicated rituals I'd have to fumble through.

Not now, though. Last year she didn't bother fasting at all until the Jelai flooded and she ran out of groceries. Killing two birds with one stone, she told me triumphantly down the telephone. Making the most of things. She's good at that, using up bits and ends of rags, of food and left-over flowers. She's good at shrines.

Her brother Anil's shrine has even more marigolds scattered on it than Rajan's. She takes Anil more seriously, blood being thicker than marriage certificates, after all. And since he never learnt to speak he wouldn't have even answered back; a point in his favour. Ammuma's stories about Anil change depending on her mood; they shift and contradict and turn into different tales entirely. I know he was killed in the war, like Rajan. But Anil, Ammuma's always said, didn't deserve it.

There's a fresh-cut flower and a bowl of sweets in front of Francesca's shrine. *Your Amma always did love sweets*, Ammuma says to me every Diwali, down crackly phone lines and clear-as-a-bell phone lines and phone lines that echo with sadness. And now I'm back here, topping up Amma's bowl of sweets myself. Francesca looks about thirteen in her photo, and it's strange to think I was born only a few years after it was taken. Francesca pregnant with no husband in sight, and who knows the tears and tantrums there were over that. And then three more feverish days and she was dead. Sixteen years old, with her stomach still swollen from baby weight she never had a chance to lose.

I put the picture back firmly. Bad enough having to deal with my memories on this visit, without bargaining for Ammuma's, too. Everything in here seems eerie, like a kind of trick photograph. With my Canadian eye it's exotic and overdone, like a photograph on the wall of a travel agency. But with my Malaysian eye it's real life.

I turn away, and to my surprise there's one more rickety table. It's been pushed in at the back of the room and there's a shadowy photograph on it. I pick the photograph up and tilt it closer to the light from the open door. My hands start to shake. It isn't. It *isn't*.

But it is. I know this photograph. It used to hang on my bedroom wall, fifteen years ago. It was taken at the kampong school just a mile away: rows of children arranged on benches with our hands tucked behind our backs. We're all teenagers and sulky with it, wearing pressed uniforms crisp as cellophane. I'm in the middle, my hair in two plaits, Tom's in the back row with a smile and a bowl-cut, and then – yes, in the front. There she is, sitting cross-legged. Wrists covered in ballpoint tattoos and nails chipped from a game of five-stones in the playground. Peony.

6.   The Princesses Set to War: 1926

In the year she turns eleven, Mary correctly spells the word *import-ance*. It's the end-of-year class test, and this achievement should have lifted her into the standard above. In that rarefied atmos-phere up there, they read Dickens instead of *Alice in Wonderland*; they parse sentences instead of telling stories. They are, in short, much better educated than Mary is right now and much better behaved.

'Well done, Mary,' Sister Hilda tells her. 'Now, the definition, please. Importance means . . .'

Mary hesitates. If she had read her Dickens already, if she already knew how to diagram sentences – in short, if she were bet-ter educated and better behaved – she'd say that importance is a state of mind. It's her temper, and the impossibility of controlling it. It's her yearning, unbearable desire to be grown up. Her bitten nails, the fried watermelon seeds she'll eat alone in the garden and her luckiest five-stone that she keeps in her desk. She'd offered that stone to Anil yesterday, if only he'd talk. But of course, he didn't.

'Mary?' Sister Hilda prompts.

'I don't know,' Mary answers, and seals her fate for the next school year.

Sixty years in the future Mary will still have the temper, if not the bitten nails. She'll be more than grown up; she'll be old, which she never truly believed would happen, and is worse than she'd ever expected, and she'll be alone again. When she tells this story to a bothersome grandchild, she'll get the tenses wrong and the participles mixed up, because she never did learn to diagram sen-tences. And she'll add a friend in, when she tells it later, to make it all bearable. A small friend, because Mary doesn't – yet – meddle too much with truth. The kind of friend she might easily have missed in all that excitement. The kind who couldn't do much harm.

*

'I'm sure Anil won't die,' Cecelia tells Mary helpfully as she pokes her head over the garden wall. Five years after they first met, Cecelia and Mary are still best friends. But ever since the district got its government doctor – Rajan's father, Dr Balakrishnan, bringing along his wife and two daughters and his tricky, sneaking son – the two girls have been eyeing each other with suspicion. Something's happened.

To be precise, a lot has happened since then; Kuala Lipis now has a railway station, the Straits Chinese are agitating for political power and the Malay sultans are making treaties left, right and centre with the British to make sure they don't get it. The Chettiar Indians are quietly lending money, the Kuomintang are recruiting Communists, and two years ago Rajan Balakrishnan clasped hands with Cecelia Lim in a flame-of-the-forest tree.

But most importantly, Mary and Cecelia have lost their bond. They used to be almost two-in-one, to the extent that Mary's measles bloomed on Cecelia's skin and Cecelia's mild typhoid half-killed Mary. Witchcraft, the bomohs would have said. But now Mary and Cecelia's connection has faded and they're just two ordinary girls. Plain, sturdy. Healthy, no thanks to those bomohs.

As for Rajan himself, he's a slippery character; head of his class with a heartbreaking smile. He has a habit of winkling people's innocent secrets out of them and puffing those indiscretions up into monstrosities. Thanks to Rajan's loose tongue, Mrs Abdul's weakness for cigars swells into an opiate habit and the beef in Ah Chen's satay is rumoured to come from stray dogs. His classmates aren't spared either: when little Pok Mat defeats Rajan in a spelling test at school, he's astonished to find himself carpeted for apparently gambling on cockfights he's never even seen. Most of Rajan's stories are harmless enough, although little Pok Mat sobs all afternoon following his beating, and is carpeted again for disturbing the class.

Rajan can be charming, though, when he chooses. Cecelia and Mary are both half in love, taking every opportunity to slip a hand into his or finish his homework. At any other time Mary's father, Stephen, would have put his foot down – Mary's getting older, she's always been wilful, and soon it won't be homework books she's opening for Rajan – but Stephen has other things on his mind. Anil is getting worse.

Mary's mother, Radhika, on the other hand, is perfectly capable of worrying over both children at once. It's true that, despite being five years old, Anil barely moves and shows no inclination to babble. But it's also true that Mary – and she *must*, Radhika complains to her friends, she really *must* stop Mary seeing so much of that Cecelia girl, not to credit market gossip but these Chinese tarts, eh? Sexy at nine years old and pregnant by twelve, isn't it? – can still coax a smile out of her brother.

But that's not enough to satisfy Stephen. He's been disappointed in Anil since the day he was born – undersized, squalling, so dark skinned that only an Indian name seemed to suit. And to make it worse, the boy still doesn't talk, so today Stephen has booked an appointment in the top hospital in KL. He and Radhika will get to the bottom of this, he's resolved, will force some words out of Anil and some backbone in. They'll be gone until tomorrow and as a special treat Mary's been allowed to have Cecelia stay the night. The two girls are going to stay in the house by themselves tonight, with a lovely cold dinner and a stone bottle of orangeade. To make up for things, Radhika's explained vaguely, and left Mary with the confused impression that Cecelia's somewhat of a consolation prize. Shop soiled, so to speak.

She's not the only one in the kampong to think that, either. Cecelia's been spending entire afternoons sitting in the flame-of-the-forest tree with Rajan, picking up bad habits. By now she's tried some of Rajan's cigarettes, she's tried some of his bad language, and she's certainly outdone him in spreading rumours. If

Rajan's stories were harmless then Cecelia's certainly aren't, and by now there are more than a few broken marriages after she's lied about seeing an embrace under the mango trees or a kiss behind the fish stalls.

It's not so much the lies, but how Cecelia tells them. She has a penetrating voice, the kind that's loudest when she's whispering. And so when she sits placidly at her mother's stall in the market-place and whispers to Amir-from-the-market that *she's* heard he feels more urges for his prize-winning goats than for his own wife, the whole marketplace hears. Not that Cecelia minds; she just gives her White Rabbit candy another chew, and says that if Amir buys her another bag of sweets she won't tell anyone else. And when the little Varghese girls refuse to play marbles with Cecelia, she whispers so noisily to their mother that her daughters have lice – actual lice crawling in their shining plaits – that all of Lipis knows about it, and Mrs Varghese is forced to spend the rest of the night shingling the girls' beautiful hair.

So, given Cecelia's inclinations for half-truths, it's hardly a surprise that Mary doesn't believe her when Cecelia says Anil won't die.

'How can you know that?' she sniffs.

'Rajan told me,' Cecelia answers. 'They're not going to do any-thing at the hospital. There isn't anything they *can* do.'

She sits down cross-legged on the grass just as wheels rattle up to the front of the house. A rickshaw's been hired to take Mary's parents with Anil to the train station. They'll be whisked to a KL hospital where a tired doctor will peer down Anil's throat, tap on his knees and pronounce him perfectly fit in everything but his brain. That doctor will be overworked and seeing a quiet child will be quite a relief for him.

'They *can* do something,' Mary insists. 'Anil's going to get better.'

'Rajan said you'd say that.' Cecelia beams, wriggling her plump shoulders under the lace of her second-best dress. She looks sweet in that dress, yellow cotton that's been trimmed with a bit of ribbon and the hem turned up above her fat little knees. She looks so sweet, in fact, that Mary starts to bristle.

'Why were you talking to Rajan, anyway?' she demands.

Cecelia shrugs again and gives her a charming smile. Neither girl is quite as much in love as she thinks, but they won't let the other one win. They're at an age to fight over anything, and the more vicious the better.

'Oh, I see him quite a lot these days,' Cecelia confides, oily with hormones and malice. 'He comes to my house, you know.' She examines her fingernails, scratches one of those rosy knees. 'My mother says she can hardly keep him away.'

Cecelia's mother, Yoke Yee, married late in life after working as a brothel-girl in the mountains of Shanxi province and spending her days doing finger-knitting to make ends meet. Yoke Yee's a cookhouse worker now and she wants something better for Cecelia. 'You know what'll happen if you don't marry,' she's told her daughter, 'you'll end up with sores on your fingers and God-knows-what everywhere else.' So Cecelia obediently invites the village boys home for tea, pressing them to take another bourbon cream, a vanilla wafer, a scarf from the finger-knitting she does on those afternoons she's not ruining her reputation in the flame trees. And then, when Yoke Yee walks out of the room, Cecelia presses the boys to kisses and liberties.

'You oughtn't to hang over Rajan so much,' Mary says coldly. 'He hates girls who do that.'

Cecelia flushes, tosses her head. 'Don't be jealous,' she says. 'Just because he doesn't visit *you*.'

This doesn't go down well with Mary. She's cross; she's worried about Anil and she's secretly jealous of that yellow lace dress that she thinks would look a lot nicer on her own slim frame.

'Leave Rajan alone,' she orders Cecelia. 'He's told me all about what you get up to with boys, and we think it's – just silly! As though he'd have anything to do with a . . . with a *Chinese jam tart*.'

Inaccurate, perhaps – Mary's been listening at doors – but

49

heartfelt. Just for good measure, too, she spits on the ground by Cecelia's feet. It's a gesture she's learnt from the beggar children and rubber-estate brats she admires, and she thinks it rather daring.

Cecelia pauses, raises one eyebrow. 'Eew,' she says, brushing her dainty skirts. 'That's disgusting.'

She rises neatly and walks into Mary's house, flicking grass off that coveted lace skirt. Mary isn't often at a loss for words and it only takes a few seconds before she's bounding up to the back door cursing. She jabs at the handle, tugs and twists, and it's only then she understands exactly what's happened. Cecelia's locked her out.

*

Three hours later, the sun's plummeted below the horizon and a brisk wind's sprung up. The air tastes of tin and grit and the ground has a soggy slap to it. Mary's crouched in the half-built annexes at the end of the garden, the ones her father put up with a few nails and some hope. She's given up trying to sleep, and she's thinking up diabolical revenges for Cecelia. She'll climb up the bougainvillaea and *strangle* her; she'll slip oleander leaves into Cecelia's morning cups of milk, she'll pull her hair out and steal her yellow dress.

Perhaps Mary will do these things, now or in some other time. Perhaps Cecelia – who, after all, by Mary's account (and what other account could there be sixty years later?) might not even have been there at all – will walk away, happy and healthy, to live to a great age and bring up her own ungrateful grandchildren. But before any of this can happen there's a noise, echoing over the sound of distant rain. It's a tidal noise, one she recognizes from her afternoons playing crocodile-bait down by the river. It's the noise of riverbanks breaking away, of surprised raindrops that had expected to fall on dry land. Mary panics, scrambles up onto a pile of wood and then one bare foot slips down again and this time she feels water.

The Jelai river, slinking past the garden wall, has oozed over its banks and begun to crawl up the path. It licks Mary's heels in a friendly sort of way in passing; it takes a breath, it swells, it darkens, and then it surges over Pahang in a riptide flood.

Amir wakes with water halfway down his mouth, and his first thought is for his prize goats. Mrs Varghese slaps at the waves, frantic, desperate to find her girls in that muck. If she'd left their hair alone she could have dived for them – dragged them out by their plaits – but as it is they're swept away, one by one, their shaven heads dipping underwater and out of reach.

In the annexe Mary scrambles from the woodpile onto an old almirah Stephen's been using to keep his tools in. Everything's pitch black – no electricity in those days, and kerosene lamps aren't much good under five feet of water – with the wind kicking little smacks from the surface. The water's rising faster than she could have thought possible, and she stands on her toes to press her face against the spiky attap roof. Not much chance of help on a night like this, not when nobody even knows she's there. Something heavy buffets against her legs, nudging her again and again. A piece of driftwood, a catfish, a drowned woman; it could be any of these and Mary gives a little scream. She's about to slip under the water, her lips pursed upwards to the tiny gap where the roof still holds a cushion of air, when she hears a voice.

'Help . . . help!'

She recognizes it, that voice that's as loud in a whisper as her own is in a shout. It's Cecelia, nearly hoarse but still crying out somewhere in the main house. Before she can react the annexe roof shudders, rocks as something grinds over it. Above her head, there's a slap of oars.

'Who's shouting? We've come! Hello, is anyone there?' It's Dr Balakrishnan, somewhere out in that darkness.

'It's me! It's Mary!'

A hand plunges in through the hole in the roof, grabs Mary by the scruff of her neck and hauls her out. Lucky for Mary that she's thin, without any of Cecelia's firm flesh. She comes out with barely a scratch.

'Ai, girl! You were shouting to wake the dead. So loud!'

Dr Balakrishnan stands by the boat's mast, where a kerosene lamp dances and glows. The light's attracting creatures to the surface, fish and phosphorescent squid and something large and snappish that lurks beneath the hull. Amir-from-the-market's huddled in the prow, his arm around the only goat left. Back in the kampung his daughters still cling to the stilts of their house, along with one of the convent nuns and the youngest Varghese girl, all of them abandoned for goats or gold or a prettier sister. It's not easy, being a woman in these times and Mary's lucky to have got out at all.

'We heard shouting.' It's Rajan, folded into a spindly bundle of legs and elbows, slopping water out of the boat using an old tin bucket. 'You're lucky we were here.'

'But I wasn't shout –' Mary stops.

She wasn't shouting, of course, and even if she had been she probably wouldn't have been heard. She's not Cecelia, with her vocal reach that can cut through a crowded marketplace. Cecelia, who's been screaming for an hour and now – right now, right when it matters – suddenly finds her throat's too sore to make any noise at all.

'Is there anyone else here, Mary?' Dr Balakrishnan steers the boat in a tight circle. The wind's whipping up, and Mary can see a mass of leeches and spiky-shelled insects struggling in the ankle-deep water at her feet. Add in one more person – say, a plump sort of person, a small friend, perhaps, the kind you might easily miss in all the excitement – and the boat will certainly capsize.

Mary thinks about Cecelia, who is her best friend and yet so quarrelsome – as Mary puts it – and hurtful. She really, truly ought to be scolded, but Mary wouldn't say a word against her and so she doesn't say a word at all. She shuts her lips tight and squats down next to Rajan, rubbing her eyes with her fists. Above their heads the lantern bounces and glares, casting a lurid glow over the drifting tree trunks and occasional splash of a sea creature out of its element. Dr Balakrishnan sets the boat heading due east, to the flood evacuation centres and away.

In later years this will be known as the Great Flood of 1926. Whole villages will be inundated and – according to local stories – simply carry on their lives underwater, quarrelling and farming and brushing the gills their children soon develop. Corpses will bob in becalmed waters for weeks, rotting away until the graveyards can be bailed out.

On the other hand, Cecelia will survive. Not quite the same, not quite a friend, and through the long, stalking years, Mary will learn to regret this night. Amir's daughters will survive, too, and the youngest Varghese girl, and most of the rest of the kampong. Not the convent nun, clinging to a house stilt. Her eyes will have been turned to the heavens and so she won't see the large, snappish thing swimming underneath her in the water. She won't draw her feet up and so will plummet down, dragged underwater by the rubbery lips of a monstrous catfish, the sort to live out the last hundred years of its life in an unknown ditch under the schoolroom.

But Cecelia will survive. More's the pity, Mary would say. Survival, to Mary, is something you earn.

The prayer room feels claustrophobic and heavy, as though the air's run out. I'm still holding Peony's picture, and an echoing clang from outside nearly makes me drop it. Somebody's thrown open the compound gate, not even stopping to latch it again. Quick footsteps cross the yard, then pause at the verandah steps. After a second they start to climb, and I realize I'm holding my breath. Ammuma's stories come back to me – the froggish monster, the spidery drowned women – and then the prayer-room doorway darkens and I see Tom.

'Durga?' His lips are wet, and I can see the tiny shreds of dried skin clinging to them. There's a scab of dried blood where he's pulled some of the skin off, and he looks worried. Scared.

'They paged me last night at the hospital, to admit Mary-Auntie. A cookery fire . . .'

'No,' I start to say, but he isn't listening.

'I went to the ward just now, and talked to Rao. He said it wasn't a cookery fire. It was the fireworks.'

He stumbles forward into the prayer room, wrapping his arms around my shoulders. It feels clumsy, somewhere between a hug and a fall.

'I promised you the market ones were good quality. I thought they were, honestly. I didn't know, I thought – God, I might have killed you both.'

His throat pulses against my chin, involving me with the rhythm of his breath. I start to shake as I lean into him. Inside, I'm calm – a little still and cold, as though I've drunk ice-water in the dark – but that doesn't seem to matter. There's an ache where Tom's body presses against mine, a thread being drawn from my stomach. I drop the photograph and it lands with a thud. Peony, face down on the floor.

'I'm so sorry.' His voice is muffled. This isn't the kind of thing you say out loud, not if you're Tom.

I should tell him it wasn't his fireworks at all, which are still in the dining room where I left them. But I can't get any words out. Tom huddles against me and there's a catch in his breath. I hug him back, and he's a swoop of muscle in my arms. Hips and shoulder blades and the softness of a stomach bulge hidden under his clothes. Perhaps he has changed, after all.

'It isn't your fault,' I say, under my breath. *This time*, Peony adds.

He keeps whispering, breathing out guilt as he slips his hands along my collarbone and rubs his lips over mine. Exhaling all that guilt makes room for something else that envelops us as we lie on the floor of the prayer room, two forked and shaking curls with all our fat rolls and strange sprouting hairs on display. Two monsters, holding tighter and tighter and never letting go.

*

Mother Agnes once gave us a biology lesson. Ahead of her time, most probably; nuns didn't approve of that kind of thing in the 1960s. But Mother Agnes was special. She was born without a tongue and brought up in a convent; it took more than a touch of disapproval to stop her. She'd drawn pictures on the board, I remember, chalk outlines of male and female bodies. *It looks like a pitcher plant!* Peony had giggled. *I'm never getting married.*

Which goes to show that at least one of us got things right.

*

Tom puts his clothes on again in a shamefaced rush, as though he hadn't quite noticed they'd come off. He moves shyly, turning his back when he gets to the vest-and-socks stage. Something about him in the light from the prayer-room doorway reminds me of Deepak. Nothing obvious, nothing I could explain. Tom's smooth where Deepak was rough. Tom's paler, Tom has more hair, and Tom's ribs are heavy and solid. Deepak was slender and Deepak was balding and Deepak managed, somehow, to look me in the eye as he told me he was married.

My eyes flicker to Tom's bare wedding finger as he ties his shoe-laces. Good shoes – nicer than Deepak used to wear – and that sharp suit on top of them too. His hair springs up, light brown and thick as sugar cane. I remember him combing it over his forehead when we were fifteen, schoolboy Tom trying to be John Lennon and only managing Ringo Starr. And the smell of him, the sweat, the salt-and-deodorant that's on my skin, too.

I crouch to put on my underwear that lies puddled on the floor. He picks up a marigold fallen from one of the shrines and brushes it against my breast. It's an oddly intimate, tender gesture and I shiver.

'I'm going to wash,' I tell him awkwardly. 'Do you want to . . . to come?' I don't know why I ask. Deepak and I used to shower together, stripping naked under great cascades of scalding water in my hygienic Ontario bathroom. I don't want that with Tom, or perhaps I do but it looks like I'm not going to be given the choice. He's got his shoes on already, and he's zipped and buttoned away.

'I can't stay long, actually,' he says. 'Maybe just a cup of coffee?'

We walk through into the darkened front room. In the gloom Tom takes my hand between both of his. It feels sweet: a teenage sort of gesture, although as a teenager he'd have done nothing of the sort. He was always far more interested in Peony. That thought makes me jumpy, overflowing with a silly kind of excitement that's too young for me.

I want to be aloof and sarcastic, just like Peony was. I want to let him make the moves. But my clothes are crumpled, my hair's in my eyes and he's already made all the moves on offer, if the last hour's anything to go by. *Not your finest moment*, I tell myself, but I feel a shudder of joy and wonder whether it just might have been.

'I can't believe it's been fifteen years since we last saw each other,' I say. 'You don't even know about –' About Deepak, about Canada, about the way Peony's smile flickers out at me from mirrors '– about anything!'

He laughs, then puts an arm around my shoulder. He has to stoop, since our heights don't match any more. They always used to, I remember, and Peony was a scant centimetre shorter. She would have stayed short, I think spitefully. She would have had to stretch to kiss him now, if she'd managed it at all.

'You'll have your work cut out with the cleaning up,' he tells me. 'Was the fire all in the side wing? Once it's aired out the smoke shouldn't be this bad.'

Tom, I remember, likes to advise. He walks ahead of me to the dining room and opens the back door. While his back's turned I grab the bag of fireworks from the dining-room table. The kitchen almirah's right next to me, and I shove the bag high up on the top shelf. He turns round a second afterwards, as though he'd heard. There's guilt squatting in the room with us, stringy as spit.

'So Ammuma didn't tell you I was coming back to Malaysia?' I ask quickly. I keep my face turned away from him, pretending to be very busy with cups and plates in the kitchen.

Tom laughs, sitting down in a chair with his legs straddled wide. 'Of course not. She wouldn't talk about you, Durga. You *have* forgotten things.'

He's right. Even if he weren't Tom and I weren't me – even without Peony's shadow stitched to our feet – Ammuma wouldn't have discussed me with him. The best thing you can hear about a girl is nothing at all, she always used to say.

'She didn't tell me you'd come back either,' I say, rubbing dish soap onto a plate slightly harder than necessary. Tom just smiles.

'So, do you have any . . . family here?' I ask. Wives, girlfriends; women I won't name for fear of conjuring them up. *Cowardy-custard*, I hear Peony jeer.

He doesn't reply, not at first. He scrapes that chair over the floor, tips it back and then back again – in another moment he'll be in the almirah with the fireworks – and says, 'Well, Mary-Auntie's like family to me.'

No lovers, then, no ex-girlfriends left alive. Tom's the sort to prefer a midnight dash, underwear in his pocket as he slips out of the door. I can see it, Tom running for his life and me with one of my hands clasped round the verandah ironwork and the other flailing in mid-air, grabbing for whatever I can get. Undignified, to say the least. That thought brings Peony's face back to me, smiling out of that strange photograph behind the shrines.

'Tom,' I say slowly. 'I want to ask you about something. In the prayer room, just now –'

He looks up warily and I see he's misunderstood. He's expecting recriminations and arguments. He's expecting expectations.

'In the prayer room – it was very . . . nice, Durga. Honestly.'

Nice. I store that one away to wring bitterness out of later. In any case he's already pushing forward with a conversation that's going to go just how he'd like.

'Now, let me give you a hand,' he says busily. 'You're doing that coffee all wrong.'

I give in. It's cowardly, but I can't bring myself to say her name. And so the coffee carries us safely over the next few minutes, with both of us pretending to share a fascination with brewing times. There are little fusses with filters and granules – Tom, unsurprisingly, has firm opinions on the way this should all be done – and whether or not the milk is fresh. He directs me to bring water, sugar, a teaspoon and tells me where to find them, too.

When I was growing up the kitchen was Vellaswamy-cook's domain. Karthika took over three years ago, when Ammuma stopped being able to manage. She's hung copper pans on the mud-green walls and there's a dim, aqueous chill over the place. When I open the cupboards in search of coffee I can see they're almost empty: nothing but mud-clumped stalks of kai lan, Milo, Maggi-noodles and Nutella.

'Do you think this is all Ammuma eats?' I ask, distracted. It's so different from Canadian-style refrigerators, full of frozen meat

58

and plastic-labelled vegetables. 'I don't know what Karthika's been spending the money on.'

Karthika used to cook, until last year. She went missing for six months, then turned up one day with a baby and still no wedding ring or kum-kum in her hair. Ammuma won't stand for her touching the food any more, so nowadays Karthika comes in to scrub the toilets and bathrooms. Ammuma's begun to call her the night-soil man, with a fine disregard for detail.

'I hope you're not nagging at Karthika,' Tom says, opening the top cupboard for mugs. 'She's quite sensitive, you know, Durga.'

I stare at him. But she's the servant-girl: the phrase comes almost instinctively. 'Since when did you care so much about her?' I ask instead, and he laughs.

It's the first time I've seen him really smile – a genuine, unpractised grin – and it smooths over the edge of irritation I've been feeling. He looks fifteen again when he smiles, and that gives me courage. I don't want to chatter about servants and coffee and food with him. I want to talk about us, about guilt and growing up. About Peony. He's the only one who'd ever understand, after all. He's the other set of footprints on my desert island.

'Tom,' I say, moving closer to him. 'When you first came back, was it strange? Remembering her?'

He raises an eyebrow, puzzled.

'Peony, I mean.' Her name sends a little shock through the air and I plunge on. 'Because I see her everywhere. It's like she hasn't gone, like she's been here all along just waiting for me to come back. Ammuma's even put a picture of her in the prayer room.'

He coughs. I wonder if he's going to tell me to forget it. To forget *her. It's just a picture, Durga; she was just Peony.* He might even say that it wasn't our fault she drowned, a fact which is both true and useless.

'That picture,' he says, fidgeting with his mug. He adjusts the collar of his sharp-ironed shirt and takes another gulp of coffee.

'Mary-Auntie didn't put it there.' He sounds very English all of a sudden, very foreign. 'I found it last year, in your bedroom.'

'In my bedroom? What, my bedroom *here*?'

A stupid question. He doesn't look at me and turns to the sink instead. He turns the tap on, waiting for the choke of air and water to pulse its way through.

'Why would you do that? What for?'

He leans towards me. 'So she doesn't get forgotten.' He sounds suddenly intense. 'She matters, Durga. Peony *matters*.'

I can feel the increase in heat, feel the skin on my arm prickle as the hairs rise to meet him. Water trickles off his arm and lands, blood-heat, on the back of my hand.

'She died because of us,' he says. 'Because of our stupid game. It's our fault.'

'Tom, I feel the same, honestly –'

'No, you don't! You ran off to Canada for ten years and you couldn't be bothered to come back till now. You forgot all about her.'

'I didn't!'

He's wrong, I want to tell him, wrong in every possible way. I stayed here for three years after Peony died, and every single day she was there in the stink of the swamp and the shadowed evenings. When I first went to Canada her face showed up in every snowfall and now I'm back here in Pahang she's lurking behind my bedroom mirror.

'I remember her *all the time*, Tom. You can't just assume –'

He shakes his head. 'Mary-Auntie's the same. When I mention Peony she just folds her lips tight – yes, exactly the same way you're doing now. Acting like she wasn't important.'

Which, coming from Tom, is certainly something. It wasn't me, after all, who ran away back to England immediately after the inquest. Who got to start all over again a thousand miles away without anyone whispering 'That's her!' in school.

'Who said you know anything about how I feel?' I burst out. 'How dare you turn up here and try to be some sort of big-man boss when . . . when – you haven't even seen me for fifteen years!'

'Durga, I –'

'You always think everything needs to be dragged out and talked about! You always want to be the one in charge!'

Who died and made you God? Peony asks. *Oh wait*, she says, *I know this one.*

Tom tries to calm me down, but it just makes things worse. I tell him that's not how things work here, and push his arms away. Just because we don't talk about something doesn't mean it's been forgotten, I insist. So why doesn't he just fuck off – go on, Tom, just leave – and go and be pretentious and self-absorbed with someone who can be bothered to listen.

'I thought you just said I shouldn't talk so much?' There's such an infuriating expression in his bright blue eyes that for a second I could nearly slap him. My hand's raised – in another life, in my ordered, sweet-talking Canadian life I wouldn't be able to believe myself – and then the compound bell rings.

We stop, rooted to the spot. After a few seconds it rings again, with a cheery ding-DING-ding-DING-DING. I drop my hand and we look away, both of us rearranging foolish faces.

'It's Mother Agnes,' I say.

I recognize her ring. She visits Ammuma a few times each week and since I've been back she's come here every day. She used to be our schoolteacher – born without a tongue but with plenty of opinions, Ammuma said, to make up for it. She stopped teaching a few years ago, and these days she looks as out of place as I feel.

I look over at Tom. Perhaps it's exhaustion or the throbbing ache in my head, but even the slight tucks of his chin seem beautiful to me. Skin like a fish, they say here about Europeans, but those creases below his neck look entrancing. Suddenly, I can't catch my breath.

'I'll leave,' he says. 'I'll let you talk to Agnes.'

Our fight's left me on edge. I'm trembling, with his sweat still on my skin where he held my arm. The lemon-sourness of it makes me want to lick at my own wrists, or bite at his.

'You don't need to go,' I say quickly. 'She's been here every day, she's just collecting donations for her left-behinds. She won't stay long.'

Mother Agnes took up charity a few years ago, after she left teaching. She works with the left-behinds, as Ammuma calls them. They're women who slipped through the cracks after the war and the Emergency, who live with their straggling families on the outskirts of the jungle near Lipis. They've no schooling, no future, and they're all – according to Ammuma – as bad as each other.

The bell rings again – ding-DING – and Tom steps back from the kitchen window, as though he doesn't quite want to be seen.

'Go on,' he says, giving me a little push towards the door. 'Agnes will want to ask about the fire anyway. And if she sees us together she'll only gossip, you know that.'

'What do you mean? Stop pushing me.' My head's starting to pound. I'm realizing how tired I am still. I could sleep for weeks. For months, for long enough for my hair and teeth to grow till they swallow me whole. Till I turn into one of Ammuma's froggish monsters, right here on the kitchen floor.

'Are you worried about being seen with me, is that it?' I ask.

Just like when we were twelve, I want to say, and you carved Peony's name on the outside of the desk and mine on the inside. Just like when you kissed her and not me on the first day of school, just like you always copied off her maths tests and not mine even though she got all her fractions wrong. I rub my eyes, pressing huge white circles into the blackness behind them.

'Of course not,' he says heartily. 'I want to see you again. But not here, though,' he adds. 'Somewhere private.'

There's an unpleasant, used-twice-over ring to that. Deepak used to say it too. I put that thought away, lock it up tight where it can't do any harm.

'Sunday, when you come to pick up Mary-Auntie,' he goes on, 'come to the hospital reception and ask for me.'

He pulls me closer, gives me a dry, squashed kiss, then breaks away. He hurries through the dining room to the back door just as

Mother Agnes rings the compound bell again. By leaning close to the window I can see her, standing there with her quiet mouth and her scandal-filled notebooks. I turn my back instead, looking out of the back door and watching Tom leave. It isn't so hard, not this time round.

After Peony's accident, I barely went outside for weeks. Mother Agnes came to see me, bringing school lessons and homework. She was the one to tell me Tom's family had left. His parents had packed in the night, she wrote to me; they'd run back to England and left behind whatever they couldn't carry. A single shoe. A watercolour picture. A pair of spectacles, as though they couldn't bear to look out through them again. Forced out at dawn, they must have thought bitterly, and after all they'd done for Malaysia. *Biting the hand that feeds them*, Mrs Harcourt would have wept and I can't say I blame her. Table manners, like languages, rarely travel well.

The bell's stopped ringing. Mother Agnes must have given up. I turn back to the sink and take my time wiping the dishes dry. The palms of my hands underwater are almost as pale as Tom's.

Skins are like stories, Mother Agnes used to say, *what matters is what's underneath*. A cheerful little proverb, but Ammuma had her own take on it. Peel the skin back, she said, and look for the fangs. I leave Tom's mug by the side, his name turned outwards. And then I pick up my anonymous white cup and drop it straight in the sink from as high as I can reach. It smashes with a satisfying crack and a slop of pale-brown coffee, and I wonder if Mother Agnes's left-behinds felt like this all along.

8.   The King and Queen Have Their Say: 1927

There's a type of mathematics called category theory. It's the mathematics of mathematics; the mathematics that describes everything else. The last resort.

It's also the simplest. A category is a collection of objects (say a Catherine wheel, a granddaughter, a grandmother and a drowned teenage ghost). And in every category there are relationships between the objects. Guilt, for example, links a granddaughter and a ghost. Or love: a dangerous arrow between mothers and daughters, one that might turn out to have too sharp a point.

Functors are one step further. A functor takes one category and turns it into a different one entirely. Swap out Durga for Mary, Peony for Cecelia. Swap Ammuma's dead daughter for a tiger-prince and his frog; the story's the same however you slice it.

There are different objects in your new category, if you dare to face up to them:

Smoke, thick enough to chew.

A banyan swamp, waiting patiently for the splash.

A gritty, billowing punch of ash or a smear of greenish slime on your dress. And then, of course, you might add in ambulances, inquests or worn-out young doctors, all with tempers and arrows of their own.

Some relationships are too hard to define. They pop up where you'd least expect. They're there; you just can't see them through the smoke.

*

Mother Agnes taught a generation of us mathematics, silently counting and adding up and taking away. She took her classes out into the playground; had them exchanging marbles for sweets and then swapping them back. If Sita gives Nadeem five apples, and Nadeem gives four away to Asha, how many nights will Sita cry herself to sleep? Divide by two, take away the number you first thought of and count up whether anyone really loved her at all.

★

If you're Mary at eleven years old, you don't put your faith in mathematics. Not once you've already survived one flood. Not once your parents have brought your brother home with the news that there's nothing the doctors can do. Any attempt at treatment would be too expensive, in any case. The numbers don't add up. If you're Mary, you might have had quite enough of numbers. You might want to give up on logic and work some bomoh magic of your own. Tell the story your own way.

Which is exactly what she's trying to do one evening, three months after the flood. The river's gone down by now and left the ground spongy, soft enough to swallow anything from a footprint to a village. Tiny green frogs spring from overturned trees, and the banyan swamp seethes with the flicker of tadpoles and leeches. Everything in the garden smells of rotting leaves and blocked sewers. Mary's in the middle of it all, kneeling in the flower bed.

She's playing dangerous games amongst those canna lilies, whispering spells she's made up herself. She's stolen a crucifix; she's scavenged chicken bones; she's taken magic words from her *Cinderella* and *Alice in Wonderland* books. But nothing's happened. So Mary's going to play her trump card, her mathematics of last resort. She's going to retell her parents' entire marriage. Take the story into her own hands, and see if she can't make it turn out better.

If Cecelia were around, she might have talked Mary out of it. But after the flood Yoke Yee forbade her daughter to see Mary again. (See what you get, Mary? With all your stories?) Mary, despite this, considers herself the injured party. Hasn't she been asked, again and again, about that turbulent night? And hasn't she insisted sweetly, again and again, that she'd simply forgotten Cecelia was there? At eleven, Mary's a picture of innocence and the grown-ups, a foot above her virtuous head, immediately agree to believe her. And if they have doubts – private, pit-of-the-night doubts – well, they keep it to themselves.

So Mary's trotted on under the gathering storms, concocting her games by herself. Today, though, Rajan's come to visit. He's fourteen now, tricky as a civet-cat and what he believes about that night of the flood, Mary will never know. He's leaning on the garden wall and watching Mary with a glint in his lazy eyes. She squats down, engrossed in positioning the scruffy blue rabbit she's brought out from her old toy box. Her Sarah-doll is here too, the wooden one with fully bendable limbs. Mary's too old to play with them, really, but right now she's poised above them; her grubby knees are spread, her incisors are glinting, and everything is about to become her fault.

'Appa,' she whispers. The rabbit, now christened, has become her father, Stephen, and she sets him down on a patch of swampy mud. It seeps into his blue fur, leaving him instantly stained and bedraggled. Stephen will never have much luck with dirt after this, will spend the rest of his life sending shirts to the laundry where Letchumani's father will turn in desperation to saltpetre and cuttlefish bile – firework ingredients if ever there were – to bleach them clean. Mary, you see, is already inclined to meddle.

While she's doing that, Rajan grabs the Sarah-doll, bending her into obscene positions and smirking at the sight of her spread-eagled limbs. He's old for his age, Rajan, and he's already persuaded Mary several times to shed her clothes and play doctor down here on the rotting leaf-mould. His probing fingers glide over the Sarah-doll until Mary feels her stomach hum inside as though someone's loosed a Catherine wheel between her legs.

'Put her down,' she demands.

Because the Sarah-doll will be her mother, Radhika, and Radhika's a well-brought-up girl. She can sing, her English is flawless, her legs are fully bendable and – thinks Mary doubtfully – perhaps she's hardly going to be impressed by a tatty blue rabbit with its ear half off.

Nevertheless, Mary hops Stephen up and over a bed of tufty fern and he leaps out into the sunlit flowers of Kerala, and back in time fifteen years. The doll and rabbit catch sight of each other and stop, bewildered by this sudden transformation.

'I – good morning.' Stephen knows he shouldn't address an unaccompanied girl; his Manchester engineering firm spent an extravagant sum on training him before letting him loose on the Empire. But he's hot; he finds the Kerala sun strangely penetrating as it soaks into his fine silky hair and steams his brain. Sweat trickles down his back and pools at his hips and all he'd like to do is get inside, away from all this liquid warmth. Into a cool, scraped-out burrow, he thinks vaguely and wonders why.

'Can you tell me the way back to Trichur?' he asks.

Radhika smiles. She's been watching Stephen come up over that grassy hill for a while now; she knows exactly how he can best get back to Trichur because she's followed him from there in the first place. She's clever, Radhika, with her arms and legs.

She's also – and this part is Mary's invention, an extra egg to her mix of fairy tale and memory – the reason Stephen's out in this heat at all. He left Trichur an hour ago, full of his English desire to take a good country walk. And in the middle of the cool backstreets near the outskirts of Trichur, he saw a white-walled villa barred with an iron gate. Unlike the baking dryness of the neighbouring houses, this one stood in cool, tar-black shadows that dripped like syrup from the coconut trees. A verandah ran around it, fenced in with lacy ironwork as delicate as frost. And behind that frost he saw Radhika.

Or at least, if Stephen's scrupulously truthful, he saw slices of Radhika through the iron gate: a round arm, a face, a lock of hair over a teal-blue sari. Nobody could feel passion for slices of a girl, but that dizzying shade of blue is a different matter. It's a wistful colour, a colour to remind Stephen of sun and sky and first love in Blackpool. A colour that doesn't wear well, not that Stephen would know. He fell in love with Radhika's clothes first, and only now, an hour later, does he start to appreciate her oiled hair and the way her bare feet swirl tiny, alert puffs of dust from between her toes. The thought of those toes excites him beyond bearing, and he leaks a little stuffing.

'Stop it!' Mary glares at Rajan, who's taken over her game and is tweaking the toys into compromising positions. Mary would like this to be a love story, a tiger-prince and his warrior princess, whose son will be flawless. She'd like hearts and henna, she'd like sweets and sangeet. She'd like a happy ending, because that's the whole point.

But it's too late; Rajan grabs the toy rabbit from her. He strokes its ears with a cool, firm grip; he smears mud in places no self-respecting rabbit would allow. Then he fluffs up its fur, leaves it staring and excited, and tumbles it down with the Sarah-doll into a damp hollow where the earth smells thick with sap. So – thanks to Rajan – Stephen and Radhika will think of lust instead of love and out of that lust will come sex and out of sex will come Mary and her removable clothes in the canna lilies. Rajan thinks ahead.

Under Rajan's sneaking fingers, Radhika obediently lifts her arm to point the way back and Stephen's mouth dries up. There's a small rip under the sleeve of her sari blouse, showing him an armpit creased with baby-fat and hair springing loose in tempting curls. The path she's pointing out is hardly more than a jungle trail, a sort of fold in the lushness of all that growth. No doubt it's full of hidden dangers, but Stephen summons up his courage. He takes her arm, bows, and offers to guide her along a path she knows perfectly well already.

*

Told the way Mary wants, her parents' courtship would be awash with nobility. Mary's fond of fairy tales, and she's done her reading. She knows that princes and princesses always get their happy endings. Their perfect children.

Rajan's different; he's a doctor's child, after all. He knows about blood, about bones, about shit and gristle and everything that holds a person together. If he weren't so good-looking he'd be terrifying. Perhaps he is, as he takes the toys from Mary's hands with a charming smile. Under his command her stories start to spin a little out of control, and her happy ending's looking further and further away.

*

Stephen, after his first meeting with Radhika, is determined to do the honourable thing. He's going to ask her for her hand in marriage. Two weeks later he hops up to her clean white house, his proposal already rehearsed. He calls a cheery greeting to the chauffeur, dark-skinned Joseph, oiling the last flecks of dirt from the gleaming sides of a bright red limousine.

'No, I only want *my* toys in the game. Not yours,' Mary objects, screwing up her face. She doesn't mind the bright red model car Rajan's brought along, but that flesh-coloured stick that he's set next to it is another thing entirely.

'It's a man's . . . you know,' Rajan tells her boldly. 'My father *amputated* it from a patient, after a leech stuck to it during the flood. It swelled up until my father had to cut it off.'

In fact, that purpling lump is only a rubber model that his father keeps as a prop for anatomy exams. It fascinates Mary. It's so different from Anil's harmless finger-length waggle at bath-time and different, too, from that enticing stir between Rajan's legs when she plays the doctor-and-nurse game. That game is certainly becoming serious – becoming thicker and hairier by the month – but it's nothing to this fleshy fistful.

'It can be the chauffeur,' Rajan says. 'Someone's got to drive the car.'

And indeed, somebody does. Because Radhika's mother and father welcome Stephen into the house with open arms. Over the next few weeks, Radhika's parents will embrace Stephen as part of their family, sending that hapless driver to tailors, to sweetshop owners and jewellers and bankers in preparation for their daughter's wedding. They love Stephen, they trim the dirt from his paws and the kinks from his fur, and give their daughter up into his hands.

But the fly in the ointment – the silverfish in the teal-blue sari – is that same driver. Joseph's a shy man with the instincts of a monk who's been employed by Radhika's parents for the last fifteen years. He keeps his eyes down when he passes girls, he takes ice-baths in winter and rice porridge in summer. He binds his loins with tight, swaddled cloths and tries to put lust out of his mind altogether, and despite all this he still throbs at every moment with a searing, carnal passion.

Unfortunately, Stephen himself doesn't. On his wedding night he's certainly panting, overcome with the night's heat and humidity and the sight of Radhika as creamy and sweet as toffee under her iridescent wrappings. At the same time, though, he can't help feeling a stab of regret when she slips out of her clothes. That sari was so colourful; it was ice-creams and innocence and suntan lotion on milky, freckled arms, and Stephen feels quite nostalgic over it. Naked, Radhika's desire is forceful, dripping and quite unladylike. Stephen does his best, which isn't quite enough, and the two roll apart in mutual frustration. Over the next few weeks he flails with an increasing desperation in bed each night, then rises red-eyed and irritable in the mornings to shower and go to work. Radhika prepares his lunch and waves goodbye without ever changing her threadwork frown. She hadn't been expecting a lack of passion in her marriage, and wonders if it's all her fault. She's started to doubt her body; her flexible limbs have stiffened and that frown is now definitely a scowl. She's begun to prefer reading magazines to books; she talks with a rather dreadful cheerfulness and she eats a little too much in the evenings. Life, it seems, has passed Radhika by.

It isn't until an ordinary day of marketing and housekeeping that things begin to change. She's leaning back on the leather seats of Joseph's car on the way to temple, fanning herself and spreading her thighs to catch the cool air. Joseph averts his eyes as he drives past a group of prim, tucked-in schoolgirls, and catches sight of Radhika in his rear-view mirror. She's neither prim nor tucked-in; she sprawls across the back seat with her legs splayed and a drop of sweat running down the valley of her breasts. Joseph loses control. He brakes, wrenches the car into a dusty dip where buffalo wallow in the summer and hurls himself onto the back seat.

It's a turbulent, thrusting moment; all biting and licking and eyes wide-open. Radhika surfaces for air, spreadeagled on the back seat with her clothes ripped off and her mouth swollen from kisses. Her limbs are bending and her smile's coming back and she's almost on the verge of happiness.

'What are you doing? That's disgusting! Give her back!'

Mary's wandered off to the swamp at the bottom of the garden, scratching at her ankle under one sloppy sock. She's not interested in all this sex and lust, not yet, although she did feel a stir of interest as she watched Rajan's fingers glide over that flesh-coloured prop. She wouldn't have minded touching it herself (and it would have done you no harm, Mary, being rubber through-and-through and a sight less dangerous than the alternatives) but she didn't want to say. So by the time she sees what Rajan's up to, he's already involved her toys in some distinctly adult behaviour.

'Stop it!' She's been playing skip-hop with some flattened rocks, and without thinking, she hurls one of them straight at Rajan's head. The rock smacks straight into his forehead, splitting the skin open and sending a trickle of blood down onto the toys. It isn't a horrific cut, nothing that a bit of mercurochrome and a bandage won't heal. But a few drops land in the toy car, on the very spot where Radhika's virginity has left a crimson spatter on the upholstery.

And, of course, that crimson spatter is going to spell trouble. Blood on the back seat can only mean one thing, when there's a wife who's still a virgin. Even more so when there's a chauffeur with lustful tendencies he's tamping down like a firework. Stephen finds that giveaway blood on the back seat of the car on a

71

sunny summer's evening, and he leaps to conclusions that are regrettably correct. Hands are raised, voices are raised, tempers are raised. Six months later, he and Radhika will leave for Malaya in a welter of tearful apologies and unspoken resentments.

'You've ruined my game,' Mary says. 'You've ruined the magic.'

And so he has. Mary's been trying to start again, to rewrite history and hope it turns out better this time. But the problem with history is that it gets its own way, somehow or other. And now, thanks to Rajan, Mary's right back where she started with two miserable parents and a little brother who can't speak. Or perhaps not quite where she started, because from now on she'll know to keep a tight grip on her stories. Dead daughters and absent granddaughters and speechless schoolteachers notwithstanding, Mary's going to fight history every step of the way.

'Your schoolteacher was born without a tongue? How on earth did she teach?'

It's Sangeeta, latching on to the least important part of yesterday. She's comforting to talk to, but the longer the conversation goes on, the stranger I feel. Her Canadian accent, a radio playing Madonna in the background, even the muffled sounds from the tennis courts outside her apartment. It's all familiar, but it doesn't fit into *now*. It's like something I've seen in a movie. I settle back onto the old cotton sofa where I used to read comic books, and prop the telephone receiver against my shoulder.

'She wrote on the board. Threw chalk, if we were talking. It wasn't really a problem, she was just Mother Agnes. Anyway,' I add, 'she doesn't teach now. She does charity.'

'Oh yes, you said.' Sangeeta opens one of the Cokes she's always drinking. I can hear the hiss and snap of the chilled can. 'The left-alones or something?'

'Left-behinds. Fallen women, I guess you'd call them. A lot of them were girls who never got to go back to school when everything reopened at the end of the war. Or girls who got raped, or took up with Japanese soldiers.'

Disgraces, in other words. Sangeeta – who prides herself on being a bit of a disgrace too – clicks her tongue.

'Those poor women.'

Sangeeta sympathizes most easily with victims, with frail and fragile women a safe distance away. But men can be left-behinds too, though it's harder to explain. Sons who never got over the war, perhaps, or fathers who didn't even try. They're not a lost generation, because *lost* implies finding, *lost* implies the possibility of a happy ending. The left-behinds, on the other hand, have been completely erased. Out here, people will look you in the eye and say loudly they never had a daughter, never had a son, no father at all. A neighbour, perhaps, or a cousin – they'll unbend so far as to admit one of them might have disappeared, but they'll keep their howling behind closed doors. Grief strolls undercover in Pahang.

'So anyway, tell me about this Tom guy. You knew him when you were a kid?'

She's most interested in Tom, of course. He's real, with his beginnings all nicely explicable. He doesn't need a history lesson to be understood.

'Best thing you could do,' she'd said roundly when I told her I'd had sex with him. But I'm not so sure. In Canada it might be fine to replace Deepak straight away – Sangeeta's own boyfriends come in such quick succession that occasionally they've overlapped – but not here. Things don't move slower here, whatever Sangeeta thinks. Virtue, for example, goes quicker than you can think.

'Do you think it'll go anywhere with you guys?'

I don't know, I tell her, staring at a chik-chak scampering across the wall. This conversation's hard work for us both. So many good intentions, but none of them quite getting across.

'Still, it's great to hear your grandmother's doing good,' Sangeeta says cheerfully. 'She's being discharged tomorrow, right?'

'I hope so,' I say. 'I left a message with the university in KL. I said I'd be there on Tuesday at least, maybe Monday.'

She laughs. 'You're neurotic about that job. Like that postdoc – Peter? From last year here, the one who barely left his office. I kept finding him asleep under his desk at 4 a.m. surrounded by McDonald's wrappers.'

I do remember, though quite what Sangeeta was doing in Peter's office at 4 a.m. herself was never explained. She's the kind for assignations, for secret meetings with unsuitable men, and I've half-suspected she might have been under the desk with Peter and the cheeseburgers herself.

When we talk about her instead, the scratchiness between us dies down. This is something we have words for, at least. Sangeeta's had a paper accepted; she's got another one planned. She's had an argument with her current boyfriend, something complicated about a sports game that ended with Sangeeta going off to a bar with the entire losing side. 'He said I could at least have picked the winners!' she complains, and laughs in lovely, clean lines. She tells me about an outside world humming with hockey matches and love matches and when she rings off, I feel brighter than I've done in days.

I look at myself in the hall mirror and see a face that's softer than I remember. No monsters creeping round the edges of that skin, no leprosy, not even any crow's feet. Just a few aches from rolling under Tom on the prayer-room floor, and I grin at my reflection. I tie my hair up in a plait, put my prettiest skirt and blouse on. I'd wear emerald trousers if I had them, I'd wear Cutex nail polish and a John Lennon haircut. It's that sort of a day.

I fill two buckets of water at the sink and hunt around for one of Karthika's scrubbing brushes. We'll need to scrub the walls down, as high as we can reach, and drag the wooden benches and settees out into the compound yard to air. Luckily, the fire was caught and held in the closed-off wings that nobody ever goes into, but everything still stinks of smoke. Upstairs, the door leading to those shut-up corridors is blackened and cool. I try not to think of what's behind it. Mountains of soft ash and clinker. Remains, destruction. Things that used to be things, before I stepped in.

I dip the scrubbing brush in the water and let it trail a dribbling stream behind me until I get to the stairs. Scrubbing helps, a little, and as the smoke moves from the walls to the dirty water in my bucket I start to feel happy again. Perhaps this is something that can be fixed after all.

After an hour I stop, emptying my last bucket outside. The Jelai's subsided back behind its banks, after being subdued upstream with sandbanks and earth walls. Licking its wounds; it'll be back. In the meantime, though, it's quiet and a stiff breeze swoops over it and takes the smoke from the rooms.

I stack the buckets by the kitchen door and go back to the scrubbed-clean stairs. Ammuma's being discharged tomorrow, and I'll need to find somewhere for her to sleep. Her room's coated in a deep grey soot, and even if it were intact I don't know if she can manage stairs. I remember she always used to keep sleeping mats in the box room upstairs, and on the way there I stop to peer through a circular window set at ankle-height on the landing. It's the only one in the house with glass instead of wooden shutters and it was once my favourite place in the world. I used to sit here to do my arithmetic homework, when that was all I had to worry about.

Looking through it now, I see Ammuma's had covers nailed over both the wells outside. She used to tell stories about ghost women living in those wells, long-haired girls still clutching broken crockery or the sarong kebayas they were trying to wash. Perhaps they're the reason for the covers; ghost women aren't the sort of thing you want popping out at you, not at an age when your own reflection can give you a nasty turn.

The box room's a tiny partition off Ammuma's room, next to the attic ladder. I push the door open and the sleeping mats are right there, piled against three rickety shelves. It looks like she's been storing hardware in here too. Two of the shelves jostle with bottles of glue, screwdrivers and plastic tubs full of batteries.

The third shelf is empty, except for a clean plastic bag with something sticking out of it. I peer closer at it, and nearly scream. It's hair – a hank of hair – and then I see it's attached to a china doll inside the bag. The doll's brown-skinned and Indian, in a glittery blue satin sari. It has brown glass eyes and it's moulded into a cross-legged shape like someone about to pray. They used to sell these dolls in the shops in Lipis, I remember. I haven't seen one in years.

There's a sudden clatter downstairs and I jump. 'Hello?'

'Mary-Madam?'

It's Karthika, arriving for the day. Of course, I remember, she has a baby now – she must have bought this toy for him. I hurry out of the box room, closing the door behind me.

Karthika's downstairs, wearing a red nylon skirt and a yellow blouse too big for her. She looks awkward, lumpish and bulging at her waist. Pregnant again, I think, and clamp down on the thought.

She's dragging her mop into the hall bathroom with its scoop-bucket shower and squat toilet.

'Oh, Karthika – please don't – don't worry about cleaning that bathroom today,' I tell her. 'We'll need to scrub upstairs and air the furniture out in the yard. I'm sorry, I hope that's OK . . .'

Her mouth hangs open, with a sullen question flat on her tongue. I'm still uneasy with her after four days back here. She was part of my world, like Ammuma and the kitchen cats, and now I can't even remember how to talk to her. I'm too tentative – I ask her if she'd mind doing things – and she resents it. She prefers Ammuma, who scolds and blames impartially. A girl knows where she is with Ammuma.

'Mary-Madam isn't here?' she asks.

'No,' I say, and she drops her mop and walks away into the kitchen. Her bare feet slap on the hall floor. She doesn't ask any more questions; it's all the same to her whether Ammuma's in KL or buried in the canna lilies. She's learnt to set boundaries, to keep out of things.

She wasn't always like this. I remember her arriving bundled on Vellaswamy-cook's hip, back when I was four years old. In those days she was all smiles and chubby arms, stealing off with my favourite dolls. And I remember pre-teenage Karthika, too, giggling with me as she Blu-tacked magazine movie-star pictures to the kitchen walls. But this grown-up Karthika is a blinking, resentful shadow in a blouse a size too big. She got herself pregnant – worse, she got herself talked about. *Could be her own father, own brother*, Ammuma told me over the phone last year. *These Tamils, ar, live like kampong cats*. There'd have been a certain smacking of lips over it, a licking of chops.

After a few seconds I hear the grainy sound of Milo being spooned out. Ammuma would slap her for that, would smack the Milo tin from her hands and throw the spoon onto the rubbish. I walk into the kitchen and she doesn't look up. She's sucking dry Milo off the spoon and holding the tin clutched tight. I want to tell her I'm on her side, to ask if she remembers those baby days when she roosted herself down next to the water buckets and made faces at me through the kitchen window. Possibly she doesn't; the memory has a slippery quality to it. A fragility, as though it might not stand up to recollection.

'Would you like biscuits, Karthika?' I ask. 'Or soft drink? Tea?'

I see her shoulder blades tense. 'What you wanting, Durga-Miss?' she asks in Tamil. 'You wanting me to clean it?'

She points at a thickening line of ants under the table and slips the Milo tin further under her arm. 'You have to clear, first.' She folds her other arm over her slack belly and nods at the table.

'No, I mean, I wasn't going to ask . . .'

I trail off, and we both stare down at the table. It's littered with things I picked up as I pottered about yesterday. Books, gold dupatta thread, a pair of tarnished earrings that had once been favourites. Some of them might even be the same trinkets Karthika and I once played dress-up with; licking sequins and clapping them to our earring studs as make-believe jewels that were shinier than any Karthika owned. We were friends of a sort, for as long as the sequins stuck.

'Here, Durga-Miss.' Karthika gets heavily to her feet, picking up her Milo tin and spoon. 'I show you how.'

She gathers a few spoons up from the table. Ostentatiously, exaggerating each gesture: this is how you keep a house clean, Durga-Miss. If you had one to clean, that is. By Karthika's lights I'm one step behind her; no house, no husband and not even a baby to show for it.

'See, I'll wash.' She takes the spoons to the stone sink then stops abruptly. Her ashy elbows brace outwards under her slippery yellow blouse.

'Wrong mug you used, Durga-Miss?'

She holds up Tom's coffee mug from yesterday. I've left it in the sink, not being quite ready to scrub the print of his lips off.

'Oh! That was . . . a friend of mine. He came for coffee,' I say.

Karthika raises her eyebrows. 'Tom-Mister was here?'

'Oh, you know . . . of course you do. Yes, he was here.' Of course she knows Tom.

I reach out to take the mug from her but she doesn't let go, not until our fingers meet on the cold china handle. She pulls away then, glaring up at me from mutinous eyebrows and muttering a sullen apology for touching.

'When did he come?' she asks. She doesn't look at me, just picks at a scab on her chin as though the answer either matters far too much or not at all.

'Yesterday,' I say again. I give her a tentative, appeasing smile, the way I've seen rich ladies do to beggars in the Ontario train station.

'There was a fire,' I say. 'That's what made all the smoke, all this stuff we've got to clean up.' Pointing at the walls and the floor in a kind of dumb show. I can tell I'm too loud, too excruciatingly patient and I tumble into sarcasm. 'You did *notice*?'

'Sorry, Durga-Miss.' She shakes her head, half-insolent and wholly polite. It's not her job to notice things.

'I took Mary-Madam to hospital, and Tom came here afterwards,' I explain. It sounds reasonable, put like that, but Karthika bristles, puffing herself like a fighting cock.

'You shouldn't see him alone, Durga-Miss,' she says with a veiled prudishness. 'Mary-Madam wouldn't like.'

'That's enough,' I tell her, more sharply than I'd meant. 'You don't know anything about it.'

'I know Tom-Mister,' she snaps back. 'He sees me, too, he likes to see me, Durga-Miss. He visits me too, not Mary-Madam only.'

She says this with a sly smile, standing there barefoot in her oversized blouse and picking at her teeth. It's hard to tell what she means; Karthika's English isn't good, and after ten years my

Tamil's worse. *To visit*, she said, or perhaps – but surely not? – to *stay with*. To involve; a reflexive verb that implies choice. You got yourself into this, on your own head be it.

She turns her back, dumping the plates into the sink and scrubbing them viciously. I set the mug back down on the table. Tom was holding this only yesterday, I think. Before we kissed, after we had sex. Before Karthika greased her smile all over the memory.

'Clean all this up, please,' I tell her, raising my voice. 'This kitchen's too filthy to cook in.'

She doesn't reply. She used to eat our leftovers, I remember, always one meal behind us and never mind where it was cooked. I've whipsawed from too lenient to too harsh; I'm out of place and she knows it. Quarrelling with the servant-girl, just like a foreigner would.

I take a deep breath.

'Karthika,' I say. 'I found that doll of yours. In the box room. Is it for your . . . the baby?'

She shakes her head. 'No, Durga-Miss. I don't know what you mean.'

'The doll, Karthika. The one in the box room. In the plastic bag?'

'Not mine,' she says again. 'I don't know this doll. Ask Mary-Madam.'

And then she turns her back, busying herself with the kitchen. She picks everything up; turns the cups round and moves the plates an inch to the left. She isn't dusting or reorganizing; she's just leaving her mark. It's a kind of graffiti: *I was here*. She's proving herself, in front of me.

I step back into the dining room and I can see her shoulders relax. I've brushed against the almirah door and it's swung open. The thought of Tom's bag of fireworks on the top shelf comes to me, and I reach up to push it further back. I wouldn't put it past Karthika to pry.

I shove the bag back amongst the left-over cutlery and tin cups, pushing a little too hard. It falls, rockets and pop-pops spilling out onto the floor in a scatter of bright plastic. Some paper falls out too – a permit, so he did have one all along – and something that looks like a small notebook. It's a pink autograph book, a child's toy. It's decorated with pastel angels which I recognize from Sanrio adverts as Little Twin Stars. It looks new but the cover's stained with dirt and towards the back the pages feel sticky and clumped.

I turn it over, puzzled, and open the inside cover. There's a piece of paper glued there and inscribed in Ammuma's swooping handwriting. This Book Belongs To: And then, below, a name.

Francesca Panikkar.

Kampung Ulu, Pahang

Malaysia, Earth, THE WORLD

I stop. My heart feels suddenly louder, a thumping drum against my ears. My mother, my Amma. Francesca.

I stand like that for a moment, until the sound of Karthika's noisy washing-up brings me back. Ammuma used to keep a tin of Francesca's toys and books in the box room – the Amma-tin, I used to call it – and perhaps this is something from that collection. But I'm nearly sure that it fell from Tom's bag, not the almirah shelf. I frown and turn to the front cover to read the address again.

Kampung Ulu. *Peony*, my mind hisses, but I tamp that down. Kampung Ulu's only an hour away from here, but Francesca – unlike Peony – wouldn't ever have gone there. When my mother was young enough to have a book like this Malaya would have been under Japanese occupation. And then after the war, during the Emergency, Kampung Ulu was in the middle of the black areas. Nowhere you'd go on a pleasure trip.

I look at it again, more doubtfully this time. I remember all Francesca's books in the Amma-tin being faded, but this one looks brand new. Perhaps it's been preserved for all those years, hidden away here from silverfish and moths on the very topmost shelf. But no, it can't have been. Little Twin Stars is modern. It wasn't around when my mother was small. It wasn't around when she died, come to that.

I shiver. This is a new book, one which never belonged to Francesca at all. Ammuma must have asked Tom to buy it, just like the bowl of sweets and the flowers on the shrine. It's an offering. It's a present. It's a reason to write her daughter's name.

I close the cover slowly. There's a curl of guilt inside me, shifting and layered as milk ice. When I was a child I'd always assumed Francesca was mine: *my* mother. I'd never thought about her being a daughter too. And then I flew off to Canada, leaving Ammuma alone with her ghosts. Well, she's got her revenge, at least. I have my own ghost now – Peony, behind my eyes and under my skin – and I can finally see what Ammuma must have known all along. Francesca and Peony are the holes in our story; the silence between our words.

There's a sudden cry from the kitchen and I jump. It's high-pitched, and doesn't sound like Karthika. I shove the book and the fireworks back into the almirah, latch it tight and hurry through the doorway. Karthika's still standing by the sink. The soles of her feet are flat on the cool concrete floor and her shoulders gleam where her blouse has slipped off. She's holding a baby, strapped tight to her body under that oversized yellow shirt.

She doesn't look at me as I come in, setting the child down onto the ground with a queer, head-ducking defiance. He's a scrap of feet and fists swaddled in cloth and I feel a rush of pity for her. A hundred years ago Karthika could have explained a baby away with no harm to her reputation: the father was a prince; the father was a ghost; the father was an orang minyak, an oily skinned jungle spirit who terrified young girls at night. But not nowadays. Pahang's always had time for stories, but these days the villains are girls like Karthika themselves. The baby howls, beating at the floor with tiny, furious slaps from inside his wrappings. She pulls the swaddlings away from him and lets him crawl out of the kitchen before giving me a sly, slipping smile.

He's not what I expected. Karthika's skin is ashy and dark, but the child has blunt-nosed features and skin pale as rice-paper. It looks like Ammuma was wrong about one thing, at least; Karthika's found herself a lover as far removed as possible from her brother or her uncles. This baby looks like a Mat Salleh. He's almost white.

'Karthika? He's . . .'

'He's what, Durga-Miss?'

Not what I expected. Our eyes meet and she knows just what I'm thinking. I don't need words to tell her that a half-white baby must have spelt trouble for someone like her. She doesn't need words to understand it either. That baby has a story behind it, and one that won't have a happy ending.

Karthika hangs her wet tea-towel over the tap carefully, then turns away from me and walks out without a word.

'Rajneesh!' she calls.

The baby's crawled through the front room and out onto the verandah. I watch from the front-room doorway as he totters over to the prayer-room door. Karthika strolls over, her footsteps loud, and bumps the prayer-room door open with her hip. Rajneesh thrusts one hand out to the sweets in front of Francesca's shrine, but she doesn't even look down at him. She's watching me instead.

'Your great-great-grandmother slept in there, Rajneesh. In the prayer room.' She says this loudly, in Malay, slow enough that I'll understand. 'You're not allowed in there, not now. Durga-Miss thinks I've been leaving dolls and toys around for you. She thinks you *have* toys.'

'Karthika . . .'

'But your great-great-grandmother went in there, Rajneesh. With Mary-Madam's father, to sleep.' She raises her voice, buttoning up her blouse with a sneer. 'She was a pelacur. She had a baby, a little one just like you.'

A pelacur, she says. A whore.

It nearly – incongruously and unforgivably – makes me smile. Karthika first told me about that wicked great-grandmother of hers when she was barely older than Rajneesh herself. She'd overheard it, hanging around Vellaswamy-cook's knees in his village while the adults talked. It became our delicious secret, this knotting together of grandparents and great-grandparents in an olden-days romance.

As we got older though, it turned into an injustice. *We ought to be sisters*, Karthika started telling me, *I've just as much right here as you*. Ammuma banished her from the dining table to eat with Vellaswamy-cook off a tin plate in the compound yard, but that didn't stop her from talking when we were alone. It ought to be *her* playing with the toys and dolls, Karthika used to say, it ought to be *her* putting out the puja offerings and giving the servant-girl some watered-down Milo. Ammuma slapped her for that, sending her dinner on its tin plate flying.

'Don't listen to her,' Ammuma warned me sternly after that. 'There's no relationship, nothing that counts in the blood and in the bone. She's not your sister. She's trouble, through and through.'

Go back fifty-odd years and Mary's in trouble of her own. She's fifteen years old, it's the morning of her Junior Cambridge exam and things have taken a difficult turn. It's a dull and heavy day, with a jungle haze thick as twice-boiled sugar. Mary's sitting in the nursery – the latest nursery, a green and sappy room at the end of a hallway that Stephen keeps adding to and lengthening – and she's clutching Anil's hand. At nine years old Anil still doesn't speak much, but he's learnt to hold his breath when things don't go his way. His face purples, darkens, takes on the waxy look of dead flesh. He's rejecting everything from the outside world, even its air.

Radhika's finally given up on him and handed the entire problem of motherhood over to her own daughter. *You deal with him, Mary*, she murmurs nowadays, and turns away. These days she sees much more of the servant-girl than her own children. The servant-girl is a runaway, a teenager called Paavai who turned up begging one evening and never left. Paavai sleeps in the room just off the verandah, when she isn't wanted by Radhika to wash dishes or clean out the drains. She smells of blood, of meat that's been left to ferment and coins that have tarnished. Of bomoh magic, Mary thinks fearfully. She doesn't trust Paavai, not day-Paavai who shovels out the chamber-pot or night-Paavai who giggles behind closed doors.

Mary and Anil have become much closer in the last few years. Mary visits the nursery every morning before school, easing Anil into the dawn by reciting lists of kings, of historic victories and longest rivers and the twelve-times table. On this particular morning, she tucks the mosquito net up over his bed and only realizes she's late when she catches sight of her father's watch hooked over a twig by the windowsill.

Stephen has a habit of taking off his watch and cufflinks while he works, tapping a floorboard here and hammering a wall-panel there. The house has become his hobby. He could go to the newly opened Pahang Club instead, a haven for Europeans to drink gin pahits and bemoan the state of the rubber market. But Stephen, with his Indian wife, his not-quite-pretty daughter and his silent son, doesn't fit in with the Pahang Club. So instead he hammers away at his house, shirtsleeves rolled high. He ignores Mary, and barely even notices Anil. But Anil loves his father nonetheless and scuttles from room to room each evening in search of him. Nowadays Mary often finds her brother sleeping in a corridor she could swear she's never even seen, with his undersized fists forlornly clutching a watch and cufflinks.

Mary picks up the watch and blows a kiss to her brother's bed. It's nine o'clock, and she hoists herself hurriedly out of the window. It's not ladylike, but these days – with new corridors curling round the place, with fathers and sons lost between one room and the next, with mothers and wives and servant-girls squabbling on the verandah – well, quite frankly, it's easier to get out from a window than find the front door.

Mary hurries away from the house, trampling ferns and touch-me-nots as she runs down the jungle path towards school. Leaves fall into her collar and itchy pitul seeds cling to her skirt, but she doesn't have time to shake them off. She's late, and by now all the other children will have gathered on the edge of the padang for the Junior Cambridge examinations. They'll all be clutching slide rules and pencils, they'll all be murmuring formulae and dates. Mary takes a flying leap over a hidden ditch and stumbles out amongst them all onto the short-cropped grass of the padang. There's Anna Fuertes, who's fifteen years old and already promised to the convent. There are Kumar and Kaya, poverty-stricken twins from two districts away. There's Cecelia, sitting cross-legged on the grass. And there, sitting next to Cecelia and quizzing her from her mathematics book, is Rajan.

Rajan isn't taking the Junior Cambridge examination today; he already passed three years ago with flying colours and is now a first-year medical student at Raffles College in Singapore. He should be in his own classes right now, probing a tumour on a beggar-woman or helping stitch up an estate-worker's severed hand. But he's taken a leave of absence instead, and he's been spending the last few weeks attending rallies up and down the length of Malaya. Rajan, in common with hundreds of other Malayan Indians, has been bitten by the bug of nationalism. He's been marching with Tamils, with Malayalis, with Sikhs and Gujaratis – half of whom he despises and nine-tenths of whom he can't understand – for Indian rule over India, a country he's never even seen. He's dropped into Lipis for a day on his way to a rally to support Ramasamy, the Tamil nationalist preacher. And Cecelia's taking full advantage of it.

'Cecelia, I thought *we'd* be partners,' Mary bursts out. She and Cecelia always used to pair up in that tense half-hour before examinations in order to make use of the last – the very last – ounce of their failing bond. Mary would memorize the beginning of every equation and Cecelia the end, their lips moving unconsciously together. But these days, Cecelia won't play.

'I would have studied with you,' Cecelia explains. 'But you were late.'

Perhaps it's not surprising. Cecelia, like everyone else in Kuala Lipis, has come to accept that Mary didn't mean to leave her to the flood. But despite that, she's still got a lot to forgive her old friend for and she's always been the kind to hold a grudge. So now she looks right through Mary and turns away, thrusting her chemistry book and her bare knees under Rajan's nose.

'Test me again?' she asks.

Mary turns on her heel with a sob. Her skirt swirls, and some of those irritating pitul seeds fly off to land on Cecelia's bare knees. *Serves you right*, Mary thinks.

She stalks off into the schoolhouse. It's a solid building, with arched doorways and low windows. The classrooms are bright with sun, and in front of one of the doorways is a nun sitting quietly in those sunbeams. It's Sister Gerta, who's come down from the hilltop convent to help supervise the examinations today. Gerta's spent her whole life in one Malayan convent or other, wearing shirts of undyed cotton and skirts rough as gunny sacks. At twenty years old she sprouted a distressing and luxurious moustache, by twenty-five her chins overlapped and spilled down like dewlaps and now at thirty her face is peaceably ugly. She's the kindest woman Mary will ever know, and right now her eyes are brimming with sympathy at the sight of Mary's melancholy face.

'Mary! Child, you can't go in yet. That's the examination room.'

The examinations are being set up in the rooms behind Sister Gerta and two masters inside chat unintelligibly as they lay out papers for the English conversation assessment.

'Come, child, sit next to me here. Everything will be all right.'

Sister Gerta likes to console. She has a kind of grim cheerfulness, an invincible way of looking on the bright side. She gives Mary a radiant smile and bounces what looks like a bundle of rags on her lap.

'What's that?' Mary asks. She sits down, crossing her legs in their sloppy white socks. Next to Sister Gerta's thick and pasty shins, Mary's ankle bones look delicate. She admires them for a second.

'This? This is Agnes.'

Sister Gerta pulls back one of the folds of cloth on her lap, and Mary sees a little face peering out at her. Agnes looks about a year old, with a round Chinese face contorted into what ought to herald an ear-splitting scream. It ought to be loud enough to drown out the English masters, to overpower the murmur of dates and formulae from outside – if it weren't for the fact that baby Agnes apparently decides against it. She waves her fists instead, she turns purple and arches her back; she has, in fact, a thoroughly satisfying tantrum, and all completely silent.

'She doesn't make a sound, the cherub. Not one word.' Sister Gerta bounces Agnes up and down on her fat thighs, and gives Mary one of the sweetest smiles she's ever seen.

'Neither does my brother,' admits Mary with a shamefaced little shrug.

'Still, he's God's child, isn't he? And what a good sister you must be to him, too.'

Mary doesn't get much praise these days – she's at that awkward age of knuckly hands and bony knees, of strange new breasts and hips that don't stay within their bounds. She wriggles a little and blushes, letting Gerta coax out of her that she *is* looking forward to the examination being over, that she *does* like English conversational practice, that she *would* like to be a nun when she grows up. Anna Fuertes, standing at the end of the corridor, gives her a fierce glare; Anna is truly, deeply religious, and she knows all too well that impious little Mary is a sham.

Sister Gerta, on the other hand, believes Mary implicitly. All her chins beam with delight, and she digs into her scanty blouse to find a sweet and a string of rosary beads. She presses both into Mary's hands.

'For your darling little brother.'

Perhaps it's the rattle of those beads that attracts Cecelia's attention. Perhaps it's Mary's squeak of surprise. Perhaps it's bad luck, pure and simple. But whatever the cause, Cecelia's tangled black head pops through the low hall window opposite Mary.

'Mary? Rajan wants you to come and study with us.'

Cecelia herself doesn't want it, and she makes that plain enough. Her eyebrows are drawn together in a don't-you-dare glare that pins Mary to her seat. But then Rajan comes up beside her, looking curiously at both the girls. Mary looks away, but Cecelia twitches her mouth into a witchy little smile. It's an enchanting curl of her lips, calculated to tell Rajan she's the sort of girl to forgive floods and failures and every scrap of guilt that's ever flown into her best friend's heart.

And it does the trick. Rajan – who's practical, who likes his girls inclined to forgiveness and smiles – slips a groping hand under the pleats of her skirt. He frees the very last pitul from her waistband, and it drops to chafe her fat little thighs. Cecelia jumps, half-turns, and the full force of her lovely smile misses Mary and lands straight on baby Agnes.

*

Agnes has had a poor enough start in life, so far. She's only a year old, but her problems began long before she was born. Her problems began, in fact, forty years ago, when leprosy first came to Pahang. It spread slowly at first, then snaked down Mount Tahan in an epidemic. Old men and women died of it, then the young. A few of the prettier girls jumped off cliffs or down wells when they saw the first lesions on their beautiful skins, and passed the disease through the water supply to their plainer sisters. Drowned women in wells: there's always more than one explanation.

And into this welter of missing limbs and missing noses came baby Agnes, missing her tongue. Not that that had anything to do with leprosy, other than as the most unfortunate coincidence. Leprosy isn't hereditary and babies aren't born with it, but nevertheless that coincidence looked bad for Agnes. Here she was, lying on a blanket and playing with her toes, and it was anyone's bet when one of them would come off, too.

The bomohs, of course, said her birth was a message. In those years, the bomohs said everything was a message. Babies in particular, especially those with missing limbs or a frill of superfluous fingers. According to the bomohs, those babies were saying: your padi-crop will fail; your wife will run off with the satay hawker; you will die of leprosy. An offering, the bomohs said – gold perhaps, or some tender roast meat or a brand-new jacket – might just avert the catastrophe.

Agnes's parents, though, had nothing to spare. No gold, no roast meat, and the only new jacket was the one they'd bought for their precious baby daughter before they knew she would never speak. But keeping Agnes would be the utmost in bad luck, in sheer wilful carelessness. So they did the next best thing: parcelled

Agnes up and turned her into an offering herself. Not to the bomohs, but to the newly opened convent.

So Agnes, only a year old when Mary first sees her, will grow up silent and religious. Owing to the nuns' stern conviction that she was never a messenger – such a pagan idea – nothing she says will ever be believed. *A storm is coming*, she'll write on her slate, and the nuns will ignore her and go out without umbrellas. Or *Sister Margaret is stealing the communion wine*, and nothing will be done until four weeks later Sister Margaret turns up dead drunk at Mass.

And then, when Agnes gets older, she'll write: *God is telling me to build a school*. Sister Agnes – as she will be then – won't even try to convince the other nuns of the truth of this. She'll take herself off instead to a tumbledown house with blocked-up storm drains. Once there she'll sweep the floors with palm leaves, darn up the holes in the attap roof and fill the desks with children. They'll be straight-limbed children, all of them, with clear skin and no diseases at all. Because, at the same time as Mother Agnes is setting up her school, the government will start an initiative of its own.

The National Leprosy Control Programme will be born in the 1960s, designed to wipe out all those doomed, disfigured women and mutilated men. And as part of the programme, the government will import a doctor into Pahang; in fact they'll import Dr Harcourt all the way from the Liverpool School of Tropical Medicine with his wife and ten-year-old son Tom. Tom, whose John Lennon hair will flop in the heat and who'll kiss Mary's granddaughter and Mary's granddaughter's best friend and anyone else who'll let him.

11. Sunday, 12 p.m.

There are only a few spaces left in the hospital car park, all of them in the full sun. I'm baking in my best silk sari and a pair of jewelled sandals that have been in my room since I was seventeen. They've got tighter, or I've got fatter, and I can feel a roll of skin peeling off my heel. I spent an hour last night trying to wear them in, pacing up and down the hall that Karthika and I had swept clean. Time enough to talk myself into being more attracted to Tom than I am. Time enough to plan a happy ending, to decide it was love at first sight. By now I'm less certain, first sight being less reliable than hindsight.

But still, I'm excited enough to arrive early. My heart's beating faster, with a smile trembling under my skin and a splash of jewels under my dupatta. The nurse behind the reception desk gives me a friendly look. Her white uniform's too small, bulging at the seams, and her dark skin's blotched with acne. She looks like someone I can cope with, someone I could even feel sorry for in this glow of best-frock-jewels-lipstick. Poor girl; she can't help it; she's doing her best.

'Can I help you?' she asks.

'I'm here to see Tom Harcourt. I'm Durga Panikkar.'

She frowns. 'Do you work here, Miss . . . Doctor? Panikkar?'

She sounds doubtful, as well she might. Doctors don't shiver like this, like new milk over a flame. They don't pulse and breathe inside gold-embroidered saris that are just a shade too tight. Doctors, unlike mathematicians, have their bodies sternly under control.

'No, I'm a friend of his. He's expecting me.'

She gets out a clipboard, running her finger down the list. She has good nails, neat and well shaped. She's not the kind to bite at them, to worry herself to the quick. She reaches the end of the list, pauses, starts again at the top.

'I'm sorry, there isn't anything here. Are you sure he knows you're coming?'

I swallow. 'Yes . . . yes, he knows. He does know.'

'I'm sorry. I can't let you up.' Her smile's less personal now. I'm becoming a problem. 'If you take a seat, though, I can get you something to drink. Tea, coffee, biscuits?'

She sounds practised, as though she's seen all this before. Perhaps she has. Other overdressed girls, left on her hands to console with tea and cake.

'No, no, it doesn't matter. I just popped in,' I tell her. My face is hot and when I give her a smile my mouth feels large and numb. 'On the off-chance.'

She looks relieved, and now my lips and cheeks hurt but I keep on smiling. I hold my head up and walk back to the car in my stupid, pinching shoes. I can see the nurses' hostel, with washing draped over the balconies and steam rising from rice pots inside. Schoolboys are playing cricket out on the soaking fields and a few motorcycles whine past on the trunk road.

I should have known. I shouldn't have got my hopes up. It's not like me to mind so much. I'm a girl for solutions, for logic and making the best of things. Or perhaps I'm not. Perhaps now I'm back in Malaysia I'm going to turn out a different sort of woman altogether, the kind to wear jewels and silks and end up drowning in my own disappointment. How nice to have the choice.

After a few minutes I open the car door and tie my hair back with a scrunchie from the glove compartment. Scrub my face with my fingertips, smearing my eyeshadow, but there's nobody to care. I try out another big, bright smile, and then clip smartly across the car park and back to the reception desk.

'Oh – yes?' The nurse is still friendly, but with a slick of steel underneath. She's got rid of me once already.

'I'm collecting my grandmother today, too' I tell her. See, I have legitimate business. I belong. Mary Panikkar, I tell her, to be collected by Dr Durga Panikkar and the nurse's face clears. She's just opened her file when a voice comes from behind.

'Aiyoh, Durga, waiting the whole day already.'

I jump. Ammuma's in the cubicle behind the nurse's desk, concealed by a curtain. I wonder how long she's been there, if she heard me ask for Tom and get turned down. She's wearing a fresh sari made of white cotton and her hands are bandaged over the worst of her burns. On the chair next to her there's a polished cylinder with a mouthpiece. The mouthpiece has straps to hold it in place and a transparent container for storage.

'It's an oxygen cylinder. To help her breathe.'

Dr Rao pulls the curtain aside and ushers Ammuma out into the lobby. He looks even more tired than before, as though he's hanging off his own shoulder blades. He puts a hand on her arm as he tells me how to help her change the bandages. Ammuma snorts. After her time in hospital, the look on her face implies, she could perform her own tracheotomy.

'Dr Panikkar, if she . . .' Dr Rao pauses, turning away from Ammuma and lowering his voice.

'If she has trouble breathing, call the hospital straight away. Or if' – his eyes drop to her old burn scar, visible above the bandages – 'if she's confused. If she starts talking about her daughter again, or hurting herself . . .'

'Enough, so much whisper-whisper! All the same, you boys and girls, always thinking everyone's wanting to hear.' Ammuma glares at us both.

As soon as Dr Rao's out of earshot she scolds me for parking in the sun. 'With your complexion, Durga. No taking chances.'

I help her across the car park and she levers herself into the passenger seat. Her shrunken hips nestle amongst a litter of paper and dried-up pens.

'Clever, that Dr Rao boy,' Ammuma says as we pull out onto the trunk road. 'Efficient with discharge,' she says knowledgeably, rolling the word over her tongue. She likes a bit of fuss, likes the paper-and-red-tape importance of being a patient.

I don't reply. I'm thinking about what Dr Rao said, if only because that means I'm not thinking about Tom. *If she starts talking about her daughter.* I look across at Ammuma, so small in the passenger seat.

'Ammuma,' I start. 'When I was looking in the almirah I found something. A book.'

'Arre, books only with you. All this university —'

'No, an autograph book, Ammuma. It had Amma's name in it. Francesca Panikkar.'

Silence. Ammuma's staring through the windscreen with as much concentration as if she were driving herself.

'With an address. In Kampung Ulu.' She doesn't look up.

'Did you take her there sometimes, Ammuma? Is it . . . was it somewhere special? You never talk about — and I thought we could —'

'Enough of thought,' she snaps, so suddenly that I jump and miss a gear change. She's turned in her seat, glaring at me and on the attack.

'Why are you dressed all fancy-fancy? Think this is an outing, is it?'

'No, I . . . I . . .' Her anger's come out of nowhere and I'm not thinking straight. 'I was going to see someone.'

'Hah! Yes, I heard it. You asking for Tom, running after him like some girl on the street.'

'I wasn't! I mean — he invited me. He asked me to come and so I was —'

'Asked you?' she interrupts. 'When is it he's asking you to do anything?'

'He came to the house on Friday,' I start to explain, 'after you were admitted, and —'

Ammuma cuts me off again. 'Coming to the house, is it? Talking, inviting, and you let him stay alone with you?'

'No, Ammuma, he was just visiting . . .' I tail off; that's exactly what Karthika said. Visiting, staying with, *involving* himself. A picture comes into my mind: Tom twined with me on the prayer-room floor.

'And now you're dressing like a showgirl, waiting to catch a glimpse of him. Spitting into the skies, Durga, always you don't

95

think.' She bangs her hand on the car seat. 'What to do with you? Next day you'll be asking for marry with some white boy, some Mat Salleh boy, isn't it?'

Ammuma dreads me ending up like my mother: unmarried and pregnant and no better than the servant-girl. While I was in Canada she used to read me stories down the phone from the KL papers. The big city, she used to say, where girls drink and dance and hold hands with boys. She chose the stories carefully, to give her opportunities to be shocked. To say things she'd regret later.

'My own granddaughter,' she mutters, loud enough to be perfectly well heard. 'Dressing up in a skirt like underwear.'

I put my indicator on, keeping my expression even. Ammuma gives me a suspicious glance. Granddaughters are hard work, that look says, ungrateful and liable to tangle with the wrong sort. She takes the rubber mouthpiece off her lap and slips it between her lips, where it takes over her breathing for her and blurs the rest of her words.

'. . . should have taught you better.'

Should have? Would have? It's a criticism – somebody's at fault, somebody's to blame – but like all Ammuma's judgements it's easily missed. She slips them out, somewhere between one breath and the next.

*

Karthika's in the dining room when we get home, with an incense stick burning on top of the almirah. She's hunched on a chair with her legs drawn up like a chicken about to lay. There's a glance between her and Ammuma as we shuffle past to the hallway bathroom; a silent call-and-response I can't interpret. We came to a sort of truce yesterday, all our quarrels broken down under the weight of cleaning that we had to do. She didn't mention that great-grandmother of hers again. Why would she, when I'm scrubbing floors too?

'Not this bathroom, ar.' Ammuma stops at the bathroom door, her skirts gathered up ready in her arms. 'Upstairs only.'

'Ammuma, I can't manage the cylinder on the stairs.'

She sets her teeth, looks mulish. 'Upstairs only,' she repeats.

I can feel the blood coming to my face. So easy to skid into a quarrel with Ammuma, and so hard to know better. Karthika looks at me with a malicious glare – *See what I have to put up with, Durga-Miss?* – and I slip my arm under Ammuma's elbow.

'Come on, then. I'll help you.'

It's a struggle to get her upstairs. My armpits are damp with sweat by the time we manage it, and the sugar-starch at the hem of my sari's marked with stains of dust. She's lost her temper, I've kept a finger-grip on mine and Karthika's downstairs listening avidly to the whole thing.

Ammuma wants the bathroom cleaned before she'll go in, so she props herself against the door while I upend the shower bucket. Water sloshes over the floor and she pushes past me, getting her feet and skirts soaked. Too dangerous, I'd have said any other time, too slippery for an elderly lady. In this mood, though, Ammuma's more fierce than old.

'Amma!'

I jump. It's a high shriek, coming from Ammuma's bedroom. I hurry across and push the door open. It's Karthika's baby, Rajneesh, sitting on the floor with his face scrunched in outrage. The sleeping mats have been dragged out from the box room to make a little nest, and he's there in the middle holding a tiny pewter horse. It looks familiar, and after a second I recognize it as mine. It was a birthday present from Ammuma the year I turned seven. There are other toys scattered about, too – a battered velvet puppet that was once my favourite, and a feathery pen.

Rajneesh is in the middle of the toys, his face screwed up and his back arched, as though all he needs is the breath to scream. There's a deep scratch on the back of one of his arms, the edges ragged and white. In a moment it'll bleed.

'What-all is happening?' Ammuma appears at the door, still snappish with temper. 'Durga, don't bring that child up here.'

'I didn't!'

Rajneesh gets his breath and lets out another full-blooded howl. Karthika must be able to hear, but she's choosing to stay put. Ammuma ignores it all magnificently, wagging her finger and lecturing me although I can't hear a word over the screaming. I should know better, she's saying inaudibly. Giving those good toys to a kampong brat, letting the servant-girl bring him up here without so much as a by-your-leave.

'Karthika must have given him the things from my room,' I say, over the screams. 'Rajneesh, hush!'

I scoop him up, wrapping his cut arm in a fold of my best blouse. All this morning's excitement of clothes-hair-makeup seems so far away; I should have known better than to pin my hopes on a good sari and some goldwork thread. Rajneesh pushes his face into my neck, then opens his fist. Something falls to the floor with a crack.

'What?'

It's a shard of china. I toe the blankets away, and find the cross-legged Indian doll from the box room underneath. He's broken it accidentally, cutting himself on the jagged edges.

'What's that?' Ammuma snaps, and I move so that she can see.

'A doll, Ammuma. I found it in your box room yesterday. I think it's Karthika's –'

I stop. She's turned pale.

'Ammuma? Are you OK?'

'Fine, fine.' She bats my question away and shuffles closer, edging me out of the room.

'Typical servant-girl,' she adds. 'Giving him your toys, and can't even keep his own out of the house. You take him away, Durga.'

'I'll be right back, I promise. You can't stay here, Ammuma. It's dirty.' I'm almost at the door now, with Ammuma's not-quite-pushing.

'You go now, Durga,' she says again, more insistently. 'You stay downstairs, with the child. I'll tidy up.'

And the door closes in my face. Rajneesh is a damp and sobbing weight in my arms. He's stopped screaming now, but his breath still comes raggedly and he's pressing his wet face into the crook of my elbow. He wraps his legs round my waist as I carry him downstairs, then lets out a shrill yelp. He's seen Karthika through the dining-room doorway.

I set him down on the floor and he toddles towards her. She's still cross-legged on her chair and doesn't look up.

'Karthika! Didn't you hear him screaming upstairs?'

She looks up then, gives me a slow stare and closes her eyes. 'Not allowed in the bedrooms, Durga-Miss. I can't come.'

'Don't be stupid!' I'm cross, my blouse is bloodstained and there's a damp mark on my hip from Rajneesh's nappy. Karthika doesn't notice any of these things: for her, they're ordinary life.

She turns away to take something Rajneesh is handing her. It's the feathery pen that he's been clutching. She tucks it neatly into the pocket of her skirt without even turning a hair.

'That's mine!' I burst out.

She blinks up at me. Something about that monkey-like cringe irritates me and for a second I have to fight back an urge to slap her. Send her packing. A girl like that; what could anyone have expected?

'Karthika, you know you can't take anything from here. All those toys . . . and that doll of yours. Upstairs, he's broken it now. I told you not to leave it here.'

'I didn't, Durga-Miss. I wouldn't have bought a doll like that. Such poor dress, a sari for old-fashioned only.' She sneaks a glance at my own sari, then strokes her red nylon skirt complacently.

'Don't lie. And give that pen back,' I add.

She clenches her teeth and I can see her jaw move. She sits very still, then turns away.

'Karthika, give it back. Now!' I stride over to her, blocking her view, and hold out my hand. 'What do you want with it anyway?'

You can't even write. I stop myself, which is nearly as bad as saying it. She flushes and brings the pen out of her pocket. It clatters onto the table and her eyes are jealous and gleaming as it rolls across the surface. It's almost comical, how much she wants a cheap glitter pen. Almost.

'Tom-Mister says I can go into the bedrooms, anyway,' she says, with a vicious little sneer. 'He showed me yours, Durga-Miss.'

'What?'

'When you're in Canada, Durga-Miss. He showed me the bedrooms while Mary-Madam sits on the verandah.'

I stare at her. Her smile's worming back over her face. Karthika, shit-smelling and scandalous with it, in my bedroom with Tom. Nonsense, I tell myself quickly. She doesn't know what she's saying. He took her up there to clean the toilets or move the furniture. To polish the floors; Karthika on her hands and knees in front of Tom. He *wouldn't*.

'Karthika!' Ammuma calls from upstairs, making us both jump. 'Stop your chatter-chatter, paid to clean the floors, isn't it?'

Ammuma's scolding brings reality back. Carrying a servant-girl off to bed is something that only happens in Karthika's highly coloured movies. Not in real life, not in all the drabness of the here-and-now, where she can't even refuse.

I give Karthika a tentative, forgiving smile but she doesn't look at me. She unfurls her legs from under the table and hefts Rajneesh onto her hip. As she walks into the kitchen, she tugs the refrigerator open. Tupperware and bowls are piled high in there and it's full of smells I remember but can't name any more. I see fried prawns with belacan, mustard seeds, muscly rendang curry. She must have spent all morning making Ammuma's favourite dishes. There's nothing an elderly woman ought to have, but everything Ammuma wants. It's a peace offering, and something I'd never have thought of.

I reach out to the incense stick and pinch it off, feeling the quick sting of the embers. Rajneesh giggles from the kitchen, and I hear splashing in the stone sink. Karthika and I used to paddle in there, ankle deep as we sat on the windowsill. We had a name for that game – Going to Sea? Swimming Away? – but that's another thing I've forgotten.

I look over at the almirah, with Tom's bag and that Little Twin Stars notebook inside. It feels better to have the door closed, to feel it locked safely away as I climb back up the stairs. Perhaps this is how people felt after the war, like everything that used to be familiar had changed. Perhaps it's how Ammuma felt after Francesca died. And thirty years later she's still searching out books and sweets and offerings. *Would you have liked this, Fran? How about that? Will this one bring you back?* The women in my family take motherhood hard, being demanding or dead and quite frankly not much better than daughters.

Upstairs, the bedroom door's wide open and I can see through into the box room. Ammuma's in there, her oxygen cylinder propped against her leg. She's laid the smashed doll on a shelf at waist height and she's piping glue onto the shards. She doesn't look old, not now, she looks alert and strong enough to hold up the sky. The sun strikes through the charred boards of the wall in hot slices and the faint scent of incense floats up from downstairs. Everything feels very still, thick with the smell of dust and a faint undertone of ash.

As I watch, Ammuma picks up a broken sliver of the doll's face, and lays it gently back into place. She presses it down and wipes the glue off with her forefinger. She's humming softly as she picks up the next piece and muttering to herself.

'Come on . . . come on, stick tight, just there. Next one, another one . . . Making it look right, just like a princess, like a tiger-prince. Once upon a time there was a tiger-prince – there you go, stick tight – and a princess. And when the sun came up they knew they were safe – stick *tight*, won't you.'

The stairs seem to shiver under me. The princess, beautiful and dangerous. The tiger-prince, with his mouthful of teeth and tiger stripes. The froggish monster like something pulled from a riverbed. The way the sun came up, Durga-child, and then they knew that they were safe.

She used to tell me this story every night before bed. Sometimes with more characters, sometimes with a different ending, but always the same story underneath. It's the bones of a lemma, this tale, the meat and muscle of a proof. It's history, getting the last word in first.

12.   A Servant's Tale: 1930

'Once upon a time,' Mary begins, 'there was a tiger-prince.'

Eight-year-old Anil claps his hands. He's delighted for several reasons: partly because Mary's curled up with him on her lap, partly because she's telling him his favourite fairy tale, and partly because there's no room for Paavai to come and sit next to them. All three of them are in the back of the compound, in a dusty and crumbling corner under the durian tree. Anil and Mary sprawl on a raggedy seat that might once have been a piano stool, while Paavai squats nearby in the sun. She's leaning against the stone coping of the oldest well, the one with half its bricks gone for rubble. Anil stretches his legs out onto the shady seat where Paavai isn't, and babbles with joy. It doesn't take much to make him happy, unlike his sister.

'Ma-ry,' he says, carefully. He's taken to speaking, these last few months. Not very much, just the odd word or two. Mary catches his socked and kicking feet in the palm of her hand and, looking up, meets Paavai's eye.

Mary and Paavai don't get along. For a start, there's the question of just what Mary should call her. At seventeen, she's only a year or two older than Mary herself, so she can't be Paavai-Amah. She isn't Paavai-Auntie either, because the children needn't respect her, and they know it. She isn't even a servant, not really, although sometimes Radhika will wake up in a foul mood and order Paavai to perform an immense and unimaginable task. Cleaning out the wells; re-tarring the attap roof. These demands happen like lightning, usually when Radhika's heard her husband stumbling from Paavai's verandah room in the small hours. He's been doing a bit too much of that, these last few months, and the inevitable has happened. Paavai's waist has begun to thicken and her belly to bulge in an alarming and unmistakable way.

'The tiger-prince fell in love with a princess,' Mary tells Anil. 'A beautiful princess. With long hair, of course' – the two children glance at Paavai's short-cropped head – 'and creamy skin' – they giggle at the soot-blackness of Paavai's calloused knees and elbows – 'and the prettiest face in the world. So pretty she had to wear a mask so people would leave her alone.'

(Mary doesn't know it, but that mask hints at something rotten beneath her story. Leprosy or beauty, it doesn't much matter which. Both come down to fending people off.)

'The princess didn't love the tiger-prince back, though,' Mary goes on, 'so he challenged her to a duel. And if he won, he would get to marry her.'

Mary's stories all involve rape and pillage, given a shake of sugar and retold as true love. It doesn't bode well for her future, sitting there in her white dress and eyelet socks. She might be able to tell stories, but she's failed her Junior Cambridge exam and her schooldays are over. From now on, she'll have to make her own way.

'So the prince and the princess battled! And just as the tiger-prince was about to win, the princess took off her mask. And he dropped down in a faint because of how beautiful she was.'

Paavai gives a loud snort. She's pulling fibres from coconut husks and twisting them in her rubbed-raw hands to make a rope. She tugs it, testing the strength.

Paavai's been in the house a year now. When she isn't working, she slips through the darkened passages and spends hours hiding in one room or another, trying to take possession of something. Mary's found her hunched in the kitchen gnawing on a lump of sugar cane and Anil's surprised her in the moonlit bathroom staring at her own reflection. Radhika's had even worse shocks. She and Paavai are the same height and same skin colour, and when they meet unexpectedly in a dark corridor, at first Radhika thinks she's seeing her own ghost.

'The tiger-prince fainted because of how beautiful the princess was without her mask,' Mary repeats. 'And while he was fainted, he turned into a huge frog-monster! *That* was his secret, that whenever he slept he turned into a *beast*. He had a mouth like this' – Mary stretches her lips open – 'and eyes like this' – she squints her eyelids shut – 'and a little pug nose just like . . .' The two children look at Paavai and giggle.

'Time wasting, Mary-Miss. All these stories,' Paavai sneers. She flicks a length of coconut fibre up into the durian tree, making the huge spiked fruits wobble on their fleshy stalks. Dangerous, to be walking under a durian tree when the fruits are falling. Everyone says the fruits never fall in daylight hours but nevertheless, Paavai's being careless.

Mary grits her teeth, though, and doesn't say anything. She's trying to be more ladylike these last few months, and biting back any swear words that spring to her tongue. She doesn't want to be like Paavai, who swears like a soldier whenever she spills hot water on herself. Ladies don't talk like that, Mary tells Paavai loftily, and grinds her own teeth instead of cursing. All this jaw-clenching restraint has taken its toll, and Mary's teeth have grown noticeably shorter and weaker. By seventy she'll need false teeth, she'll slop biscuits against her gums; she'll suck at sambal petai that Paavai's great-granddaughter Karthika cooks for her and take her long-awaited revenge by sending the girl to mop up shit.

'Ignore Paavai,' Mary tells Anil. 'Listen, when the princess saw the tiger-prince faint and turn into this awful monster she ran to help him. She fell in love with him too!'

Anil's lost interest, though. His eyes are turned up to the durian tree. The branches should have had gunny sacks tied over them a week ago to catch the falling fruit, but Stephen hasn't bothered. Every night the weight of dew gets too heavy for the largest and ripest fruits. One by one, they droop, they tremble and they eventually come loose and hurtle down to smash into the ground or straight down the well with heavy, resounding thuds. The fruits drop every night, regular as the whistling Lipis train, and when on dry evenings the dew doesn't fall and neither do the fruits, the whole family's kept awake by the unaccustomed silence.

'Anil, Anil – listen! The princess knew her father wouldn't let her marry a monster, so she disguised the prince. She cut off his nose, and his lips and his ears.'

(Shades of leprosy again, shades of that disease that's already bounding down Mt Tahan with its slobbery face turned towards the kampong.)

'Then the princess rolled him in clay and sand so he ended up looking just like a man. And then the tiger-prince and the princess ran away, while he was disguised enough to fool everyone. They ran all night, and bits of sand kept dropping off him. The sand turned into roads and bridges and houses. By the time the sun came up they were high in the mountains, with a whole city all to themselves. And then in the sun, of course, he turned back into a tiger-prince.' She finishes triumphantly. 'And when the sun came up, they knew that they were safe.'

It seems, on the face of it, unlikely. Mary's left her prince and princess stranded in the wilderness, on top of a mountain famed for its ghosts and devils. They've got no food, and she doesn't seem to have thought that in a few days the tiger-prince will be eyeing those delicate veins in his princess's neck. That's what you get with stories; you get consequences. Mary's lovers are unlikely to get out alive.

'All nonsense, Mary-Miss.' Paavai stands up, tucking her sari high around her spindly legs. Radhika's instructed her to clear out the stones and fruit rinds that clog the bottom of the deepest well on the property, under the durian trees. It's dangerous work and really needs a team of men, but Radhika's insisted that Paavai do it alone: 'The girl's putting on weight, haven't you seen that belly of hers? She could do with the exercise.'

'Such a waste to tell stories to Anil-Mister.' Paavai hoists one leg over the stone coping and points at Anil. 'Can't understand a thing, that one.'

She wouldn't normally speak like this to the children, but she's desperately jealous. Paavai's prettier than both children put together and at least half as clever again. And yet they sit there on a padded velvet seat telling stories, while she's sent down to unclog rubbish.

'Anil-Mister ought to be in a home,' she goes on. 'Nobody will marry you, Mary-Miss. Not with something like *that* to take care of.'

And with that, Paavai drops herself down into the yawning, blackened well on the end of her coconut-fibre rope.

'You – you dirty keling, you coolie, how dare you, how dare you!' Mary's furious. She shouts herself hoarse, leaning over the well and spitting all the insults she's ever heard in Malay or English or Malayalam. Halfway through, she recollects herself and claps careful hands over Anil's ears.

Mary loves her young brother, she's fiercely protective and can't stand the thought of him being hurt. She'd never abandon him to get married, she insists. Never, she repeats, and she sounds less sure each time.

Mary's lonely, that's the real problem. After failing her Junior Cambridge she hasn't gone back to school, while Cecelia passed with flying colours and is now in the top standard. Rajan's gone back to his Singapore college, in between tearing around Pahang agitating for Indian nationalism, Malay nationalism and home rule for any other country that cares to ask for it. Mary still plays the occasional solitary game of marbles, she still wanders up to the convent on the hill to see Sister Gerta. But there's no getting away from it; Mary's ripe for marriage and nobody's come to ask.

*

Later, everyone will agree that it was dangerous to send Paavai down that well. It was unsafe, with the well-stones crumbling every time a durian fruit bounced off the coping. True, Paavai went down at noon, when durian fruits hardly ever fall. But still, everyone agrees, Stephen should have known better.

Paavai wasn't missed till twilight, by which time she'd been in the well for six hours. When she was hauled up she was limp as cloth and her mouth slopped full with water. And then there was that large, spiky bruise on her forehead, exactly the size and shape of a durian fruit. At first she didn't say a word and then she wouldn't stop. She babbled about two small heads that had appeared in the circle of light high above her when she was cleaning out the well; she chattered about seeing a durian fruit tumbling down on her, thrown by two small pairs of hands. She swore that she wouldn't stay in the house with Mary and Anil one more moment, not even if she was paid triple. Radhika – who disapproved of her being paid at all – simply shrugged. 'Then go,' Radhika said, 'and take your pregnant belly with you.' Radhika doesn't want Mary being exposed to a bad example.

*

'And when the sun came up, they knew that they were safe.'

Mary will tell Anil the story of the tiger-prince and the fighting princess again and again over the next few years. As a teenager he'll meet Paavai's son: a coffee-coloured boy called Luke, with a resemblance to Stephen that's unmistakable. When Luke turns out to know the tiger-prince story too (from his mother, because Paavai, just like Mary, is in the habit of telling tales) they'll become fast friends. Both will have their crosses to bear – mad mothers, dead mothers, mothers who never wanted to be mothers anyway – and together they'll roam the jungle, throwing stones at any nearly drowned women who cross their path.

Stories twist through the past like hair in a plait. Each strand different, weaving its own pattern and ducking out of sight just when you're following it. Like category theory, in a way. Like families. They don't stay put either.

Don't believe me? Think of your family; picture them right down to the details. Eyes, smiles, the thumbnail your brother chews. If you're lucky then you know them off by heart. If you're not, the heart won't come into it at all. (Don't cry; there'll be time for all of that later.)

They're a category, your family, and the objects are simple enough. Aunties, uncles, cousins. A grandmother, if you want to court trouble. But this category changes. Just wait and cousins turn into aunties, uncles become disgraced, babies grow up and brothers grow apart. In a few years the aunties will be dead, the uncles will have forgotten their children's names and those grandmothers will have become quite another proposition altogether. (Don't cry; it's too late for all of that now.)

All the heartache of going from then to now – all that growing up and growing old, all those first grey hairs and last cold wrinkles – that's your history, right there. Perhaps you don't like it now you've got it, perhaps you'd rather it had all turned out differently. You might dream of *if-only-I'd*, and *he-should-have-done* and *what-if-she'd-listened* – all those little pleas and quarrels. They're a category in themselves, your set of missed chances. They're how things might have been.

*

'You need to come back.'

It's Anwar Goneng. He's the head of the mathematics department in KL, a haggard Malay with an emaciated face and a bulging body that doesn't match it. When he talks he pats his mouth with a folded white handkerchief, as though he wants to clean away any residue of bad news – and it always is bad. I can hear him now, blotting up the words.

'You've had your week's leave. We were expecting you back today.'

'I'm sorry. I couldn't . . . I mean, my grandmother's been in hospital. Didn't you get my message?'

'If you need some compassionate leave, you can apply for this after your probation.' There's a bite to Anwar's words that's the furthest thing possible from compassion. 'There's a process, Dr Panikkar.'

I flinch. It would be so easy for this job to disappear in a puff of bureaucracy.

'I'll come back,' I say quickly. 'I'm sorry, I didn't realize . . .'

'Ye – es.' Anwar concedes this magisterially. His English is excruciatingly correct. 'Mistakes are easy to make. But we need you here, Dr Panikkar. The lectures, you see. The classwork.'

I twist the phone cord around my finger, letting it grow purple. Through the hall window I can see everything outside flattened under that golden light that means the afternoon rains have missed us. You don't get that light in Canada.

'I'll come tomorrow,' I say. I slide down the wall, knees to my chest amongst a tangle of telephone wires and paper clips on the floor. 'I'll leave tomorrow morning and be there in time for afternoon lectures.'

Anwar smiles. It's a dignified sort of smile and I can hear it all the way from KL. Before he hangs up he says he knew he could rely on me. It feels strange, as though I've started to turn into someone different here. Like one of Ammuma's stories, like a drowned girl becoming a ghost or a princess becoming a leper. I need to get my grip back on Dr Panikkar, while I still remember who she was.

★

The afternoon reshapes itself after that, turns into lists of tasks to be ticked off and belongings to be organized. Finding my suitcase, packing dirty clothes because there's no time to send them to Letchumani, and clean clothes because I'll have no time to do washing at home. Ammuma takes the flurry surprisingly well.

'This job of yours, Durga. Worth doing well, no point letting the goats go after they've bolted.'

She's imperious while I pack, getting me to fold and refold clothes so they don't crumple. She scolds Karthika for slopping the dishpail, then pokes around the kitchen for dirt, enjoying herself hugely. She goes in for complicated arguments, the sort that start out one-sided and finish over the kitchen table five hours later in a welter of broken crockery.

By evening the rooms are full of mosquitoes that hover in thick clouds under the furniture. The wind's too strong for them outside and the air's full of rain. When I go out to feed the chickens I see the Jelai smacking at its banks, high and so fast it's almost solid. There must be a flood further up the valley.

A big flood, too, because a few minutes later we're plunged into blackness. A power cut. There are a few scurrying, shouting minutes while Karthika and I find the hurricane lamps. They flame into frothy yellow light as I line them on the edge of the verandah. A flittering ring of insects gathers and Ammuma starts giving her bony shins vicious slaps. Under her chair a green mosquito coil crumbles to dandruff and powders my bare soles.

I'm not used to power cuts any more; they're not part of the rhythm of my life and I've forgotten how to take them in my stride. Perhaps it's something more than a power cut, I think, perhaps it's bad luck and bad omens whistled up by Ammuma's drowned women in their wells. There might be witchery in that coiling wind; there might be devilment setting the kitchen cats hissing under the table. I could frighten myself like this if I had more time, but Ammuma needs a beaten egg soaked in milk, and my suitcase still needs packing. No witchery here, just an extra pair of hands.

'Mary-Auntie! Hello, hello.'

The shout comes as I'm turning up one of the hurricane lamps. The wick flares and goes out, singeing my face and plunging the verandah into gloom. Tom. Here without so much as a by-your-leave, expecting us all to jump and flutter and burn our fingers into the bargain.

'I heard you were discharged yesterday, Mary-Auntie.' He comes up the verandah steps two at a time, with a rucksack slung over his shoulder. I relight the lamp, sending a sudden glare over my face, and he gives a start.

'Durga!'

Ammuma huffs, something between a cough and a scold, and Tom immediately turns to her. He knows how to please, kicking his shoes off – one lands in a dusty corner and lies there in all its Italian-leather glory – and sitting cross-legged by her chair. He slings his rucksack into a corner with the shoes and the dust and me. You'd almost think he's delighted to be here, sitting with his trouser-creases getting ruined and mosquitoes crawling down into his collar.

'So good to see you home again, Mary-Auntie,' he says. 'Dr Rao said you were his best patient.'

She snorts again. On the one hand she'd like to send him packing – *out into the night you go, and no thanks for sniffing around my granddaughter* – but she can't resist the urge to boast.

'Taking antibiotics,' she tells him. 'And also this cylinder. Heavy one, but already helping.'

She pats it with pride. She's brighter when she's got someone to perform for. She likes Tom, likes the gossip he brings back from work. So much more interesting than a granddaughter and her mathematics.

'One of the Varghese kids came in with measles today,' Tom tells her absently. He's patting her hand and making a big performance out of inspecting the oxygen cylinder. He takes her rubber mouthpiece and bends it back and forwards against his palm.

'One of our best, this is,' he says, and Ammuma beams. He doesn't mind humouring her — of course not, he doesn't have to live with it — and in return she softens.

'Dr Rao said this was important. And the dressing-paste also. See? Here, for the bandages. He's a good boy, this Dr Rao.'

Not half an hour ago she was fretting, sure her burns were worse and calling Dr Rao a jumped-up quack who couldn't tell rice from grass. I roll my eyes and stand up, brushing dust from the seat of my skirt.

Tom smiles at me. 'Durga can help you with the bandages, can't she?' he says.

Ammuma's head whips round. She'd nearly forgotten I was there. Huddled in the dark, getting up to who-knows-what behind her back. Going to the bad, most likely.

'Durga won't be here, lah. Going back to her job.'

There's a silence, stretching out between the three of us. I thought Tom would have said something. At the very least he could have been polite and sorry-to-hear-you're-leaving, or perhaps he could have swept me off my feet and carried me into the night. But he just coughs, rubs his jaw. I'm too heavy for carrying, that much is clear. There's too much solidity in my bones.

'Why don't I bring some tea, Ammuma?' I ask briskly.

She's pleased enough at that, asks for gem biscuits too and some of the watermelon. She doesn't want me around Tom, not even on my last night. Too risky, too easy to slip and spill my virtue everywhere.

I walk slowly to the front room. I'm not wearing my best sari any more, only an ordinary skirt and blouse crumpled from my suitcase. But underneath, where nobody can see, I'm still wearing silk. It's slippery stuff that shivers and slinks, a set of underwear I bought in Canada to wear for Deepak. It's a sunrise pink, it's the exact colour of the flush on Tom's throat and it's far more beautiful than me.

I stand still, listening to the trickle of voices from the verandah. The room's almost black, with only a weak glow filtering in from the compound at the back where Karthika's lit a fire. There's a smell of boiled sugar from the sweets Karthika cooked to be placed in front of my mother's shrine. Silverfish scuttle in the corners, and a few scorpions hang black and ponderous on the ceiling. There's nothing in here that can hurt, I tell myself – a little heartache, a little poison – if only you keep your wits about you.

'Durga?' Tom's a bulky, formless shape, coming in from the verandah. His bare feet pad on the floor with a sound as wet as buttermilk.

'Are you really going?' he asks quietly.

'I can't stay,' I tell him. There are lectures, I explain, research grants to apply for, Anwar doing double-duty teaching all my classes. They give me some logic to brace against.

'You're cross about yesterday,' Tom says. 'I know we arranged to meet, but I'm sorry, Durga, I just forgot –'

From Tom, who thinks that forgetting is a crime. *He wouldn't have forgotten Peony*, I think – and then, I'm suddenly sick of it all. Sick of the past, which Ammuma rightly says is all blood under the bridge. Sick of ghosts, who should know their place and wait their turn. I feel the heat of Tom's body next to mine and remember lying on the prayer-room floor. I remember his fingers, slippery and seeking and finding their home. There's a stir in my belly and a trembling in my thighs. And so what if I'm no better than all those girls who've gone to the bad or gone to the devil, just like Ammuma warned me about. I'm exactly like them, under the skin. Looking for happy endings, looking for proofs, looking for love in all the wrong places.

I take Tom's hands and he jumps in surprise as I bring them to my mouth. He smells of salt and curry, and his thumb rubs up against the angle of my jaw. He pulls back and I reach up and brush my hand over his neck. His shirt's starched, smelling pungent and bright as a naphtha flame. His face glimmers in a flare from the hurricane lamps on the verandah and just when I think he's going to turn away he takes my hand instead.

I tug him through the room and out into the pitch-black

corridor. The kitchen door's swinging open and a breath of wind comes in. It stinks of the Jelai. That river-swamp smell reminds me of Peony, and I drop Tom's hand with a jolt. I remember us all playing hide-and-seek here fifteen years ago. Me behind the door, Tom under the settee where his white skin wouldn't show. Peony in the attic, always the last to be found. You were good at hiding, Peony. You still are.

'Come on,' I tell him.

Karthika slams the kitchen door again as we creep past. She's burning banana leaves in the back compound. I wait until her back's turned, then pull Tom quickly past under the curve of the stairs. There's a side door to the yard, and the bolts are covered with a floss of spider webs. The path outside is luminous and milky with phosphorescence. Mud squelches under my feet and something squirms just beyond my toes.

'Durga, are you sure we –'

I lead him round the side of the house, under the durian tree. Everything's lit with a shifting, flickering light from Karthika's bonfire. We reach the annexe that spiders along the back wall, and I stop. Tom puts his shoulder to the annexe door, shoving it open against the piled-up dirt. I'm chilled, but Tom glows like that yard fire. He shuts the door behind us and it's like a weight of darkness coming down over my eyelids. In here, he could be any colour at all.

I brush my fingers over his shoulders. His heart jumps, like a clean and friendly animal nudging under his skin. I want to lick him, my tongue rough as sandpaper coating his skin. He's flesh and bone and sweat, and I want more.

He slides down the wall, pulling me onto his lap, and kisses me. I feel his legs under mine and his hands unbuttoning my blouse. He smiles at the feel of silk underneath, at the soft give of it under his fingers. I run my hands down his spine and pull at his temples, running my lips over the creaseless line. He pushes my blouse down to my waist, and then his shirt is off too, tugged over his head and dropped carelessly on the floor. I feel brand new, as though he's touching something almost at the core of me. Everything's pulsating, slippery, thin as icing drizzled into cold water, and Tom's face is close and invisible in the breathing dark. He's muttering something – a private, urgent whisper I'm not meant to hear.

'Peony.' It's a spit of cold water. 'Peony.'

'What?' I pull away. Tom startles, letting his arms drop from around me. I'm still tight-wound inside, but I can feel myself loosening, ratcheting down. Becoming slacker, back to something that feels dull and heavy inside. Back to my bones and my skin, which doesn't sing any more.

'Tom . . .'

My eyes have adjusted, or it wasn't as dark as I thought. Light comes filtering in through cracks in the door, and round the sides of the boarded-up window. I can feel my daytime face again, frown-lines re-emerging. There's a sudden sound outside, and I jump.

'Who's that?' Tom moves sharply. He pulls away from me and the air sucks at my damp stomach. *Cover yourself up*, Ammuma would say. I grab for my blouse, shaking dirt out onto my skirt.

There's another noise and a sound of footsteps outside. The far wall dims slightly as someone passes in front of the door. Stands there for a second, close-up with an ear pressed to the wall. A smell comes wafting in: pandan leaves and fish with an undercurrent of shit. Karthika.

Tom springs upright, pushing himself off the wall to wrench the door open. Light spills in from outside.

'She's gone,' he says. 'It was Karthika. Durga – come on. We need to get back.'

He holds the collar of his shirt between his teeth while he buttons it. I'm still struggling into my clothes, pulling my blouse around me and feeling the itch of dirt working its way under my breasts.

'Durga . . .' he says, one foot already out of the door. He's dressed now, and his hair isn't even ruffled. No half-naked indignity for Tom, nothing he'll regret tomorrow morning. Nothing he'll regret tonight, come to that. Clever Tom.

'Wait!' I stumble after him into the compound. The electricity must have come back on because I can see yellow light spilling onto the path. Tom pulls the door open and steps into the warm hallway with its lemon smell of overheated lightbulbs. I stop on the threshold.

'You were imagining Peony, weren't you? Not me.'

Karthika's voice comes through from the verandah, whispering frantically. Carrying tales to Ammuma and wallowing in self-righteousness.

'Durga . . .' He swallows, and his eyes dart sideways to the verandah.

'You didn't want me, did you? For God's sake, Tom, you had to pretend I was *her*?'

I fold my arms. There's a rash above my wrist, where Tom pressed me against the annexe wall.

'At least most men obsess about models, or – or girls from *Playboy*. Not fifteen-year-olds, Tom; not *dead* fifteen-year-olds.'

He looks stricken. 'Durga, don't, don't be so angry. Peony was your friend, too, remember, Peony –'

'I'm not interested in Peony!'

The words hang there. Tom looks shocked, as though he can't quite believe I've said them.

'What's all happening?' Ammuma comes stamping through from the front room. Her mouthpiece hangs down from her chin and she's dragging the oxygen cylinder on one strap. Karthika lurks behind, her head downcast. She sneaks a glance up at me and then drops her eyes again. A little bit triumphant – *hands off, Durga-Miss, what's mine is mine* – and a little bit scared at what she's done.

'I heard you all. Like some fishwives, upsetting everything.' Ammuma looks irritable, but that's all. Perhaps Karthika's said less than I thought.

'Everything's OK, Mary-Auntie.' Tom gives her a practised

smile, a 100%-and-then-some smile, but it doesn't soften her one bit.

'Ar, then time to go. It's late, no need to be all here like this, keeping us up in the middle of the night.' She puts her hands on her hips and sends Tom a sharp look. 'Too late for staying.'

Tom looks stricken. He holds out his hand, gives me a polite handshake while mumbling something about it having been nice to see me. We walk back through the front room. Karthika's scuttled away to her fire again, now she's done all the damage she can. With any luck she'll trip on her own wagging tongue, end up in the cinders or down one of the wells.

Tom slips his shoes on and turns to give me an awkward smile.

'Good luck,' he says, and then, 'Keep in touch.'

His voice sounds artificial and flat. The way goodbyes do in airports and on train stations, when everybody wants the next few minutes over and done with.

I stand on the verandah with Ammuma on my left, watching him walk away. I can't think straight; I don't know whether I'm glad to see the back of him or I'd be glad to see him back. There's a pad of bare feet and Karthika comes to stand on my right. Three Graces, three Muses, three monkeys. Take your pick, Tom. Ammuma with her watchful eyes, Karthika guilty as sin and twice as unreliable, me still in a swamp from fifteen years ago. And behind us: laughing, tangled hair, ballpoint tattoos on her fragile wrists, always and for ever, Peony.

'Truth or dare? Go on, Durga.'

We're fifteen years old, in Tom's father's car. Cars aren't exactly new in Lipis – Mother Agnes has an old shabby one – but most of them are just tin Milo things, as Ammuma says. Flimsy, lightweight. Tom's father, on the other hand, has a brand-new Nissan Sunny in the brightest, most luscious red. Tom persuaded his father to let him and Peony come for a ride in it today. Me too, but only after Peony asked.

Catching Peony's bright glance in the rear-view mirror, I look behind. She's got ink on her collar and her mouth is red and clownish where she's been chewing her cedarwood pencils.

'Truth or dare?'

'Truth,' I say.

Tom, sitting on the front seat next to me, grins. 'Right – truth, then. Durga, who would you rather kiss, Fat Ali or me?'

He's laughing. I wish lightning would come and strike me dead right now.

'Shut up, Tom.' Peony reaches round from the back seat and gives my hand a quick squeeze. 'That's a stupid one,' she says. 'Durga . . . how about – did you copy Noor's maths test?'

We're an hour away from Lipis, waiting in the car just outside Kampung Ulu. Dr Harcourt – Tom's father – parked next to the swamp and told us to stay put while he made a quick visit to the leper colony down the road. A leper colony sounds scary, but this one isn't. Not really. It's just sad. There are TB patients in it, too, and some poor people who were born wrong and can't talk or move. Mad Ahmad lives there too, and he was in the San before it burnt down fifteen years ago. The remains of the San are just across the swamp – I can see one of the burnt-out buildings from here – and that *is* scary, just a little bit.

'Yes,' I say. 'I copied Noor's answers.'

I didn't, in fact – she'd got half of them wrong – but I want to join in. Make it exciting. Make *me* exciting.

'Liar,' Tom says. 'You're such a goody-goody, Durga. You'd never.'

'I'm not lying! I'm not!'

'Leave her alone, Tom.' Peony rolls her eyes, and that's that. Tom always listens to her. 'Your turn, and don't come up with anything strange. Durga and I won't play if you do.'

Playing Truth or Dare was Peony's idea. All the best ideas are. Tom keeps going too far with it, though. Teasing me about Ali, who's chubby with a stupid little fuzz-moustache. As if I'd want to kiss *him*.

'Truth or dare?'

'Dare.' Peony always picks dare. Tom grins.

'Cross the swamp to the San,' he says, and we all look up, out of the windscreen. The swamp's thick and black. Overhead is the biggest banyan tree in Pahang. The roots curve and swoop overhead to make a cave where Dr Harcourt's parked, and the water hums with dragonflies and mosquitoes. The colony's on the other side.

'And then sing "Locks on the Gates" three times,' he adds.

'No way!' Peony's eyes go round and wide. 'That's not fair.'

'That's dangerous,' I say, although nobody's listening. 'Mad Ahmad might hear. It isn't funny, Tom.'

Mad Ahmad was the only person they rescued from the San when it burnt down. Even though that was fifteen years ago, but he still isn't normal. Some afternoons they say he walks right out of the leper colony and goes back to the tumbledown San, where he thinks he belongs.

'Locks on the gates,' Tom sing-songs, 'and bars on the doors.'

'Don't!' I push him.

Locks on the Gates is a chasing game. One person's the lunatic from the San and the others are the guards. *Locks on the gates*, we sing, *and bars on the doors. Coming to get you, ready or not!* I'm not sup-posed to play it, though. Ammuma heard me once and lost her temper. She *hates* that game, she told me, but then she hugged me and didn't let go for ages.

'You know they never found some of the bodies, don't you?' Tom says. 'After the San burnt down? Some of the loonies escaped and set fire to the place. And they've never caught them.'

I stare across at the burnt-out San. I don't believe Tom, but I'm not going to say anything. One time he waited after school and hid behind the surau to jump out and scare Peony. He never tries to scare me.

'Don't be silly.' I sound prim and stupid. Tom rolls his eyes.

'I'll do it,' Peony says suddenly. 'I'll cross on the banyan roots.'

The roots stick up from the water like witch's teeth, and I shud-der. She gives us both a wink, aimed exactly between us, and bounces out of the car. She makes it look easy, jumping from one root to another with her pleated skirt flying and her socks slipping down. She's wearing a friendship bracelet on her wrist made from red wool, and I'm wearing the other. Friends for ever, that means.

Tom gives me a sideways glance as we watch her. A smirk sneaks in around the side of his mouth.

'She's showing off, isn't she?' he says.

I giggle. Peony *is* showing off, sleek hair glinting in the sun as she stands on one leg and sucks at a mosquito bite.

'Locks on the gates!' she calls, cupping her hands around her mouth. Nothing moves.

'I don't know why girls always show off,' Tom says, looking at me hard. 'I suppose they think boys will like them more.'

I chew at one of my nails – I bite my right forefinger, just like Peony; we're always the same – and giggle again. I'm not sure what to say.

'Perhaps – I mean, I don't know. I'm sure you're right.'

'I'm sorry I called you a goody-goody. You're not, Durga. You're . . .'

He reaches out and twines his fingers around mine, pulling my hand down from my mouth. His other hand creeps up onto my knee, then inches higher. My legs are bare and brown in the hot sun, and Tom seems suddenly very close. I can smell his sweat, his disinfected insect bites, the cologne he buys from the sundry store.

'Hey!'

Peony bangs on the windscreen and we jump. Her face is screwed up into a scowl and she looks cross; really cross. Tom whips his hand off my leg and edges away from me along the seat.

'When you've quite finished.' Peony climbs back into the car, banging the door shut.

She's in a temper, tugging on the seatbelt that Mr Harcourt rigged up for the backseat. She snaps it around her waist with a vicious click and drums her fingers on the window glass.

Tom and I look down at our laps, awkward and quiet. I can feel sweat springing from my armpits and trickling down my stomach. Peony, with her skirt rolled high and her milky legs swung up on the seat, looks daggers at us in the mirror. I pluck at my friendship bracelet.

'It's your turn, Peony,' I say in a small voice. 'For Truth or Dare?'

She takes a deep breath and pushes her hair back. The seatbelt pulls her shirt tight against her chest and her skirt falls back down her thighs. Tom's eyes meet hers in the rear-view mirror and neither of them moves.

'All right . . . Tom. Truth or dare?' she says.

'Dare.' Tom's voice breaks. He coughs, wipes his mouth with the back of his hand and Peony smiles.

'Kiss whichever one of us you like the best,' she says. 'Me or Durga.'

'Peony!' She doesn't look at me, just lies back with a lazy stretch of her legs.

'Go on, Tom,' she says. 'Choose.'

I sneak a glance at Tom. His jaw's clenched and his eyes are bright. I force a big smile onto my face.

'Brilliant, Peony! Go on, Tom, you have to choose.'

He wipes his mouth again and locks eyes with Peony in the mirror. Without breaking his stare he reaches over to me. He wraps his arm around my waist and pulls me next to him. My bare legs rip off the hot leather seat. I yelp, and then giggle but neither of them looks up. Tom lifts me half onto his lap, with the brake lever digging into my legs. He lifts my head, his eyes still fixed on the mirror, and touches his lips to mine. His mouth is soft and sticky with Vaseline. He tastes of the pandan cake we ate on the drive here.

It's me! I want to shout. I want to break away from Tom and laugh at Peony's stunned face – *See, Peony, it isn't you, it isn't always you* – but Tom's not even looking. He's staring over my shoulder into the rear-view mirror. Even as his tongue flickers to mine, he never once looks away from Peony.

I wriggle loose and my leg pushes against the brake lever. It creaks and grates down a notch. Tom shifts too, and then the car begins to roll forward.

'Tom!'

He snatches at the steering wheel. The car turns, lurches again and starts to tilt. Two side wheels sink down over the bank as he pulls at the steering wheel.

'The brake! The brake!'

We both grab for it together, pulling upwards, but it's too late.

'Pull it harder!' Peony screams, but we're already teetering on the edge and sliding sideways. A banyan root thuds against my window, smashing it, and the car topples over. We smack into the muddy water with a giant slap. Tom and I cannon against each other and I can hear Peony screaming still. Tom's shouting too, and I'm pressed against the upside-down roof. I can't see anything but mud, slopping halfway up the windows. I kick my legs out and grip the edge of the shattered window. We're completely underwater now, my face is hurting and my lungs cramp and spasm. *It's cold*, I think irrelevantly; who would have thought this swamp could get so cold? And then another kick and I've pulled myself out through the window opening. From here, it's almost beautiful. It doesn't look real, all that silt suspended in the greenish water and the San casting a huge black shadow over it. There are shafts of sunlight tangled up with the ribbons of water-weed and one pale hand pressed against the closed rear window of the car. Peony.

I break through the surface, sobbing. I must have been screaming for a long time, because my chest feels flattened and dry inside. I can't even take a breath at first. Tom's come up, too, further out in the swamp. He's clinging to one of the banyan roots.

'Get my father,' he gasps, and dives down again.

He's going down to Peony, of course. He'll dive and dive again as I clamber up the bank and stagger towards the path. 'Dr Harcourt,' I'll whisper, while my breath gives out and I tumble to my knees over and over. The leper colony's half a mile down the road, and by the time I reach it Tom will have dived a hundred times, a thousand times, and Peony's hand will have peeled away from the window to lie limp in the brackish water. And though I don't know it yet, I'll always – even fifteen years later – be able to taste that pandan cake and a slick of Vaseline on my tongue.

I don't sleep that night. Perhaps nobody does. Karthika stays overnight, folded in on herself in a corner with Rajneesh swaddled tight as a steamed bun. She won't meet my eyes. Don't worry, Karthika, I want to tell her. From now on you're welcome to Tom, to top-doctor-lawyer Tom with his handsome suits and pale skin. It's fifteen-year-old Tom I was after all along, it's jackstones and first kisses, and love before other people got in the way.

At some point the rains get heavier. The drains are overflowing, Ammuma calls, and Karthika needs to clear them. So out Karthika goes into the blackness, wiping her nose on the back of her hand and with Rajneesh tied under her soaking blouse. I can see her bent double, slapping at the puddles with a palm-frond broom. She stops eventually; there's no way anyone can clear those drains fast enough tonight. She leaves wet footprints as she squats in the dirtiest, dustiest corner of the verandah. Rajneesh babbles once or twice, then falls asleep neatly and quickly. Like his mother, he knows better than to take up much space.

Ammuma copes best out of all of us. She doesn't even mention Tom; Karthika must have been too mealy mouthed to get her point across. Instead, she finds me a spare carrier bag to hold snacks for the drive to KL tomorrow. She reminds me how bad the traffic gets on the Gua Musang road, and she even finds a map and plots out different routes.

Around midnight she asks me to put some sleeping mats for her in the prayer room. It's peaceful in there, amongst the flowers and coins and smell of incense that's soaked into the walls. A little bit of glitter, a few old friends. Not much to ask for, when you look at it that way. I wonder who she sees at night when she first closes her eyes. Francesca? Me? *Nobody*, she'd say if I asked. Nothing, an empty space like the middle of a wedding ring or a life-preserver or a whirlpool. All these things are the same, according to mathematics.

I go upstairs and gather the sleeping mats together from where Rajneesh was sitting yesterday in the middle of Ammuma's bedroom. The door to the box room's firmly closed and the key's gone, for the first time I can remember.

And then I slump in Ammuma's rattan chair. I'm not ready to sleep and I'm secretly glad to hear Karthika's smothered snores. Ammuma's snoring too, but much less decorously. Like me, she's used to sleeping by herself.

After an hour or so Ammuma's snores start to turn to words. At first it sounds like she's telling a bedtime story again – I hear tiger-princes in her snorts, and princesses in the silvery, delicate intakes of breath. But no. It's not a bedtime story; it's a warning. For me, for Karthika, for Peony; if it weren't thirty years too late it'd be for my mother, too. *Take care, you unwed girls,* she warns. *Take care, you streetwalkers and kampong brats and university lecturers: you'll come to the stickiest of ends.*

16.   And One Princess Remains: 1934

It's a shame nobody ever gave Cecelia that advice. Stay away from boys, stay away from temptation and danger and the lure of missed chances. But Cecelia wouldn't have listened. She's nineteen years old – plump and beaming, head of the matriculating class – when she turns up at the convent one evening in 1934. Mary's sitting inside with Sister Gerta, their hair stirred by the fan. It's that luminous and untrustworthy hour just before the rains, when the light's in the air and not in the sky. The convent lies dim and quiet, with only a few hushed footfalls and the trembling glimmer of a hurricane lamp to show anyone's there at all.

Mary's been spending a lot of her time at the convent lately. She likes the clean, white orderliness of it all and she likes being wanted. She hasn't converted to Christianity yet, and that means she still has an unsaved soul to offer. Sister Gerta licks her lips over that soul. More than once Mary's woken from her narrow mosquito-netted convent bed to see Gerta sprinkling her with a basin of holy water, in case Mary's dreaming of baptism. Mary wakes each morning at the convent in a damp and blessed bed but happier than she's ever been before.

It's a different story when she goes back home, though. Her mother's now wholly lost in her betel nuts and gin. Each night Radhika traipses barefoot through the scrub jungle, coming back to the house at dawn with her feet swollen and bleeding. She's trying to find her way back home, or back to something better. Poor Radhika, she's always been slow to give up hope.

Stephen's miserable too. Since Paavai left four years ago Stephen's been in a state of rage. He takes it out on the house, spending every night renovating and remodelling by the light of a smoky carbide lamp. When Radhika finally returns in the grey and ashy dawns, she could be forgiven for not recognizing the place at all. Stephen blames this house for everything, and traces his personal disasters to its corners and nooks. The puddles under the verandah are Radhika's smile; murky and unknowable. The sloping windowsills and overhanging vines are Anil's mind; blurred and shadowed beyond all hope. The dark corridors, the precarious ceilings, the rooms without windows and others without doors, well, they're the easiest of all. They're Stephen's own mistakes, in a very literal sense.

With a family like that, it's no surprise that Mary prefers to spend her time at the convent. These days, she only goes back home to talk to Anil. He's grown handsome and tall, with an eye for pretty girls. He's only thirteen years old, but if he knew what hearts were then he'd break them. Mary loves him more with every passing year.

'Mary, dear.' Gerta puts her embroidery down and looks across at Mary through the humid, breathless evening. 'I'm just going to prepare Agnes her supper. She'll be in here whining about how she's hungry soon.'

It's a joke Mary and Gerta share, this gentle pretence that Agnes could talk – could nag and whine and complain – if only she wanted to. Agnes is eight now and she's sweet and sturdy, but she's never said a word. Nevertheless, Gerta lives in a permanent and excoriating atmosphere of hope. If Our Lord can get off his cross and walk, she says, then Agnes will one day speak without a tongue.

Sister Gerta lumbers out of the room, heading for the convent kitchen. As soon as her skirts have twitched out of the door a tangled black head pops up outside the window and a hand waves frantically to Mary. It's Cecelia, looking exactly as she did last time Mary saw her. She's bent in at a window, she's baring her sharp little teeth in a friendly smile and she's about to cause trouble.

'Cecelia!' It's so dark that Mary can barely see Cecelia's face through the open window, just the lace of her dress glimmering in the firefly dusk. Cecelia and Mary have lost touch almost completely in the last few years. While Mary's been busying herself with needlework, Cecelia's been expanding her worldly education. She's been kissing boys in the back row of the Empire cinema, she's been sucking on cigarettes and stealing nips of alcohol from hipflasks. She's shallow, she's tacky, she's soiled and tawdry, and Mary's missed her more than she can say.

'Cecelia! I haven't seen you since –' Mary hesitates. Since the examinations, she was going to say. Every time she thinks of her failed Junior Cambridge exam she grows bitter. She isn't used to failure yet.

'Oh, I *know*, everything's so rushed these days, there simply isn't *time*.'

Cecelia sounds brittle and sophisticated. Mary's nearly in awe of her, this girl who used to be her best friend. She's heard the rumours about Cecelia, of course. Over the last few months the girl's become far too eager to grow up, to get herself a lover and ask questions later. Anybody who comes to Cecelia's house is fair game, and more than once a happily married postman or delivery boy has found himself standing by the gate with Cecelia's busy little hands sneaking around his waist under the pretence of helping him carry a parcel. Cecelia's out for a husband, or the nearest she can get.

'Come up to the hilltop,' she tells Mary. 'I want to talk. I want to tell you everything.'

Mary's surprised by this. They've barely spoken in the last few years, but now Cecelia's acting as though they're still best friends. She always did have an *everything* to tell, Mary thinks. Mary herself, sitting on a convent chair with her hair uncombed and her legs gawky under an outgrown dress, can't compete.

'How's dear little Anil?' Cecelia asks after the girls start walking up the hill. Mary isn't sure how to answer. Anil isn't all that little, for a start, and she doesn't want to risk him getting in Cecelia's lip-smacking way. Perhaps that's why Cecelia wants to be friends again, she thinks. She's been biding her time, that's all, until Anil grew up.

(Mary will later concede that she was wrong about Cecelia, that after being left to sink or swim in the flood of 1926, all Cecelia wants is to keep her distance from Mary's family. Only later, in her seventh decade and as distant from herself as Cecelia ever was, will my grandmother admit that she might – just might – have made a mistake.)

'I've something exciting to tell you,' Cecelia giggles. The two girls sit down on the grassy hilltop. It's nearly dark by now, and they can see the lights of Lipis below them. It's market night, and the busy bazaar is glaring.

'It's about Rajan,' Cecelia says, then adds carelessly, 'Have you seen much of him?'

Mary shakes her head. These days Rajan's a fully fledged doctor, a junior member of a government hospital across the valley. He's a political firebrand, too, and he's already spent a few nights in jail for protesting against laws that restrict rice cultivation to the Malays. Rajan doesn't want to cultivate rice – he doesn't know the first thing about it – but it's the principle of the thing, he says. He's big on principles, on equality of income and of opportunity. He's told Mary all about this, leaning out of the window of his father's Daimler while she walks to market with a fish basket over her arm.

'Well, *I've* seen quite a lot of him,' Cecelia says, gloating rather. 'We've been . . . well, we're thinking of . . .'

Cecelia hesitates. In fact, she isn't sure what exactly Rajan's been thinking of. The matter's been weighing on Cecelia's mind, waking her at three a.m. (as a durian falls in Mary's compound, as a bomoh creeps along a jungle path, as Japanese soldiers in Manchuria begin to cast glances at the Malay peninsula). And Cecelia certainly has good reason for being nervous. If Rajan doesn't start thinking of marriage soon, she could be in a very awkward position indeed.

'You mean . . . you're engaged?' Mary feels bitterness welling into her mouth. So this is why Cecelia's come to visit her. She hasn't come to make up; she hasn't come to be friends again or even to be enemies. She's come to gloat.

'He actually proposed to you?'

Mary looks at Cecelia carefully. Cecelia's lying back on the hilly grass with her knees apart and her white-frocked stomach a little higher, a little rounder than Mary remembers. A little too full to be explained away.

'Cecelia! You haven't! You *didn't*!'

It's undeniable, though. Cecelia is pregnant. For a second Mary's horrified – oh, poor Cecelia, she thinks in a moment of pure sympathy; what has she done?

'It's Rajan's, of course,' Cecelia says. 'We're getting married.'

That curdles Mary's sympathy. And the worst of it is, she believes Cecelia. There's a glow about her tonight, a radiant and blossoming beauty because she's carrying her lover's child. And that's a problem – that's a real problem – because Mary has always held out a forlorn hope that she herself might one day be Rajan's wife. In the chill of the convent nights Mary's imagined lying skin-to-skin with Rajan. She's imagined kissing him, licking him; in her convent bed and her imagination Mary's gone at least as far as Cecelia. She's foreseen lust and love and strolls hand-in-hand under the bougainvillaea bushes.

Now, though, it seems all that will belong to Cecelia. In a hot, hurting moment Mary sees Rajan and Cecelia living in a luxury bungalow with a tribe of half-Indian, half-Chinese babies who look Malay and can therefore move in any world they want. She sees Rajan content at last, and Cecelia on his lap with a little cat-smile. And Mary sees herself, too, for ever making do with a cold convent cot and a family who've no time for her; making do with a mild-mannered future of compassion and good works.

'You *trollop*, Cecelia! You dirty little *whore*!' Mary's good temper and good works, it's clear, are going to have to wait.

Cecelia sets her small teeth. 'Don't be jealous,' she answers. 'You never loved him anyway. Not properly; not the way I do.'

She lays a palm on her stomach and strokes dreamily. It's a clear enough message: Mary might have sailed over the floodwaters with Rajan once, but now Cecelia's snagged him like a fishing net.

Something about that gesture prises Mary open, sparking the tiniest, slightest flicker of her old bond with Cecelia. As the other girl pats her stomach, Mary feels something move inside her own. A wriggling little tadpole, fastened onto her liver and heart. *Jatuh hati* – falling liver – is what the Malays say for falling in love; and that's exactly what Mary feels. A swooping, dizzying feeling, because Cecelia has the real thing – Rajan's wriggling tadpole and liverish love – and Mary cannot stand that, cannot stand it at all.

'You should be happy for me,' Cecelia says with a provoking little smile. 'We're best friends.'

It's those last words that decide Mary for good and all. Best friends don't steal each other's imaginary boyfriends and imaginary futures, no matter how much in love they are. Best friends are supporting characters, not heroines of another story.

'I'll *show* you,' Mary bursts out, and then she's gone, sprinting down the hill road in her outgrown lace-up shoes. She's racing past the convent, she's running past the scatter of houses washed halfway up the hillside. And before Cecelia can even puff herself upright, Mary's down on the main road and heading to the night market.

When Mary reaches the night market she stops, breathing hard. Half of Lipis is in there, selling goats and meat and fruit and fireworks to the other half. News and scandal fly about in the brightly lit walkways, with every transaction being accompanied by its own morsel of gossip. Market ladies chatter over washing-up pans behind cook stalls, and jewellery makers stoop over fragments of metal to swap rumours with mining magnates. The noise is deafening, and from where she stands panting out here in the dark Mary can feel the wind of all those words.

And young Mary knows the power of words. She sets her teeth and tucks her hair neatly behind her ears. Stopping only to polish her shoes on the back of her grubby socks, she steps in through the market door and leans over a stall to whisper delicately in the ear of one of the market ladies.

'Cecelia Lim's going to have a baby,' she murmurs, 'and she says the father could be anybody. Just *anybody*.'

She hears the market lady's puff of surprise at being given this secret, this chewy and tender morsel of gossip. And then Mary takes a prim pace forward and stretches up to hiss the same thing to a group of Tamil rubber workers, who spit secrets as fast as betel-nut juice. She can hear fresh whisperings start behind her, swelled by the clicking of tongues. By the time Mary's walked all the way through the market, Cecelia's reputation will be in tatters. Cecelia will be condemned as reckless – her second baby, isn't it; *I* heard it was her third and a different father for all of 'em – and dismissed as a hussy who's got what's coming to her.

'What a bad wife she'll make,' Mary purrs to nobody in particular, and looking through the crowd sees Mrs Balakrishnan – Rajan's mother – prick up her suspicious ears on the other side of the market. Mrs Balakrishnan frowns, swivels, leans forward to catch the whispers and looks black as thunder. Rajan *won't* be marrying a bad wife, Mary resolves, with a comfortable lack of foresight. Not if she has anything to do with it.

17.   Tuesday, 8 a.m.

The courtyard's almost invisible behind sheeting water when I wake. Huge raindrops slam down onto the verandah roof and wet my feet with fine, bouncing spray. The prayer room's been swept and the candles relit, with Ammuma's sleeping mats piled up in a corner of the verandah. The clock in the hall finishes its chiming: eight o'clock. Time to go.

Karthika comes out onto the verandah as I shake the stiffness from my legs. She's dragging a bucket full of dirty water, with her skirt tucked high between her legs. Her bare feet leave splay-toed prints on the concrete floor. She heaves the bucket to the edge of the verandah and spills water in an arc. Without turning round, she takes a deep breath.

'Durga-Miss . . .' she says, then stops. She's frightened, I realize. She's scared I've spent the night chewing over what happened with Tom; gnawing my way through shock and anger until now I'm after revenge.

'Sorry, Durga-Miss,' she says. She looks down into the empty bucket, standing on one leg. She cradles the other foot like a stork against her bulging knee. She's swaddled Rajneesh under her flimsy blouse. 'About last night, so sorry. A mistake is all. A mistake.'

That shuts me up. Karthika's cleverer than I thought. She's learnt to apologize, to grovel, to make excuses before anyone's asked for them. She'd like to be vicious but if she can't, she'll be fragile.

'You're always meddling,' I snap. 'You go into my bedroom, you give Rajneesh my things. You tell lies about my . . . about Tom-Mister.'

Karthika looks taken aback. 'No, Durga-Miss. I didn't. I didn't *any* of it.'

'You're just jealous. You want to meddle in my life because –'

Because yours went wrong. That peaked face, all nose and eye sockets, watching from above a mop as I went off to school. Those thin fingers picking fish from the bones I'd left on my plate.

'No, Durga-Miss,' she insists, more earnestly than I'd expect. 'Not jealous.'

She looks down, and I can't believe it, but there's a blush creeping up her cheek. 'Me and Tom-Mister are hati . . . in love. He says he wants to marry.'

'He *what*?'

She smiles, unabashed and clear-eyed and greedy as any well-brought-up young lady. 'Look, Durga-Miss,' she insists. '*Look.*'

She starts undoing the buttons on her blouse. Rajneesh lies tightly swaddled against her ribs and I can see only the pale rind of his forehead. She pulls her blouse further apart to show me his skin gleaming against her flat brown breasts.

'See how fair? Like Tom-Mister . . . just like.' Her voice trails off. Gets quieter, more hesitant, as though for the first time she's hearing just how it sounds. He's Tom's son, she's saying, and I feel sick. Queasy, as the truth slips down like a cold pebble. He's Tom's blood and bone – foisted on her – in my bedroom, most probably. How did they do it without Ammuma hearing? Did she want him like I did? Did she not want him at all? She's my little sister, for what that's worth.

'So you can stop saying this, all of it,' she finishes, with a sudden tawdry bravery. 'I'm not jealous, no need of jealous. Tom-Mister loves me. He says it *serious*.'

'Karthika . . .'

And in the middle of this horror, it's somehow funny. *She looks so small, so fierce. So much like a servant-girl*, the old Durga would have thought.

'Karthika, Tom isn't – you don't really believe Tom's going to marry you?'

She doesn't reply. Perhaps she hasn't understood; she's not at home in English, where her elbows stick out and nothing quite fits. And I'm angry, all of a sudden. At Tom, at myself. At Karthika, who's had what I haven't and got what I'd have loved to refuse.

'You'd better stop saying things like that. You need to be modest, in your position.'

She stares at me, then her face suddenly crumples and she slams her foot against the empty bucket. Her thick toenails crack against the rim and it tumbles away. She balls her fists up in the folds of her too-large red nylon skirt and turns her back on me. I can guess what she's thinking. Modesty's no good to her; won't turn sequins into real gold or a red nylon skirt into a threadwork sari. Won't turn her into a girl who could have any man she wanted, instead of a girl who's already had several she didn't.

She stamps over to the sleeping mats, her lower lip pushed out and her eyebrows arrowed. Ammuma would say that I shouldn't encourage her by talking to her. Give her an inch, Ammuma says, and she'll take it, too.

As Karthika pulls the mats together I see something in the corner, a shapeless flop of canvas against the wall. Tom's bag. I quickly grab it as she stamps out of the room. The canvas straps are dark and stiff with sweat and cologne. Last night comes back to me with an ache in my belly. His fingers on my skin. A lick of his sweat on my tongue. And then Karthika, peering through the door with her eyes bright and vicious as a movie pontianak.

I hold the bag up, breathing in its smell. There's an address tag on it, a hospital-issued paper strip, with TOM HARCOURT in bold black letters. The address is Jalan Seroja, one of the streets on the outskirts of Lipis.

'Aiyoh, Durga,' Ammuma's voice makes me jump. 'Should be going already.'

She's standing by the verandah entrance watching me. 'Got packed, is it? Some bag for home?'

'Yes . . . yes. For home.' As I say it, I realize I'm going to keep it. I'm going to prop this bag up in the corner of my KL apartment where it'll slump against the wall and point out my thickening waist and tiny crow's feet. It's going to be the first thing I see when

I walk in and when I wake up. When Deepak calls to tell me he misses me so much that he's had to start sleeping with his wife again, then Tom's bag and I will huddle together and remind each other about all our bad decisions.

'You're ready to go?' Ammuma peers up at me, her eyes bright. She hands me a box, wrapped and smelling of food. Keema, mutton curry, brinjal pureed with yoghurt and oozing in its Tupperware. 'Won't have time to buy lunch at university.'

She pushes the food at me – *Take, take* – and then settles herself into her rattan chair. 'Will miss you,' she says quietly.

She looks tired, sitting tipped sideways with her head resting on her arm. The scar on her forearm looks red, like it always does when she's exhausted. A memory comes back to me of the hospital, her face all yellow bone and her smoke-sore voice.

'Ammuma,' I say, then stop.

I want to tell her I know she misses Francesca. I want to tell her I miss Peony. I want her to admit that china dolls won't help, nor autograph books – nor raking up the past, come to that. Perhaps that's what I've come back to learn; the ghosts in Malaysia are for good. They're fragile monsters, these nothings of ours.

Ammuma just shakes her head. 'Aiyoh, Durga, always so worry. Of course you should go.'

'You'll keep putting the dressings on?' I wrench myself back to the present. 'And take the antibiotics. They're in those little boxes for each day. You will remember, won't you?'

'Yes, yes, the antibiotics.' She rolls the word around in her mouth, pleased despite herself. She likes all the fuss of her dressings, the little bottles and finger-dabs of liniment. So far from the Minyak Angin Cap Kapak and Tiger Balm that she usually uses, or the Benedictine Karthika buys from the Chinese grocers.

'And if there's anything, then you just ring. Any time is fine, Ammuma, the office or at home or . . .'

'Durga.' She interrupts, putting her two palms on either side of my face. She smells like herself again, like Nivea and sandalwood soap. She drops a dry, hard kiss on my cheek then pushes me away.

She's on edge. Wanting to get going. Wanting me out so that she can settle down and miss me.

I go upstairs to change my clothes before I leave. Everything's sharper today, as though I'm finally feeling at home. I'm starting to remember details that were hardly worth forgetting to begin with. The lace collar on my favourite yellow dress, the dread of school on hot, fresh mornings when I'd forgotten my homework, reading comics while Vellaswamy-cook made lunch. Tomorrow, I think, I'll be back in KL. Buying yellow blouses that don't flatter me, and watching the sky for Superman.

Ammuma waves me off from the verandah. At first the car won't start, then it lurches forward. Unmarked assignments spill out of my bag into the footwell. They'll get dirty and there'll be complaints from students, objections that I've missed out a mark. I watch Ammuma recede into the background. She's a white blur in the darkness of the verandah, and I'm leaving all my memories behind and looking forward, with a kind of joy, to complaints about marking.

*

Halfway to Lipis the traffic starts to thicken. The morning's turned hot and damp as a mouth, and my hands leave palm prints on the steering wheel. Cars crawl along and motorcycles inch up the sides of the road. Everybody looks worried behind the glass of their windscreens. The traffic stops, and a family of children burst shrieking from their car. We're not moving anyway, but a taxi driver waves at them – *Get back in there!* – with an impatient hand. Two cars nudge at each other's bumpers and rage threatens to overflow.

The sky's an ugly yellow, lumped with clouds that mean business. I can hear thunder rolling somewhere down in the valleys, and a wind like ripping cloth. A flicker of blue light comes from somewhere further down the road and all of us pause. The mother holding a naked baby. The father with food spilling from his hands. The taxi driver, now expressionless as a movie star. Into this sudden quiet comes a police motorcycle, working its way back against the traffic.

'Turn round!' he's shouting. 'Go back!'

Nobody moves, of course. There's nowhere to go. We all sit, stupid and frozen behind glass with our tongues stopped in their chatter. My window's down and the breeze stirs the papers scattered over the car floor. A drop of rain falls through with a single, ominous plop.

'There are floods.' The policeman's stopping at intervals up the line, shouting through his cupped hands. His eyes pop slightly, and his thick neck strains under his turban. 'The road's blocked. Go back!'

'Blocked?' someone shouts.

'Everywhere?'

'To KL? To *KL*?'

The policeman doesn't stop. A dismayed chatter rises behind him.

There must be a way to get to KL, they're saying. Most of these people aren't locals: they're tourists or businessmen or simply lost. There must be a way out of Pahang, they're insisting. It isn't the sort of place you stay.

But there isn't another road. The floods have come up fast, bubbling over from wells and drains, and we're stuck. There's a headache growing behind my eyes. All around me cars are slowly turning round, backing and filling and making their way along the grassy middle verge. The family dump themselves back into their car seats and the father begins to sound his horn in short, vindictive bursts. The back of my neck pinches, as though someone's dragged the skin tight. I start the car again, my toes curled tight in their sandals. I wrench the steering wheel around – horns and shouting, 'Look where you're going!' – and the rear-view mirror shows me a long, strung-out bracelet of traffic wrapped tight around Kuala Lipis.

★

It's two hours before the traffic eases. People have peeled off to villages and flood evacuation centres, their tail lights red and affronted. I've been looking for a place to pull over for ten minutes, but all the verges are full of motorcycles and broken-down cars. I'm exhausted. I can feel my blouse clinging tight with sweat, and my thighs chafed by the leather car seat. One strip of white line crawls past under my car, then another and another. Someone takes pity, waves me through to the side of the road. Through the windows the drivers look goggle-eyed, staring right through me.

Up ahead there's a huge banyan tree, nearly as big as the one out near the Kampung Ulu swamp. There's a streetlight tangled in its roots. Ghosts lurk in those roots, Ammuma used to say, devils and jungle spirits and plain old murderers waiting to knife you with their parangs. I turn off the engine anyway, and rest my head on the steering wheel. The murderers will have to take their chances.

When I open my eyes again, I see Tom's bag slumped in the footwell. Karthika's sneery little smile comes back to me. *He loves me, Durga-Miss,* she said, and I could almost envy her. At least she has something to be wrong about.

Jalan Seroja isn't far from here, only a few streets over. Practically on the way home. If this were one of Ammuma's stories, Tom would be waiting for me there. He'd appear from behind a palm tree or abseiling down a wall. He'd carry me into the jungle with a knife between his teeth and my hair arranged to show off my cheekbones. There'd be a map, an escape route. Burn after reading. Swallow in case of emergency. Look before you leap, which good story heroines never do.

An oniony smell rises from my armpits as I tug the bag up onto the seat. None of that's going to happen – I don't have the cheekbones and won't get the happy ending – but perhaps Tom and I can sit down anyway. Talk about his son; talk about my sister. Have a cup of tea and fish out some drowned women from their wells and swamps. I want to be friends, which should be easier than lovers and might just last.

And where do I come into it? Peony whispers inside my head, flicking that tangled hair from her sleepless eyes. I have an answer this time, though: she doesn't. *Because you're dead, Peony, you're dead and that's all there is to it.*

★

Jalan Seroja is a long street, running out past the high bridge. The water's brown and choppy underneath, and I can see palm-oil plantations in the distance. All those stubby trees whipping their shocks of hair about. I wonder what it's like to live out there, with the stink of char in your nostrils all the time. It's solid enough to slice, to cut and cube and chew till shreds of it hang in your teeth.

The address is just off the main road, down a private drive. A large bungalow stands at the end, two storeys and whitewashed clean behind high iron gates. It has an air of drawing itself up off the ground, refusing to get the tips of its feet dirty. I can see banana plants over the wall, and a froth of bougainvillaea.

The wind picks up as I climb out of the car. The telephone wires are vibrating overhead, as though there's a tumbling current up there. Mother Agnes used to say those high-up winds brought ghosts, the kind to slide in through your ears and turn your thoughts inside out. I shake my head; pull myself together. I've had quite enough of ghosts for today.

Inside the compound yard I see a woman bending over a terra-cotta flowerpot. She's white, large-hipped, in a pink cotton sundress. Her toenails are polished green and her hair's blonde, almost white in the sun. Next to her is a bright red convertible, a more-money-than-sense car in the luckiest of colours. My stomach starts to dip.

'Yes?' There's a slight Australian lift to her voice, a gluey blur as though she's stuffed her mouth with meat.

'I'm Dr Panikkar,' I hear myself say. 'I'm looking for Tom.'

'Tom?' She stands up and brushes her hands on the seat of her dress. She straddles the path and nudges a flowerpot behind her with her strong calf.

'Are you from the hospital?' she asks. She gives me a close-lipped smile and adds, 'I'm Alice.'

I shake my head. 'No, no, I'm from KL. Not the hospital.'

She tips her head back, watching me. Good eyebrows, the kind you inherit with skin like that and the diamond bracelet that's tight around her wrist.

'Sorry,' she says. 'Tom's not here.'

'Oh.' I swallow. 'Is he coming back? I wasn't expecting . . .' Her.

She gives me a hard stare. 'They aren't, generally,' she says, so quietly I might miss it.

She watches me watching her hands – bare, no ring – and the ghost of a smirk flits over her face. She stands there in front of Tom's house just exactly as though she belongs. And she does. She's a wife. She's a mate. She's fifteen years wrapped up in a pink-print dress and she's been here all along, if I'd only had the sense to see.

'Did you say Panicker?' she asks suddenly. She slurs it, mashing the edges of the name. I turn into *one who panics*, in Alice's mouth.

'Yes.'

'You know Mary Panicker then? Lives out past Kuala Lipis?'

'She's my grandmother.' I can hear my voice grate, but Alice takes no notice.

She comes closer, pushing her gleaming hair back. 'I hope you don't mind me saying it, but she needs a lot more support, you know. She has Tom out there all the time, fetching her groceries or taking her on trips to Kampung Ulu and Pulu and Wulu or wherever. Ridiculous names,' she adds, nearly under her breath.

'Kampung Ulu?' A gust of wind ruffles my hair and sends the bougainvillaea stalks chattering against the wall.

Alice looks impatient. 'Something like that. She's got him driving her out there every month.'

'I'm sorry . . .'

Alice's nose wrinkles like a cat given food it won't eat. She sighs. 'I'll tell him you came by.'

She's already turning away. The cloth of her dress pulls tight against her haunches as she steps over her flowerpots. Anyone else would tug it down, with the embarrassed shuffle of a fat woman seen from behind. Not Alice. She swings her legs out, her thighs slapping together, and climbs the house steps without a single glance back.

I feel battered, as though I've been in high seas or a rolling barrel. I walk slowly back to the car, letting Tom's bag fall on the passenger seat. I've come all the way to Pahang and ended up just where I started. A two-minute Maggi-noodle mistress. Handy at the time. Not like Alice, who fits. Alice, who's tamed the jungle into terracotta pots and sundress prints. It'll take more than a flood to get her out; the Jelai and I don't stand a chance.

18.   A Prince and Princess Marry: 1935

Three months after the rumours about Cecelia begin, the satay man turns up at Mary's house.

'Cecelia Lim's left home,' he tells her. 'In disgrace.'

Mary, her lips coated with peanut sauce, stares. She thinks he's joking, at first. But the satay man gazes blandly back at her, hands her a stick of mutton and shrugs his shoulders. The Lim girl or the Panikkar girl; they're all the same to him.

Because Mary, without knowing it, has started a wildfire of gossip. She didn't mean to, of course. She'd expected a few whispers in the marketplace, an unkind glance or two sent Cecelia's way. A few small hurts, enough to get her own back – and Rajan, too, into the bargain. If she'd kept her ears open, if she'd known how bad the gossip had got, she might have stood up for her old best friend. But Mary hasn't been to the marketplace since it all began, and she hasn't heard a thing. She's spent these three months quietly, sewing with the nuns or reading in one of her father's endless corridors. Mary's been nestled in lonely, forgiving places, and she's forgotten how much a reputation matters.

So this news comes as a shock. But she rallies, takes a bite of her mutton and pulls herself together. She knows better than to give in to her feelings.

'Best thing that could have happened,' she tells the satay man sturdily.

Sometimes, she thinks, *you have to be cruel to be kind*. And when the satay man's news spreads, Mary's glad to have heard it first. Cecelia and her growing stomach, it turns out, have boarded a bus to KL and they won't be looking back. The market ladies lick their lips over it, of course. They blame Cecelia's mother, Cecelia's friends and her schoolteacher and even Solomon Varghese and his brother-in-law Amir. Solomon and Amir are regarded doubtfully anyway; they take long walks hand-in-hand through the jungle, and exchange hot-eyed whispers through keyholes. After steadfastly making love to each Varghese sister, it seems Amir's finally found peace in the arms of the brother. Typical, the market ladies huff; the only faithful lovers in Lipis are the boys.

But Mary can't bring herself to be completely sorry Cecelia's gone, not quite. Because since Cecelia rode away on that bus, Rajan's been paying Mary some definite attention. He turns up every day with his curling moustache and split-legged stethoscope and gives her confident, unregrettable kisses. Rajan moves quickly, and he's certainly got over Cecelia. Like everyone in Lipis, he'd heard the rumours about her, and he dropped her like a stone. Rajan, unlike Mary, believes in being cruel to be cruel.

And so Mary isn't surprised to spot him waving at her one sunny morning soon after she turns twenty. She's climbed into the casuarina tree to be alone with her thoughts. Mary's fined down over the last few years, and there's a suggestion of something needle-like about her. Something hard, like a casuarina, and breakable. Liable to draw blood.

'Mary, darling! How are you?' Rajan pulls himself up from the ground to the branch Mary's sitting on. 'Marooned between earth and sky . . .'

Mary rubs her forehead irritably. Rajan's been doing this a lot, lately, coming out with snippets of poetry and lines from plays. Asking her what she thinks of T. S. Eliot, of women's rights and the state Europe's in. He's filling her mind with education, and Mary doesn't like it. Poetry reminds her of her failed Junior Cambridge exam, and any mention of women and their rights brings back the image of Cecelia, giggling on a convent hilltop.

'I'm well, thank you,' she says. Despite all her regrets, Mary still wants Rajan very, very much. It's partly the musk of sex he exudes whenever he moves. It's partly the thought that something good has to come out of Cecelia's exile, otherwise what was the point? And it's partly Mary's own father, who's put up the sort of opposition that makes Mary wild with rage.

'No daughter of mine,' Stephen has thundered, 'is going to marry the son of an Indian quack!'

Stephen's become thinner over the years, his eyes are redder and these days he barely bothers to finish building new rooms in his house before tearing them down. He's disintegrating rapidly, becoming a remittance man whose Manchester family want nothing more than for him to stay in Malaya out of everybody's way. The only person who still loves Stephen is fourteen-year-old Anil, who loyally sleeps in one new room after another as his father builds them, but Stephen barely notices him, and most mornings Anil wakes to the sight of a blue sky and his father dismantling the roof. For Mary, it's worse. She's not yet twenty-one; she still needs Stephen's permission to marry and she doubts very much she'll get it.

'You're looking spiffy, old girl,' Rajan says. The slang is a recent affectation, as are the waistcoat and soft hat, an attempt to slather colonialism over his dark skin. He pulls himself up onto the branch and squeezes close to her broderie-anglaise skirt.

Mary gives him a sharp look. It's flattering to have Rajan's full attention, but every time she looks at him she sees wan-eyed, round-faced Cecelia. And she can't leave that thought alone.

'Do you miss her?' Mary asks, compulsively. 'Cecelia?'

Rajan knows by now to ignore these questions of Mary's. 'Come for a walk with me,' he says, and takes her hand.

The pair of them slip down out of the tree to land on the padang grass. A few children are playing cricket on the padang, and their screeching laughter echoes over the field.

'How sweet,' Mary says, although she thinks nothing of the sort. 'I love children, don't you?'

Rajan beams. He considers this an entirely proper view for a woman. He slips his arm around her waist, guiding her onto a jungle path. They brush aside ferns and low, sliding stalks of rattan. A leech fastens onto Mary's ankle, filling with blood. She feels hot and itchy, like she might want to cry. Something momentous is about to happen, or perhaps it already has.

Rajan turns to her in that dappled light and puts his hand behind her head. He pulls her close to kiss her and she feels light and air-filled, as though balloons are colliding inside her belly. The blood rushes to her lips, leaving the rest of her drained and empty. Her fingertips go white and she shifts uneasily from one foot to another, knocking the leech off her ankle in a spatter of crimson blood.

Rajan pulls her dress off her shoulders, kissing the tip of each collarbone. His own clothes are coming off too, and Mary shudders. She pulls him to her, then gives a little scream as he drops to one knee. He looks up at her, half-naked, his shirt-tail hanging loose and one sock flashing pristine white against the mud. He's holding a ring, and Mary fights back a desire to giggle. She'd always assumed proposals would be fully dressed affairs. The sort you might tell a granddaughter about.

'Mary. Will you marry me?'

When Rajan slides the ring onto her finger her heart beats faster, drumming its heels. That drumming warns Mary that she's on the verge of disaster, that this is the biggest decision of her life and she must make it now. She thinks of lonely, celibate Sister Gerta; she thinks of trudging to market with a heavy fish basket; she thinks of her future shut up with an incomprehensible mother and an intolerable father and of growing old with nobody to rescue her. And then – because Mary's open-minded and sees all sides of a question – she thinks of Cecelia, lonely exiled Cecelia who was Rajan's true love. She thinks of Anil, and how her marriage would leave him alone to face the frailties and doubts of the world. And then, too, she thinks of a durian fruit hurtling down towards a dark-skinned servant-woman who predicted just this dilemma. Bearing all that in mind – and bearing in mind that Mary at twenty is still very young, that she thinks she's in love and that she has a history of impulsive decisions – she looks up at Rajan to answer.

'Come here, Mrs Doctor Balakrishnan!'

It's too late; he's taken her silence for agreement. He surges to his feet for a gluey, satisfied kiss. His trousers are still at half-mast, her blouse is still around her waist and whatever she was about to answer has been lost in a press of lips and bodies.

In half an hour's time they'll walk back on that jungle trail. Mary will be carrying her shoes in one hand and a spray of bougainvillaea in another. The flowers don't suit her; their colour clashes with her pale skin and she looks washed out and tired. She'll look much better in orange blossom, in photos the colour of old tea and a finger-tip veil. She'll look brave and pure and ardent, as only a young bride should, and for the rest of her life she'll wonder what might have happened if Rajan had waited just a heartbeat longer.

*

'Mary. Mary,' Anil croons. She's left Rajan at the top of the drive and come back to find Anil sitting on the verandah. He's rocking himself in a raw and shining new rattan chair and she runs to him, takes him in her arms and feels him wriggle away. He stares at her ankle, where the blood's soaking through her sock, and his eyes widen.

'It's just a leech,' she says, and then – because this should be a celebration, because she needs to share the news with someone – 'Anil, I'm getting married!'

Tradition and the law say Rajan should have asked Stephen for her hand in marriage first, they both know that. But tradition also says the mothers should have arranged the match, Radhika and Mrs Balakrishnan putting their glossy heads together over tea and sweets. Plotting so much money in return for Mary's fair skin, so much kicked back for Rajan's unsavoury political leanings. Perhaps the wedding wouldn't have come off after all; Radhika might have smiled sadly, gulped her gin and kept her daughter well out of it all. Perhaps Rajan himself would have taken fright. He might have learnt about Mary's true character; he might have heard whispers in the markets and five-foot-ways that Cecelia Lim was never that bad, and Mary Panikkar knew it.

But since Mary and Rajan have arranged it for themselves, there's nothing to stand in their way. 'I'm getting married, Anil! But you can come and visit me,' she adds. 'It won't be a bit like Paavai said, I promise . . .'

It's no use. Anil doesn't talk much, which leaves him plenty more room for thinking, and right now he can see through Mary's protestations. Rajan won't stand for a halfwit brother-in-law hanging around, and this might be one of the last few moments Anil will be alone with his sister. So he pushes her away, jumps off the chair in tears and races down the steps and into the jungle.

Who knows what he was thinking, this strange, quiet great-uncle of mine? Anil, who's always been more complicated than anyone's given him credit for, is the kind to fling himself away from trouble. The kind of boy to see it coming, to put his head down and run as fast as he can from this vision of the future, until he runs slap-bang into Paavai's son Luke, kicking a stone down the jungle path.

'Where are you going?' Luke asks mildly.

Luke and Anil look extraordinarily alike, although Anil's four-teen and Luke is only four. They're both coffee-coloured, sturdy, with Stephen's grey eyes and huddled neck.

'Mary!' Anil bursts out. 'Mary . . . marry, Mary.'

Luke frowns. He doesn't understand, but he can tell his best friend is terrified.

'Anil-Uncle,' he says. 'You and me sit down there.'

He tugs Anil, now quieter and calmer, along the dappled trail. It's the same path that Mary and Rajan walked earlier and their footsteps are still plain for Anil to see in the mud. He follows them, head down and eyes wide, and then stops abruptly. There's a splash of blood mixed in with the leaves.

Anil yelps; the blood is so red, and it's soaked into the ground. The leaf underneath squirms and pulses and throbs with a sicken-ing rhythm. If Anil stopped to think, he'd realize it's only the leech that had been on Mary's ankle, unceremoniously pushed off by the toe of her patent-leather shoe, and spilling out its last meal as it fell to the jungle floor. Anil should know this, of course, but in his panic he forgets. Luke gives a little scream, and clings to Anil with all the strength of his four-year-old fingers.

'Blood, Anil-Uncle! It's hantu – it's ghosts. It's *bloodsuckers*!'

Luke cowers back against Anil's legs. He's a superstitious child, and Paavai's filled his head with tales about drowned women, about lepers and jungle spirits and pontianaks. No wonder he's confused. The two of them clutch at each other's hands and back slowly away from that throbbing crimson puddle.

'Ghosts,' Anil repeats thoughtfully. 'Devils.'

Anil will continue to whisper this all night. He'll still be whispering it in the sleepless dawn when Mary rolls over in her convent bed, thrusts her fists with grim determination between her legs and begins to plan her wedding day.

Because against all expectations, Stephen has agreed to the marriage: Mary and Rajan will marry in two short months' time. It'll be an extravagant wedding with music and snake charmers, with Mary in her jewelled gown and her mother's rubies. Radhika will sniff back tears and Stephen will escape from the dancing to sit in his lonely study and brood over the newspapers and his letters. And after that, Mary and Rajan will move – for ever, Mary thinks, because at twenty everything is for ever – across the Kinta Valley.

After Mary's gone, there'll be nobody to calm Anil's fears and hush his talk of devils. The state of Europe will get worse in those years, women's rights won't count for much and T. S. Eliot for even less. Stephen – reading about Europe in flames, about men shot against the wall and his own brother's death from shrapnel while driving an ambulance in France – will never tell his son that devils don't exist. Radhika, learning in an airmail letter of famine riots and madness in her hometown, will lock herself into her bedroom and scream quietly for days.

All of this will get into Anil's dreams. He'll see splashes of blood in his sleep; he'll see leeches and snakes that have charmed his sister away. He'll submerge himself in books he can barely read. He'll learn about Chinese ghosts and Malay tricksters, about vampires and demons that flap their wings about the roof at night. He'll open his mind to a world he can't see or touch; he'll lose what language he has and gain a reckless, useless sort of bravery instead. With his mind open and his mouth firmly shut, it won't be long before he makes the worst decision of his young life.

19.   Tuesday, 3 p.m.

It takes all afternoon to make it back from Tom's house to Ammuma's. The roads south are still blocked, and there are only a few cars left on the roads. The clouds have thickened, and look like they mean business.

'Durga!'

The smell of chai and spices drifts out from the verandah, where Ammuma's sitting with Mother Agnes. They have their heads together over a pile of cheap postcards, scrawled over in clumsy writing. Ammuma told me the left-behinds have taken to dropping their letters at Mother Agnes's house to save the postage. It's a point of pride with Agnes never to let them down and so she picks the letters up every day. By the time Arif-the-postman arrives here she's stamped every letter and told Ammuma every secret in them. Ammuma won't read them herself; she'll only give them a shake and smooth them down. She used to be a postmistress herself and nobody – she says now over Mother Agnes's head with a scalding calm – likes to get crumpled news.

Mother Agnes is scribbling in her red exercise book – private, those crimson pages, for secrets and confidences only – but drops it when she sees me. She snatches up her blue-for-friendship book instead.

Durga! she writes.

She's in a satin-green kebaya and her eyebrows are plucked into pencil-thin lines. She heaves to her feet as I climb the stairs, bringing me into a powdered hug that smells of perfume and ink. Mother Agnes moves like a much larger woman, always leaving room for extra flesh.

'What is it, Durga? All this coming-going, forgetting something is it?' Ammuma leans forward. She looks more animated than she did this morning, her eyes bright with secrets.

'All the roads are closed,' I say. 'Floods, out by Gua Musang.'

Mother Agnes turns to Ammuma with a triumphant look. She scribbles another line in her blue exercise book.

I told you, Mary. They have us on evacuation alert in my village.

Ammuma clicks her teeth impatiently. 'Your village is in a swamp. Shouldn't have built there to begin with.'

Ammuma drops her slurs when she talks to Agnes, those *lahs* and *arres* that pepper her speech normally. Agnes is, after all, a schoolteacher and mustn't give herself airs.

'You ring your job.' She turns to me. 'Tell them what-all is happened.'

My stomach tightens. When I was at Tom's house I'd forgotten about work. But now Anwar looms at the other end of the phone line, a gathering thundercloud garnished with a scrap of white handkerchief.

The phone lines may be down, Mother Agnes writes. She scrawls her letters larger than normal, breathing sympathy from every pen stroke.

I bite at one of my nails. 'They can't be, surely. Not already.'

Ammuma's voice follows me as I walk quickly through the front room, dropping Tom's rucksack by the hall phone. 'Don't be foolish, Agnes. Worrying the child.'

But when I pick the receiver up there's nothing but silence. Not even static, or the clicking of a connection trying to be made. I put the phone down and scrub at my face with my fingertips. Nothing to be done. In a few hours Anwar will be standing in the office doorway staring at my empty chair, disapproval breaking like waves on the rock of his nose.

I turn away, feeling my headache tighten. The kitchen radio's on, which means Ammuma's sent Karthika home.

'. . . urgent evacuation will be arranged.' The radio announcer sounds unflurried, all soft-serve voice and rounded vowels. 'Residents of Pahang should keep alert for flood updates.'

'Ammuma!' I scramble back to the verandah. 'Ammuma, did you hear? The radio was saying we might be evacuated.'

She snorts, dropping her dignity for a palate-cleansing, phlegmy distaste. 'Only down Raub, it is,' she says. *What else can you expect?* she implies.

Be patient, Durga, Mother Agnes agrees. Out here nobody takes disasters that seriously. Floods, storms, race riots: when Canada would be in flames, Pahang barely looks up from its dinner.

'Remember the last time, ar. Not doing that again.'

Ammuma's smile is humourless. She was last evacuated in 1971, when the government set up tents after the huge Pahang floods. Better off at home, Ammuma decided after two days, and demanded the use of a rescue dinghy instead. They'd let her, too; Ammuma outside being less trouble than Ammuma in.

'Durga, you stay here tonight,' Ammuma says. 'No point coming-going like this,' she adds. 'Tomorrow all the roads will open, isn't it?'

She looks tired, Mother Agnes scribbles.

'Sleeping in a chair only last night,' Ammuma says self-righteously. 'Dark circles on her eyes now.'

Mother Agnes looks up at me with a sympathetic smile and pushes one of the postcards across the table.

Read this, Durga, she writes in her red exercise book, trying to cheer me up. *This girl's gone to the bad and no mistake.*

That red book bulges with gossip and scraps of paper. She pushes it back inside the straining waist of her skin-tight sarong kebaya. The more rumours she swaps the fatter it gets, tight against her waistband, and soon she's going to have to change her tailor or let her girls go to the bad without anyone knowing at all.

'No need for Durga to see all that.' Ammuma slaps her hand down on the postcard and gives Mother Agnes a warning look. She flicks the postcard back across the table, humping her shoulders so I can't see.

'All this nonsense, and on the back of a postcard too,' she mutters. 'No morals, these left-behinds of yours.'

I slip out through the front room and into the dining room,

where I unlatch the almirah door. I pull out Tom's bag of fireworks from where it nestles on the top shelf. It feels like a hundred years ago that I put it there. Ammuma's voice rattles on from the verandah, and I walk slowly back through the hall to where I dropped his rucksack. There's an ache deep inside me, a tearless and gulping ache as I gather all I have of Tom into my two hands.

Upstairs the bedrooms still stink of smoke. Karthika aired everything out, but the odour still seeps in from the locked side wings. I sit cross-legged on my bare mattress with my feet leaving dirty marks. Everything's quiet, and the radio's chatter drifts up from below.

I unzip the rucksack slowly, imagining Alice's capable fingers zipping and folding and clicking things shut. Inside there's an empty crocodile file and a dirty lunchbox. Nothing here except the gone-and-forgotten sniff of reheated noodles. No wedding ring, for example. No family photos, no declarations of undying love for Alice or Peony or Karthika. None for me, come to that.

I touch the fireworks packets, jumbled into their bright market-bag. He must have gone to some effort, I realize for the first time; he must have made a special trip. That thought brings back the ache, and so I pick up the autograph book instead. It's tucked into the very top of the bag, and I leaf through it to that front page again.

Francesca Panikkar,
Kampung Ulu, Pahang
Malaysia, Earth, THE WORLD

Kampung Ulu. Alice had talked about it too; she'd said Tom was taking Ammuma there. I frown, tracing the letters with my finger. They remind me of something, a long-ago something from when I was tiny. Francesca's old books that Ammuma used to keep in the Amma-tin.

I get to my feet very quietly. The Amma-tin was an old biscuit tin that used to be kept on a box-room shelf. Ammuma would take it out on special days, when she seemed heavy with sadness. She'd show me strings of beads or a tiny ornament. A teddy bear; a picture-book with pop-up animals inside, and a name and address written in the front cover. *Francesca Panikkar*. I remember pointing at it and asking scornfully why anyone would bother to write THE WORLD after her address. As if there'd be *another* world, I remember saying with my tiny arms folded and a sneer in my voice. And I remember Ammuma slapping me and taking the book away.

I pad softly out of my bedroom. Ammuma and Mother Agnes are still well away with their gossip, ears and eyes closed to everything but the smack of scandal. They don't hear as I creep out into Ammuma's bedroom, placing my bare feet edge-down so the floorboards don't creak.

Karthika's swept the floors upstairs scrupulously clean, leaving a line of dust straight across Ammuma's bedroom door. Underneath the smoke I can smell Tiger Balm and sandalwood, mixed with the antibiotic dressings from the hospital. The box-room door's closed and the key is gone.

I push my hands up through my hair and step back to look around the room. The box room's never been closed before, and I've no idea where Ammuma would put the key. Despite the fire damage, the room's surprisingly neat. She's got a place for everything: an almirah for cardigans, a dressing table for medicines, a bedside cupboard for things best kept hidden away.

I crouch down in front of the cupboard. It's on the side of the room that was protected from the fire, and apart from a coating of ash it doesn't look damaged at all. There was an identical cupboard in my room when I was younger. They're cheap plywood drawers from the sundry store and the lock on mine broke after a few months. You could only open it by smacking it hard enough to dislodge the latch, and so I kept all my secrets in there. Diaries, detention slips, maths tests where I hadn't topped the class. Ammuma had far too much respect for the furniture to break in.

I put my hands on Ammuma's cupboard, rocking slightly, then clip the door sharply with the edge of my palm. The movement comes back to me. Once, twice and then the door swings open. Inside there are a few earrings without backs, a tube of hand

156

cream, a watch strap half-rotted away in the humidity. And the box-room key, large and brass, on a leather thong.

The box-room door opens reluctantly, pushing against swollen floorboards. There's a strange, filtered light in here as though oiled paper's been laid over all the windows. The floor's littered with curls of dried-up centipedes, and dust from years ago.

There are two large trunks in the far corner. I remember these: Ammuma kept my Christmas and Diwali presents in there because I wasn't big enough to open the lids. I used to stand on the attic ladder and watch her over the partition wall as she knelt here with an armful of packages. *Not yet, Durga*, she'd say, without even bothering to look up. *Have some patience, child*. And then – on a good day – she'd take out the Amma-tin from the bottom of one of the trunks, and call me down.

The trunks are smaller than I remember, bound with iron and faced about with teak wood. Under my fingertips the wood feels spongy, as though it's got old without anyone noticing. I kneel down, just as Ammuma used to do, and shove at the lid of the closest trunk. It opens smoothly. Perhaps it wasn't ever as heavy as I thought.

It's filled with bulging plastic bags. I pick one up at random and hold it up to the light. It's been marked with thick black pen: *Francesca Birthday*. Inside are trinkets wrapped in cellophane: glass bangles, some pink hair slides and a feather clip. Another one's labelled *Francesca Christmas*. There are dolls in this one, all dressed in silk and satin like princesses. The cross-legged Indian doll lies on top. Ammuma's carefully mended it so you can barely see where the cracks were. I didn't know she had the patience for such painstaking work any more. There are picture books, coloured pencils, costume jewellery wrapped in red-and-gold paper. *To Francesca*, read the gift tags taped to every package.

Francesca. For a second it feels as though there's somebody else here; someone who's been walking a pace behind me ever since I came to Pahang. I'd thought she would be Peony, but it's never that simple. She's Peony, she's Francesca, she's a baby with a Little

Twin Stars book and she's a teenager with a best friend for ever. She's all the missing girls of Pahang rolled into one.

For a brief, hallucinatory second I wonder whether my mother might really still be alive. Whether she could be living quite calmly by the Kampung Ulu swamp – fifty years old by now; large as life and twice as unnatural.

'Amma?' I whisper, and the sound of my own voice shocks me back to reality. These aren't gifts for a fifty-year-old woman. Like the autograph book, these are gifts for the child she used to be. I can see the Amma-tin at the bottom of the trunk, dark-blue, with Huntley & Palmers in red writing. I hesitate. Locked up inside that rusted lid is a daughter, after all. No weightier than a breath, perhaps, but she's there for all that.

I take the tin out onto my lap and pry the lid off. There's a pop-up book lying on top, just like I knew there would be. Animals spring out from its pages: crocodiles with softened teeth and fish turned damp with age.

Francesca Panikkar, the inside cover reads.

Ipoh, Perak, Malaya, Earth, THE WORLD

It's Ammuma's elegant handwriting. The same as the lettering in the autograph book, crisp as a ruled line. There isn't much else in the Amma-tin. A few strings of beads, with the thread nearly rotted away. A wooden toy cat, long-since stroked into smoothness. An unbearable pair of tiny pink socks and a roll of plain black cloth. The cloth's wrapped around something slippery and yielding, and my fingers know what it is before I've even opened it. A small plait of hair slides out. It's been carefully preserved, tied with a pink satin ribbon.

I know this plait of hair, although Ammuma never showed it to me even on her saddest days. It explains a lot, for its size. Why Ammuma might still be buying gifts for a long-vanished four-year-old daughter. How she must have felt, the night she cut that daughter's hair off, and what the alternative might have been. Which is to say, not much of one at all.

20.   The Princess Lost: 1941

The birth of Mary's daughter was difficult, as first births generally are. Mary was alone in the echoing and expensive house in Ipoh except for an indifferent midwife. But then, she'd been alone nearly every day since moving to Ipoh. Rajan spent all hours working in the general hospital, and Mary herself had always found it hard to make friends.

So it was the midwife who helped her crawl between the bed and the marble floor, who held her hand through the pains. There weren't any aunties or grandmothers or quiet, caring friends. When Francesca opened her eyes on the world for the first time, it held nothing but her mother.

The next three years were hard ones for Mary. Rajan plunged eyebrows-deep into political scheming, bringing home firebrand friends and conspirators well into the small hours. These friends squatted out on the marble verandah – Mary'd moved up in the world; she had a marble verandah instead of a concrete one, she drank her tea out of a bone-china cup and wasn't a bit grateful for it. The friends smoked on that verandah and muttered out of the corners of their mouths. *War*, these friends muttered, and *Japan* and more and more they muttered *invasion*.

And then, before Mary knows it, it's 1941. Francesca's three years old with a charming lisp and two dimples in her chin and a howl that can stand plates on end. And those plates are empty, more often than not. Rice is rationed these days, as is milk and salt. Mary has very little spare to feed Rajan's friends but they're not, by now, the type of men to sit around a dining table. A few of the more cautious ones have already sent their wives to Australia or India or even Singapore, which is impregnable and which will never, ever fall. Occasionally the visitors include a few British soldiers, grim and over-clean men who make three-year-old Francesca cry and wriggle in Mary's arms at the sight of their pale skin.

'What a good thing you never met your grandfather,' Mary tells her daughter, thinking of Stephen's blustery red face. Stephen would never have approved of such a rebellious girl-child; didn't approve, in fact, when he had one.

Mary hasn't seen her parents since the wedding. She's exchanged letters, of course, the sort of buttoned-up, good penmanship letters that don't say anything at all. Her father's replies – Radhika, by now, is too far gone in betel-nut dreams to do anything so mundane as write to her daughter – talk about the weather. The expected rain. The expected heat. These letters are so bloodless, so lacking in muscle, that Mary's almost surprised to find the paper doesn't turn blank as soon as she's read them. Francesca will have more love than that, she resolves, and hugs her daughter tight.

'Come on, Fran,' she says. 'Leave your father in peace now.'

Truth be told, Rajan is playing an even more dangerous game these days than Mary knows. It isn't just old friends he's inviting into his house. He's inviting single-minded, single-eyed men agitating for Indian independence; he's inviting disaffected Malays who want their sultans back in Malay palaces and their rice paddies back in Malay hands. He's even on occasion invited a few meek and unthreatening Japanese men: a photographer, or a barber or a dentist. Harmless men, he would say, but no matter. Collaboration will, in any case, soon stop being a choice.

So when the rumble of planes overhead increases in frequency, when exploratory bombs start to be dropped over Ipoh and leaflets tumble down in every language known to man, Rajan's been expecting it. The general hospital has already started discharging patients in preparation for war casualties and the streets around are filled with one-legged men, with women recovering from hysterectomies and children with skin complaints. Mary goes about with pans of what little rice she can spare, and worries that Francesca will catch something awful from her new and leprous playmates.

Mary's looking thin and haggard these days, wearing herself out with war preparations. She stalks through the streets during trial blackouts, tutting over the tiniest chink of light and knocking at houses where hurricane lamps still glimmer. There aren't many of these houses, in fact, because half of Ipoh is doing the same and when one night the trial blackout is interrupted by a glorious mass of fireflies bursting into light in a nearby orchard, the brilliant streets are found to be packed with scurrying, scolding women.

But when the Japanese finally land at Kota Bharu at the end of 1941, all that preparation and worry become worthless. The British run, fleeing in their hundreds in cars and lorries. And it's not just the British running; it's Chinese, who know which way the wind is blowing, and Indians, who can sniff trouble from a mile away. One by one they slip into paddy fields with all their worldly goods tied to their backs, planning to live out the next few months in the jungle untroubled by anything but malaria and starvation. Others only run as far as their neighbour's abandoned house where they rifle the rooms for furniture and valuables. Refrigerators are migrated from wealthy mansions to huts that don't even have electricity, almirahs are shifted with the clothes still in them, and several families simply move themselves into the mansions instead and save on all the heavy lifting. It reminds Mary of the floods she saw as a child, where wives and children were abandoned in favour of goats and cold, wet coins. She knows that if she and Francesca are to make it out at all, she'll have to be braver than most.

And then one night when Rajan's been absent for twenty-four hours straight, a note in his handwriting comes to her door, delivered by one of those dubious friends. *Get out*, is all it says, and for a moment she thinks of refusing. But Mary's a hard-headed woman now, and something in those two frantic words convinces her.

As Mary gathers Francesca's belongings she hears a bullock cart go thundering past her windows. Somebody's set up a spotlight outside and it twists wildly. A beam of light bounces off her marble floors and sets the cats yowling. In that flitting light she can see others leaving too, rushing out of their houses with nothing in their hands. Across town, cooler heads are prevailing; the wives and children of British mine-owners are packing suitcases and closing up their shutters. By dawn, and all through next week and the next, cars will purr up to those British doors, silent Rolls-Royces and Daimlers smelling of leather and polished wood. As the days pass, the last wave of fleeing Europeans will jostle in their cars on the narrow streets, ramming each other off roads and the few bridges left intact. Their Rolls-Royces and Daimlers will rub together like potatoes being washed – as the Japanese will later say – while those same Japanese calmly cycle down the peninsula on borrowed bicycles. And two weeks later those bicycles will reach Ipoh and there'll be no point in Rolls-Royces or Daimlers or any cars at all, because dead people can't drive.

So Mary makes an escape of her own. By dawn she's pulled on her clothes, she's scooped up Francesca and she's walking out along the steep road that leads to Ipoh's limestone caves, twenty-five kilometres away. At each road junction she finds a dishevelled knot of people, huddled in the brown light. Fires are burning across the country and, although she asks everyone she meets, nobody's come from anywhere near Kuala Lipis. Mary isn't panicking – not yet, not yet – but in the distance she's sure she can see a column of advancing dust.

It takes Mary two days to reach the Ipoh caves. Francesca's only three and she can't walk far, so Mary makes the journey with her daughter cradled in her arms. By the time they arrive there are already people scattered through the caves, people crammed into passages and shallow scoops of rock. Mary climbs up to where the largest cave opens up to the sky and finds a cluster of worried faces.

'Hello?' she says. At first nobody answers.

'My girls. They just – took – my girls.'

Mr Thivappuram's come from across the valley. He's a bone-setter, the type of man Rajan would sneeringly call a quack. He looks lost now, his eyes red in their sockets. Mary sits down and Mr Thivappuram reaches out a smoke-stained and bruised hand to caress Francesca's head.

'What do you mean, they took them?' Mary lets go of Francesca's hand and watches her scamper around the pile of rubbish and sleeping figures.

'All the girls. When the soldiers arrived, they took all the pretty girls. Even the children.'

Nobody says anything. Mr Thivappuram's own daughters are famous beauties, two thirteen-year-olds with flower-petal mouths.

'From my village, too.' It's Mrs Chang, who's come north from her kampong because she thought her family would be safe in Ipoh. Last week she married her three plain daughters to the neighbour's boys, hoping that their status as married women would keep them from harm. But both Mrs Chang and Mr Thivappuram are here alone, with bruises and blood and no daughters at all, whether penny plain or tuppence coloured.

Mary looks over at Francesca, nestled against Mr Thivappuram more happily than she's ever been with her father. Francesca loves strangers; she'll gladly take the hand of a passing hawker or demand a cuddle from a taxi driver. When she wakes from nightmares she never calls for her Amma or her Appa, but always shouts names that Mary's never heard before, people from her storybooks or simply out of her own head. Francesca loves the unfamiliar – the strange, the different – and Mary wouldn't put it past her to walk right up to a Japanese general and ask for a piggy-back ride.

'Fran, though . . . she's too young. Of course she's too young. Isn't she?'

Mrs Chang and Mr Thivappuram look worried. Young, yes, they say, but who knows with these devils? Already rumours are flying about: rape and pillage and horrific injuries being visited on babies and grandmothers alike. Nobody is safe, Mr Thivappuram says, and looks at his empty hands.

'Francesca! Come here.' Mary claps her hands, commands her daughter away from Mr Thivappuram and into her own arms.

'Listen to me. Listen very carefully. We have to hide, do you understand? From the bad people.'

'You can't be a little girl any more,' Mr Thivappuram says suddenly, and turns to Mary. 'In the villages,' he says, 'they are chopping their daughters' hair. To make them look like boys.'

He touches Francesca's plait. There's a second of silence, then his meaning filters in and Francesca begins to scream.

'No! My hair! My hair. Amma, my hair!'

She's only three, but she kicks so fiercely that she almost escapes Mary's grasp, almost pulls free and runs all the way back home where she knows the bad soldiers have never come and her father is waiting and nobody will chop her own, her very own, hair off.

But Mary knows better. She crouches over Francesca, pinning her daughter with her knees, while down in the valley Ipoh burns. Mr Thivappuram has brought a knife, which everybody agrees, immediately, not to question. He hands it to Mary. It's clean and oiled with a blade that feels as cold as she's ever known. With Francesca squirming to get free, Mary takes her daughter's plait in one hand, pulling it tight. She slides the knife underneath, waits for a heartbeat, and slices.

As soon as her hair falls, Francesca stops screaming. She blinks, putting up her hands to feel at her shorn neck. She's had long hair all her life, ever since she can remember, and now that she feels it bobbing and short, a slow smile spreads on her face. Francesca — who loves the unfamiliar, who prefers people she's never met and places she'll never go — has found herself to be somebody completely different.

*

'Joseph!'

Now here's the sting in the tail. If Francesca's pretending to be a boy, then she needs a new name. Mary's already brought one Joseph into things when she was twelve years old and inventing her mother's indiscretions with a Kerala chauffeur. *Why not another?* she must have thought. Why not, indeed.

So here's another Joseph, a tiny three-year-old one with a ragged pink blouse and a mop of short hair. Mary's wrapped her daughter's plait in silk and stuffed it into her own pocket, until she feels ready to look at it again.

'Joseph, stay with me.'

Mary and Francesca-Joseph have come out of the caves by now. The Japanese have come down the Malayan peninsula, the British have come a cropper at Singapore, and everybody has come to their own conclusions about what life is now going to be like. Soldiers and civilians are scattered about the streets, all as worried as each other. Mary's been slapped twice for forgetting to bow to a Japanese sentry and now she keeps her eyes fixed firmly on the ground. Another soldier has shown her the photographs of his own small children and the rest have ignored her completely.

But now she's back at her sprawling, marble house and she's facing up to facts. She'd hoped to find Rajan here but there's no trace of him, and she daren't go out again to inquire at the hospital. She wanders through the spacious rooms, noting where an item of furniture's gone missing or a corridor's been strafed with machine-gun fire.

'Where's Appa?' Francesca-Joseph asks, and Mary hushes her.

This is, she suspects, a dangerous sort of question to ask. Men have certainly died in the invasion, or fled or been captured. But not men like Rajan, with his slippery good looks and his fingers in every sort of political pie. Rajan's in the jungle, Mary suspects, his face blackened and his legs encased in puttees, fighting with the Communist guerrillas. Or he's on a rubber estate, posing as a worker and inciting the Tamils to riot. He's sipping tea with a Japanese general; he's lying in a Johor brothel with Mr Thivappuram's daughters; he's everywhere and nowhere and will watch Mary for the rest of her life. *Men like Rajan don't get themselves killed,* she'll say darkly in a few decades' time. *More's the pity*, she'll add.

*

Mary and Francesca-Joseph don't stay in Ipoh long. It's hard, with no husband and not even a garden where Mary can grow vegetables. And then, too, there's her half-white skin. Eurasians are being watched across the country, being asked to register or report to Japanese holding offices that not everyone comes out of. Mary's dark enough to pass for Indian, luckily enough. There's not much of her father in Mary, except for his rages and his stubbornness and his surprisingly strong will. But she worries about being caught, about being taken away, and then what will happen to Francesca? As food gets scarcer — as Mary starts to barter for rice and Francesca to steal it — it becomes clear that there's only one solution. They'll have to go home.

Not, of course, that it'll be easy. There are travel permits to get. There are letters to be written, bribes to be paid and Francesca-Joseph's hair to be cut as short as possible. By the time Mary and Francesca are on one of the irregular buses that have just started to run to Lipis again, Mary's exhausted and very worried indeed. She doesn't know what she'll find at home, not having heard from her parents in weeks.

After a four-hour journey the bus humps itself over the mountain roads to a stop just outside Lipis. Mary's anxious to get off; she's in a fever of worry and can barely wait for the doors to open. She scoops up Francesca, settles her on her hip and begins the long trudge out to the house. The jungle's been scorched in places, cut back in others, and Mary's sure she can see flitting dark shapes in the trees. Perhaps Japanese soldiers, perhaps Communist guerrillas, and she doesn't know which would be worse. The Tiga Bintang, the three star resistance fighters, have taken some tips of their own from the Japanese and are shooting any collaborators they can get hold of.

It's dark by the time she reaches the driveway, and Francesca's long since fallen asleep. Mary pauses, shifts her daughter to her other hip and takes a deep breath. She walks into the plastered courtyard. She sees the concrete verandah and the banana trees leaning over yet another extension. She sees one of the wells she used to play near and the strange boxy prayer room. And then she sees Anil.

He's sitting in the rattan chair, curled with his knees tight to his chest. He's thin and a scar runs down his face. For a moment she can't believe that he's alive and breathing, because the house itself is dark and all about her is the smell of rotting food.

'Anil?' she calls.

Anil moves slightly in his chair and raises his head.

'Ma-ry,' he says slowly, but doesn't move.

Although Mary doesn't know it, Anil's long since given up expecting her or anybody else to come at all. Stephen and Radhika are both dead – and Anil refuses to think of that, just as Mary refuses to think of Rajan lying broken in a ditch somewhere – and Anil's been surviving on fruit and well-water. Left alone, the devils have uncorked themselves from inside his head and sauntered about the house poking their noses into things that don't concern them. He's shut them up into rooms, he's locked doors and blockaded passages until the only safe place is out on the verandah, but that hasn't put them off. So, when he sees his sister walking down the driveway – when he knows she's far away in Ipoh and irredeemably married – he can only conclude she's a devil. A Mary-devil and a little-boy devil, dressed in a bright pink shirt.

They must be ghosts, thinks Anil, *a trick of the light*. And so he doesn't move, not even when Mary runs up the stairs and pulls him into her arms. My great-uncle doesn't believe all he sees these days, and very lucky for him, too.

I wrap the plait of hair back up in a neat roll. Ammuma's never talked about those days, not straight out. She only ever mentions the war in opaque, allusive words – sometimes even in Tamil or Malay – as though if she tells it differently then this time it might turn out better.

I stare down at the trunks, crammed with tiny, tawdry presents. Here's where Ammuma's grief is, not in her words. She's been packing it up in dolls and toys, in things the war took from Francesca. And she's been taking them to Kampung Ulu. I don't know why. Perhaps because Peony died there; one dead teenage girl being very much like another when it comes to grief. Perhaps not. Perhaps no reason at all but the windy demands of ghosts.

When I put the plait back I feel something papery stuck to the side of the tin. It's a yellowed envelope, tucked in one corner. There's faded tape across the back and *Francesca* written over the front. Inside are a few photographs, tacky with damp. They don't look like they've been moved in years.

The first one's Francesca as a girl, a sepia toddler of three years old with milk-teeth and satiny plaits. And another: Francesca looking like a little boy with short-cropped hair. Teenage Francesca in a copy of the picture from Ammuma's shrine. And then, startlingly, a colour picture of almost-grown-up Francesca on the verandah downstairs. The steps look polished and swept, and Francesca's dressed up like she's going to a party. She must be fifteen or so, but she's in babyish lace and a satin-sashed party frock. Ammuma's behind her, leaning forward with her hands on Francesca's shoulders. The puckered scar on her arm looks fresh, and far worse than I'd have thought, with the skin weeping off it in great sheets. To my surprise Francesca has smaller, patchier scars splashing up her arms too. She looks more helpless than she did in her three-year-old photo. She's heavier than I expected, with her satin-covered stomach bulging out, and I wonder if I'm in that sepia world too. Biding my time.

There's one more photograph, and in this one Francesca's hugely, frankly pregnant. She's lying in a starched white bed with metal railings and her stomach curves in a solid arc out from the sheets. There's a birthday cake next to her, incongruous with its candles and scattered sweets. On the bedside table is a hairbrush, some torn wrapping paper, a brand-new doll, dressed as a princess. Ammuma sits on one side of the bed, holding Francesca's hand and smiling at the camera. She has to lean over, because Francesca's arms are scarecrowed above her head with her wrists bent out. The photograph's overexposed and it takes a moment before I understand what I'm looking at. A metal rail. The shadow of a pillow. And a pair of handcuffs, manacling my mother to the bed.

I drop the photograph. My throat swells. I can't breathe, then air scalds its way into my lungs. Francesca stares back at me from her picture. A birthday photograph, although her face gives no clue that she knows what's happening. She's blank, her mouth hanging open and a thread of spit lacing between her teeth.

I don't know how long I sit there. From downstairs I hear sounds – little, creeping life-noises – but they seem very far away. The wind, the buzz of the radio, a flutter in the corner as a cockroach crawls. Everything's melting together, blurred as though it's behind a pane of broken glass. I'm cold, cramped, my fingers clenched tight over a faded envelope and toys scattered in my lap. Ghosts everywhere I look. Ghosts everywhere I don't.

Gradually my heart slows down. I sit back on my heels, taking a deep breath. I dump the rest of the photographs back in the envelope, then examine this one more closely. There's a fascination to it, a squirming horror that could turn the whole thing into a joke, if I let it. Villains and handcuffs and Ammuma at the middle of it all.

The picture isn't very clear, but I can just make out some objects piled on the foot of the bed. I rub my thumb over the photograph. It's a pile of books, tumbling over the taut sheet. Exercise books, in a bleached-out rainbow of colours. Green, mauve, black. Blue, for friendship. Red, for secrets and confidences that she never did keep too well.

I jump up, grabbing the tin tight to my chest. 'Mother Agnes!'

The box-room door rebounds as I fling it open, leaving a dent in the plaster wall. My feet thump on the landing, shaking the house as I run downstairs. Everything's darker than it should be, and the wind's rising. As I hurry through the front room I can see a towering lump of cloud. The house seems to be pulling in on itself, shrugging me off like a flea on its skin.

'Ammuma! Mother Agnes!'

Ammuma's sitting by herself on the verandah. There are two cups on the table but everything else – letters, exercise books, Mother Agnes with her mincing plumpness – has gone.

'Already Agnes left,' Ammuma says calmly. Then, as I stare at her, 'Look, some storm we're in for.'

She nods out into the compound yard. Sweeps of rain spit across the driveway, with intervals between them like a held breath. Everything's damp, my hands sweating where I'm clutching the photograph and a strange, swooping feeling in my stomach as the pressure starts to drop.

I find my breath. 'Ammuma? I found . . .'

Her lips compress over her outsize false teeth. She's like a snake, she can taste a brewing fight from a single sip of air. 'Prying-poking, Durga? You go looking for trouble, you find it.'

She looks up at me. I'm about to hand her the photograph, but then I can't. My arm shakes, refuses to move. Once she sees it, I know, there'll be only a few seconds of my old life left. A minute or two at most, before everything changes and unravels and carries me away like a flood.

'I found this autograph book last week,' I say instead. 'In Tom's bag of fireworks. You wrote Francesca's name in it.'

Ammuma picks up the book. She stiffens slightly.

'With fireworks?' she asks, then seems to pull herself together. She shuffles further back into the chair and folds her arms. 'Gift only. For the shrine, it is.'

'No. It isn't, Ammuma. The address, you wrote Kampung Ulu.'

We both look at the book lying in her lap. 'Ammuma, was . . . was Francesca in . . .'

There's only one place near Kampung Ulu where people were handcuffed. Where there were locks on the gates. Where there were backwards boys and all-too-forward girls. The San.

Ammuma sets her mouth obstinately and picks up her cup. 'In Tom's fireworks bag?' she asks again.

'Yes, I told you. Stop pretending –'

She waves a bony hand. 'Tom-this, Tom-that, Tom-everything. Words only, isn't it, Durga? Choking like fishbones on fancy –'

'Ammuma!'

'– on fancy words. Enough –'

'Ammuma, it's –'

'– enough only to stop flirting.'

'Ammuma!'

'I told you better to stay away from him, Durga,' she says, sucking her teeth. 'All very well for the servant-girl to fall on her back,' she continues, as if to herself, 'but not so good for my grand-daughter to do the same, hanh?'

'I'm *not*.' I grab Ammuma's hands, pulling her round to look at me. Her wrists are like my mother's, splayed and delicate. My hands clench; Ammuma's bones slide under her skin. She lets out a yelp.

I want to stop. I want to let go before it's all too late and I can't change my mind. Her skin turns white under my fingers. I wonder if my thumbs will meet, crush those flaky bones to powder and ash as she vanishes and leaves me with nothing but dirty hands. There's a lusty urge to hit her, to do something I'll regret while my blood's singing and I'll never have this chance again. A curtain of rain sweeps over the roof with a noise like scattering pebbles. *Let go, let go –*

'I found this photograph, too.' I fling her hands back down into her lap. 'In the Amma-tin.'

She doesn't look up. Her hands lie limp as eels in her lap. There are two large white patches where my thumbs were clenched over her puckered scar. Every bit of me's horrified: Dr Panikkar with her how-could-I, and day-time grocery-fetching Durga wailing that I've made a mistake and sleepless night-time Durga asking what-was-I-thinking. And so, to put them all back in their place, I pick the tin up and dump it on Ammuma's lap.

'It's Francesca, isn't it? In the handcuffs.'

Ammuma looks down at the tin, plucking the photograph out. She gives it a quick glance but doesn't say anything.

'Why is she handcuffed? Did someone put her in the San? Did you? Tell me!'

Ammuma purses her lips and stares out at the rain. There's a tiny sink fixed to the side of the house, and it's jammed with twigs. Water swirls around inside, unable to drain and never getting anywhere. I recognize that look on Ammuma's face. It's a shut-door look, a stamped-foot look. It's Ammuma insisting on black when the world's saying white.

I take a deep breath and turn away from her. The verandah floor feels swollen with damp, as though it's trying to shrug me out. The banana plants around the compound walls are almost flattened, and there's a milk-coffee look to the sky. The wind rises, then stills. And then, out of nowhere, there's a tiny crunch and a seeping hiss of air.

I whirl round. Ammuma's choking. She's picked up the mask attached to her oxygen cylinder and slipped it over her head. But she must have done something to it, because it's smothering her, suffocating her. She claws at the mask straps, letting the mouth-piece slip just a fraction and then she gags again. When she finally draws in a breath, it sounds like fingernails grating on stone.

'Ammuma!'

She gives another sandpaper gasp and spits out some shreds of plastic. I lunge across the verandah and snatch up her shattered mouthpiece. The tubing pulls tight. Her face tips closer to me and for a second we stare eye to eye. The mask is sliding and wet. It's coated in saliva and some sticky, greenish fluid. The rubber nodules have been severed and there's a set of tooth marks on the tubing. She must have inhaled a fragment of the tube. I slam my palm on her back, over and over. She bends over – I'm smacking her spine with my fist – and then a small piece of rubber flies free.

Ammuma gives a rattling, whistling gasp: she can't breathe, even with the tubing gone. I jam the mouthpiece back over her lips but the mask must be broken because nothing comes through. She coughs, and this time there's more fluid. Some blood, something sticky and essential from deep in her guts.

I thrash the tubing down on the floor. Some clots fly free but the oxygen still isn't flowing, and Ammuma's gasps are whooping-cough loud. I stick my fingers in the mask to clear it. Nothing.

Ammuma's chest shudders and she convulses. Her arm flies up and points behind me. She's seeing ghosts, I think wildly: Francesca and Peony standing there with their translucent hands full of broken china and oxygen masks.

'Breathing,' she gasps, and her head lolls.

I run into the hallway and snatch up the receiver. It's still dead and I bang it down. No help, nobody to stop Ammuma drowning right here on dry land as the Jelai floods harmlessly through the back garden. I run back to the verandah and grab her mask again. I thrust my fingers deep into the mouthpiece. Jabbing at it, again and again. There's something in there, just out of reach. I jam my whole hand in, the skin scraping from my knuckles. Once more, and then I've got it. A piece of chewed rubber just like the one in her windpipe. I throw it on the ground, and feel a faint breeze of air from the tube again.

I press the mouthpiece against her face. Her lips flutter and then she takes a feeble breath. Her heart's racing under her collarbone, shallow trips that lift up her skin. After a few breaths her lips lose their blue tinge. She lifts a hand to the mouthpiece and holds it herself. It shakes with her tremors, then stills as I watch. The sweat shines on her face and there's a triumphant cast to the hollows below her cheekbones. Behind her mask, behind those dislodged porcelain fangs, Ammuma's smiling.

★

By evening she's a little better. The mask seems to be holding, although there's a patchiness to the oxygen flow that I don't like. She's getting less air with every breath. I try the phone every half hour to see if I can reach the hospital but the line's still dead.

When I tell Ammuma this she snaps her jaw in satisfaction. She can barely breathe, but she doesn't want to go into hospital. I can see it in her face, that dread of being trapped in a starched bed until she desiccates into nothing but skin and bone and the feeblest of demands. Ammuma, at least, knows where she belongs.

Between attempts, I stand at the back door. I'm exhausted, propping myself up with my hands braced on my hips. I can see clods from the riverbanks falling in with a sound like ripping cloth, and the water's thick and syrupy. The wooden house-panels jam tight against each other and the floorboards give every time I take a step. Chickens cluster under the house – stupid, the first place to flood – the cats are in the attap roof and monkeys cling bedraggled to the palm trees. I think, very hard, about the chickens and the cats and the monkeys. I count them all, and then I start again and I don't think about anything else. I could pass an afternoon like this or a week or a year. I could pass a few seconds. A minute or two, at most.

'Durga?' Ammuma calls from the verandah. She's become restless as the day closes, muttering words I can't make out.

The contents of the Amma-tin are still scattered over the table. It's dim, but I can see the photographs and the Little Twin Stars autograph book. My feet pad on the concrete floor but Ammuma doesn't even look up. She leans across and touches the photograph gently, with the very tip of her finger. The air tightens: a breeze, a breath, a shifting foundation. This house was

174

built for giving away secrets, right down to the floorboards that creak under me.

'Wanted answers, ar?' Ammuma's voice is thick, and her breath smells of rubber and old spit.

'Ammuma, I . . .'

'I don't chatter-chatter secrets for being asked, is it,' she mutters to herself. Her head sinks down between her shoulder blades. The blanket's fallen away from her scrawny legs and she stretches out her feet onto the damp floor. And then, without looking up, she exhales a rubber-and-plastic breath and asks, 'Did I ever tell you about the Kempetai, Durga?'

22. The Princess's Sacrifice: 1943

Ammuma might be a poor patient and a questionable grand-mother, she might be inclined to lie first and answer questions later, but she has a gift for storytelling.

'So imagine, Durga; 1943 is no food, is soldiers and sentries. I sing "Kimigayo", I keep my head down, isn't it? And in a few weeks only, I'm delivering letters.'

It was a pitch-black morning, she says, and she was standing outside Noor Abi's house with the post office gunny sack chafing her shoulder. Anil was waiting at the gate with their shared bicycle, having been too scared to wheel it up the overgrown path to Noor Abi's shadowy door.

Strictly speaking, Mary has no business with the post office sack at all. Anil is the official postman, a job that keeps him out of Japanese conscription into the railway gangs. Of course, Anil can't read or write, so Mary surreptitiously helps him out. She's *tidying up*, she tells him as she sorts and files and stacks the letters for delivery; she's *along for the ride*, she explains as she pedals madly uphill with Anil clinging on behind. And now she's standing at Noor Abi's door on a gritty, raw day with a letter bringing news of a death. It's not a pleasant task at all, and Mary arranges her face into a suitable sorrow before knock-ing. A respectable sorrow, befitting someone who wouldn't dream of steaming open a sackful of letters just to stick her nose in their secrets.

'I *am* sorry, Noor,' she says as the door opens.

Noor Abi is old and heavy; she's lost more sons than she can count and she's still giving birth to an infant every year. She cries over each new death, sobbing until her milk dries up and her breasts shrivel and her latest baby weans itself in disgust. Noor's sons are daredevils, and they've always had a streak of rebellion. Two are off in the jungle fighting with the Tiga Bintang, three are running rice-smuggling operations in Terengganu and one's up in Kedah launching a suicide attack on the Japanese water supplies. Noor Abi knows immediately what's in that thin white envelope. She's no postman, but she knows that bad news takes up less space than good, and nearly always comes typewritten.

'Agnes!' Noor calls. 'Find the camphor-water.'

But Agnes is there already. She's already lowering the chick blinds and setting out mourning clothes. She keeps camphorwater on hand now, ready to wash the body of the latest son to be carried back dead from the mountains.

'Hello, Agnes,' Mary says.

Agnes is working at Noor Abi's house every day, in an attempt to stretch the tiny convent rations further by looking after Noor's children. She comes forward, breathing sympathy, and scribbles a line for Mary in her exercise book.

Any news of your husband yet?

Mary swallows a flutter and plummet in her throat, and shakes her head.

'Oh, my dear . . .' Noor Abi comes out of her own monumental grief to sympathize too. 'You must be worried sick. Those Japanese . . . those Kempetai. They're – they're bastards.'

The word pops plump from her dignified lips and is immediately snatched up by Anil. Although he can talk now, he doesn't tend to except when it makes trouble.

'Bastards, bastards,' he begins to sing. 'Kempetai bastards.'

Mary hurries down the steps to hush him. Noor and Agnes stand on the porch, arm in arm and sadness trickling right to their soles. *If I could talk*, Agnes might be thinking, *I'd use my voice for something better than swearing – and I wouldn't slap people either –* as Mary cuffs Anil round the ear to keep him quiet. No, Agnes disapproves of violence, and despite her liking for Mary she feels a surge of spite. One day, she thinks, Mary will get her comeuppance.

Mary slings one leg over the bicycle and starts pedalling off with Anil perched behind. Their next delivery's at the convent, which means a hill to climb first.

'Bastard, Kempetai bastards,' Anil sings, and lights start to flicker on in the houses that line the steep street.

'Hush! People will be awake soon,' Mary hisses.

Everything starts early in Malaya these days, now all the clocks have moved on to Japanese time. Alarms ring two hours before dawn, housewives begin to cook supper while lunch is still on the table and children rush screeching out to the kampong school before even the most conscientious chickens have untucked their heads. By the time Mary and Anil reach the convent walls the whole world is astir.

'Mary?' Anil taps his sister on the shoulder as they turn in at the gate. The convent sits in the middle of the compound, surrounded by the fishbone trunks of palm trees. 'Mary, where is Joseph?'

Mary's puzzled for a second, and then remembers just in time. 'She . . . uh, *he's* at home, Anil. He's safe in bed.'

Joseph, of course, being the name little Francesca still goes by. Even here in Pahang, where the Japanese soldiers are disciplined and regimented, Mary's wary of letting anyone know Francesca's a girl. For the last couple of years, Francesca's been thoroughly enjoying her life as a boy, spending her whole days running about with a gang of tot-sized neighbourhood toughs. All Mary's half-hearted attempts to reintroduce dresses and dolls have failed, and now it seems as though she's stuck with a son. *It could be worse*, she thinks now, remembering Noor Abi. Plenty of women in Pahang are running out of sons.

'Kempetai bastards.' Anil bursts into song again and Mary frowns. The Kempetai may be bastards – and she agrees with that, though she wouldn't say it out loud – but she doesn't blame them for Rajan's disappearance. She doesn't blame the rebel Tiga Bintang fighters either, nor the Koreans who are press-ganging men into the Thai railway work. No, she blames Rajan himself. Mary suspects it's his own choice to stay away. And on his own head be the consequences, she thinks rather wildly, and shouts over her shoulder in a voice tart as pickled limes that Anil should *shut up now*.

As they wheel through the convent gate Mary wipes her forehead and shakes her aching legs. The convent's shabby these days and there are only a few nuns left. But Sister Gerta's still here, and she comes hurrying out of the front door as soon as she hears the bicycle wheels. Her skirts whip around her skinny legs and her habit billows in the snatching wind.

'Mary!' she exclaims with pleasure.

Every month since the Occupation began, Mary's heaved a bagful of letters up here for the nuns. Begging letters, all of them, asking for help or charity or prayers. There've been so many that Mary's had to stitch a special postbag for them, embroidering it with a tiny crucifix. That bag reeks of misery from the letters inside it, and if any joyful note – say, a wedding invitation – is accidentally placed there the consequences are calamitous: jilting, adultery, divorce of the groom and all his brothers. As Mary sorts those letters the envelopes stick to her fingers in a peeling, damp way that has nothing to do with the weather. The people who write them are desperate, and that's an easy thing to catch.

'Some extra ones today, Sister,' she says cheerily and Anil joins in again.

'Extra, extra, Kempetai extra bastards.'

Sister Gerta gasps. 'You should stop him. What if the soldiers hear?'

Mary, who's been trying to stop Anil for the last half hour, keeps her temper.

'He won't stop,' she says. 'But it'll be all right. There weren't any soldiers around this morning.'

'Really? You didn't see any at all? No sentries or anything?' Sister Gerta seems curiously excited by this. She leans forward, her hands clenched into the rough serge skirts that bunch around her hips.

'None at all.' Mary's about to ask why Gerta cares, when Anil suddenly falls quiet. 'See? He's stopped,' she announces with satisfaction.

'Let-ter,' Anil says carefully, and points at Sister Gerta's bunchy skirts.

'*We're* delivering the letters, Anil.' Mary's no more patient than she ever was or will be, and the scouring hilltop wind is getting on her nerves. If she doesn't quite roll her eyes at her brother then she certainly comes close, and perhaps that's why she misses the quick movement as Sister Gerta brings an envelope from her skirt pocket and imprints a kiss on it.

'Mary, will you deliver this?'

Mary looks up at the envelope in Gerta's hand. 'Will I . . . ?'

She steps forward to take a closer look at this envelope. The envelope's a delicate cream colour and it's addressed to Father Narayan, of the La Salle Boys School in Lipis.

Mary shakes her head. 'It isn't chopped.'

The envelope, scented with jasmine and rosewater, hasn't been chopped; it has no censorship stamp. That means the Japanese soldiers haven't approved the contents and it would be a crime for Mary to deliver it.

'I'm sorry, Gerta,' she says. 'We can't take it.'

Gerta looks stricken. 'Please,' she says. 'If there aren't any sentries . . . please?'

Mary's tired. She's been up since four o'clock wrangling some breakfast into her son-daughter and doing her brother's post round. She's cold, she's hungry, she has an ulcer on her leg which isn't healing. It's been a hard few months for Mary, and who can blame her for not paying quite enough attention to Gerta, standing there under the frangipanis with her skin white as dirty china and her eyes pleading.

'Just go down and get it chopped, Gerta,' she says impatiently. 'Don't be embarrassed, the censors read all sorts of things. Love letters and everything; yours can't be that bad.' (Oh, Mary. She's never been one to think things through.)

Mary hands the empty sack to Anil and turns to walk back to the bicycle. The handlebars stick, just a little, and by the time Mary's got them free, Anil and Gerta are standing side-by-side with their hands behind their backs and gigantic, cream-fed smiles on both their faces. Anil has the sack slung over one shoulder and Gerta's letter has disappeared.

'What's got into both of you?' Mary asks. 'Come on, Anil, time to go. I'm sorry we couldn't take your letter, Sister Gerta.'

But Gerta doesn't seem to mind, shrugging and smiling as she waves them both off down the hill. Mary puts her feet up on the bicycle forks and coasts, enjoying the feeling of wind beating into her face.

'Ma-ry.' Anil taps her on the shoulder as they reach the bottom of the slope. 'Go to Lipis-town? See the schoolboys?'

Anil loves everything to do with school. He never got to go, of course, but he used to press his nose to the compound gate to watch as boys in striped ties carried their boxy school satchels along the road. He's always particularly liked the yellow-and-red stripes of the La Salle school uniform, even going so far as to beg for a blazer of his very own.

Mary smiles back at him over her shoulder. 'Very well,' she calls. 'We'll go and see the school.'

She starts pedalling again and swings them onto the narrow road that leads out to the school. It's at the end of a rutted lane, with low pavilions spreading themselves out behind cricket pitches. Like many of the schools in Pahang, it isn't actually open. There aren't enough Japanese-speaking teachers, and schools aren't permitted to teach in any other language. The head, Father Narayan, fills his days by setting out unmarked blackboards and counting his chalks.

'Pity Gerta didn't have her letter chopped,' Mary calls to Anil as she pedals the bike over dried-up mud. 'We could have dropped it in to Father Narayan now –'

She breaks off. There's a Japanese sentry standing under the angsana tree by the school corner. His hat's tweaked into a stiff fold and a gun hangs from his polished belt.

Mary stops the bicycle and pulls Anil off after her. 'Bow!' she hisses, but he doesn't move.

The soldier puts his thumbs into his belt and begins to walk towards them, each leg swinging like a pendulum.

'Anil!' Mary gives him a sharp, hard pinch. The sentry's smiling, with a clear and hard grin that doesn't bode well. 'Bow!'

Anil drops his head and Mary sinks with relief into her own

bow. *Don't look at us, keep walking by*, she thinks and then just as the soldier reaches them she hears Anil draw in a breath.

'Bastards, bastards,' he sings. 'Kempetai bastards.'

The soldier stops. For a long, heart-stretching second he doesn't move. Mary's holding her breath – *don't understand English*, she's praying, *please don't understand* – and then Anil chirps again, almost to himself.

'Bastards, bastards, Kempetai –'

The soldier pulls back his fist, swinging it with a brutal punch into Anil's face. Anil crumples to the ground and a second punch from the soldier sends Mary lurching away. She lands on the bike, feeling the spokes pierce her leg and her mouth fill with tiny, clattering stones that turn out to be her own teeth. The soldier stamps down hard on Anil's head and Mary's sure she can hear something crack. She scrambles to her knees, crawls up to the soldier's flying boots.

'Please,' she says. She puts her head on the ground. 'Please,' and then there's a sudden silence.

Mary lifts her head up, blood brimming from her lips. The soldier's picked up Anil's gunny sack and is feeling inside it. He grabs at something – but there's nothing there – thinks Mary and then, a second later . . . Oh, Anil. Oh, Anil.

Because the soldier's just pulled out a delicate cream-coloured envelope, lying innocently in the post-office bag and uncensored. Unchopped. Unimaginable.

'Aha!' The soldier kicks Anil again, holds up the envelope in triumph. 'Illegal,' he screeches. 'Illegal!'

Mary screams as the soldier kicks Anil again. Blood pools on the road and on the soldier's boots, which seems to upset him. He takes a step back and slips the gun off his shoulder.

'Stupid. Foolish postboy,' he says, and brings the rifle into position. Anil lies still on the ground with his legs at an impossible angle and the soldier tightens his finger on the trigger and then –

'I did it,' Mary says. 'I put the letter in.'

23. Tuesday, 5 p.m.

Ammuma's voice gets slower and slower, till she falls silent.

'Cannot remember next,' she says, looking me in the eye. A few missing facts. A few missing brothers, and sisters, and daughters. Not worth remembering, those daughters. They're just footnotes in history.

She pulls in on herself after that, settling ostentatiously to sleep. And I go back to standing by the door, watching the sun set and the green mosquito coils shiver into fragments under the kitchen table. I shut the door and then open it again just to feel purposeful. There's a coppery tang to the air, like coins fished from a well. Perhaps the floods are going to miss us after all, sweep out to the eastern plains and leave only the stink of mud and river bones.

I don't know how long I stand there. The sun sets and the air turns salt-bright, trembling on the edge of calm. I think about Ammuma, about Peony and Francesca. About equilibrium, and tidy mathematical games which have a winning strategy for every player. In real life, it turns out, the ghosts are always a few points up.

'Ammuma?' It's almost dark now on the verandah. Shadows bleed across the concrete floor and Ammuma's sari gleams in the dusk. 'Are you awake?'

Her head lolls to the side. One eye opens in a slow, sightless blink and she lets out a windy belch. There's a rustle as papers flutter off the low table. I can't see where they land. The corners of the room are pitch black, as though the light's been wrung out with two hands.

I kneel down and pat at the floor, expecting at any moment the sizzle of an earwig or the dryness of a chik-chak or even – and the thought comes without asking – the stamp of Ammuma's heel.

My palm skims something soft. It's cloth, the black roll wrapping my mother's plait. I find the autograph book on the floor too, with the pages dog-eared. Ammuma must have been picking over it while I was in the kitchen. Rummaging through, sniffing and tasting and peering at every blank page.

Next to it I find the envelope of photographs. It's split open and the frayed edge rasps like a friendly tongue. My palms pad over gritty dust and the occasional cool sheen of a photograph that's fallen out. Perhaps there are more I haven't found: pictures blown down cracks to puzzle some young girl-cousins in thirty-fifty-a-hundred years' time. I'd wish them good luck, those futuristic flawless cousins with gleaming hair and space-age skin, but I doubt they'll need it. Women like that can look after themselves.

When I've gathered everything I can find, I bundle it all up and take it into the hall. Ammuma keeps a torch on the table in here, for days like this when the power goes out. It sends a feeble beam into the front room. The furniture leaps out at me: chairs and tables and bamboo pictures looking affronted in the sudden light.

By torchlight Francesca seems calm and unflappable in her handcuffs. She's so hugely swollen that she must have given birth not long after this photo was taken. Me. And then she died, but that can't have been like I've always thought. No clean white sheets or gentle nurses: my mother would have burnt alive in those handcuffs. Peony once showed me the news photographs about the San fire – the famous ones, in the *Straits Times*. Shadows burnt onto padded walls and faces melted to chicken fat. Ammuma refused to have those pages in the house: *Death and foolishness and God-knows-what, child, ten years ago it is now, why don't you leave it alone?* She's wary of history, Ammuma. She had a daughter, once, before all that history.

I shove the autograph book in one of my skirt pockets, and then the photograph and Amma's plait in the other pocket. I'll need these things; they're the only proofs I've got right now. The torch flickers and I cup my hand over it, blood-veins and bones showing through. I pad back through the front room to peer at Ammuma.

Her head's sunk back and her skin is loose around her exposed collarbone. No blood-veins for Ammuma, no insides showing. She keeps her secrets.

But there's someone else who doesn't. Someone who deals in gossip, which Ammuma likes, and facts, which she'd never stoop to. Someone who was there from the start, keeping order and always giving a straight answer in her coloured exercise books. *What's the height of a triangle, Mother Agnes? What does this word mean? Why did Francesca end up in the San?* Now there's a question, Mother Agnes. They don't make dictionaries big enough for that one.

Ammuma doesn't wake as I tuck the blanket up over her hips. She doesn't stir – I think – as I buckle my shoes on. Her eyes surely don't snap open and stare into the darkness behind my back. She isn't sitting there – she *couldn't* be – watching me tiptoe down the steps.

Once I'm outside I switch the torch back on. A circle of light leaps out and everything else drops dizzyingly away. The kampong track's overgrown and barely visible; nobody's taken it for years. I used to know this way so well, and now it's like seeing a familiar face turned shrunken and twisted. Ferns wrap themselves around my ankles, and spider webs plaster my face. I trip on a rattan spine, slashing my leg and landing in a mess of vines and springy little trees. Something blunders into my hair, then tugs itself free. There's a rustle behind me: footsteps or hooves or claws. I swing the torch. There's nothing there, or nothing I can see.

I gulp and push myself on. The shadows are on my heels. They're licking out from behind me, swallowing my torch and I start to run. My feet slam through rotten logs and crusts of mud. Knee-high ferns that cling and soak my legs. Something's following me, something's padding in the echoes of my heartbeat. My torch swings wildly over trees and rocks, looming out of nowhere.

And then a sense of space. Not quite light, just not-blackness. It's the edge of Mother Agnes's village, by the great padang that stretches out with a sucking emptiness. I know where I am now. I used to sit here in the afternoons, those years after Peony died and

I couldn't face school. There's a deeper blackness of shadow where a flame tree crooks over the grass. I can smell water too, and silt. The floods have been here, not long ago.

Mother Agnes's house is twenty metres away. It's a two-storey brick square, flat to the road and attached to the old school via an open walkway. Nothing frightening there, nothing but the memory of chalk and the gentle smell of childhood bullying. She keeps a scrubby little garden, with a hibiscus flattened under a pouring drainpipe.

There's no light on in any of the windows and my torch flashes over a lion's-head knocker on the door. It's solid iron and resounds through the house as I let it drop. Echoes race along the street, thump their feet over the bench by the padang and trip each other up. But the house stays dark.

Nothing else stirs either. The cluster of houses by the crossroads is locked tight; no uncles smoking outside their houses, no aunties trying to soothe sleepless children behind netted windows. And then I realize: the floods. This village lies on a swamp plain, and the Jelai rises faster here than anywhere in Pahang. Everyone's been evacuated, perhaps hours ago. All that's left is the river, in a green glassy wall at the bottom of a jungle cut.

I turn right and walk down the side path. The school's windows glint back at me and the attap roof tips its hat. Mother Agnes closed it up years ago when she stopped teaching, but those rooms are still crammed full of pigtailed ghosts. These days she uses the building for the left-behinds, as a drop-in centre or a safe place to sleep. The left-behinds are always looking for safety. They're always dropping, one way or another.

I step over the brimming drain by the side of the walkway, turning towards Mother Agnes's house. She always leaves her back door unlocked, even at night. Even during a flood evacuation. She's proud of it, makes a point of telling Ammuma just how easy it is for one of the left-behinds to come for food, or the sort of help you can't ask for in daylight. Ammuma disapproves, needless to say. She doesn't hold with help at any time of day.

I push the door open and step forward into the laundry room. It's black inside, and my eyes take a moment to adjust. The room echoes with dripping water and the sound of clothes stiffening as they dry. In the beam of my torch a cockroach rustles in the sink on its back in a centimetre of grey rinse-water. There's no electricity, and I creep cautiously through the inner door to the study, my torch held high like a baton.

The study's so empty and shabby that I recoil. There used to be a bow-legged almirah and a desk with an enviable glass-green lamp. All that's gone now, replaced with a rickety table and a stack of old *National Geographics*; Indira Gandhi and Richard Nixon covered in silverfish droppings. It looks bare in here, like a slumhouse. Like poverty.

The walls are stacked with cardboard boxes, some of them taped down and others gaping. I peer into one: books, tins of food and coffee-jars and musty clothes perfuming the air with the memory of someone else's skin. Donations for the left-behinds, and now I know where Mother Agnes's money has gone. Above her desk there's a list with doctors and bomohs, children's specialists and lawyers who'll work for free. They'd need to, I think, looking around the shabby room.

There's a neat stack of papers fanned out on the spindly table, inviting me to pry. I sit down on the bare kitchen chair and shine my torch on the top sheet. As I'd guessed, it's covered with lists for her left-behinds.

Siti, in Kampung Baha: dolls, toys. Sanitary pads.

Ali, in Kampung Baha: Toy cars. Picture-books, sweets.

Puan Hamza, in Kampung Tahan: milk powder, clothes, contraception.

TOOTHPASTE, in large letters at the top, then in smaller ones: *will they use it?* Poor Mrs Hamza; poor little Siti, half-grown with her dolls and sanitary pads. I wonder how many teeth they have between them.

At the edge of the desk there's a book pushed down against the wall. It's jammed as far into the corner as it can go, as though Mother Agnes tried to hide it in a rush before she evacuated. I work it free with guilty fingers. The pages crumple and tear, and then the book slips free. I look down, and nearly drop it. It's her red exercise book.

This book is Mother Agnes herself, all her secrets and chats and whispered little privacies. I know she uses this when she tells Ammuma her secrets, her regrets, her lumps and worries of the body. I sit there with the book in my hands. She wouldn't want me to read it, I know that, she wouldn't want *anyone* to read it. Even with floods surging at her door, Mother Agnes hid this where she thought it wouldn't be found.

I look down at the cover, and open it. This is worse than reading her diary, I understand, worse than prying through her drawers. But I'm doing it anyway, skimming over the pages. A spice of gossip here, an apprehensive confession there. *A little bleeding*, she's written, *a little pain* – and I turn the page quickly before I need to think. And then something right near the end, a recent entry, catches my eye. It looks like another one of those left-behind shopping lists – and I frown. Mother Agnes doesn't make lists in her red exercise book; she *talks*.

Sweets.

Dolls.

Socks, five packs at least.

Some clothes, a blouse or two. T-shirts.

Floss? (check Cold Storage)

Robinson's toys: light-ups? But what about batteries?

Picture-books. (Maybe pony ones? Little Twin Stars?)

Little Twin Stars. That gives me a jolt. I turn the page with fingers that are unaccountably sweaty, and see what's written on the other side.

Francesca Panikkar, in Kampung Ulu

*

I'm cold. My lips feel numb and goosebumps are sprouting on my legs like mosquito bites. It feels like hours that I've been sitting here, staring at that page. Floss, I could recite. Socks, five packs at least. Francesca Panikkar, in Kampung Ulu.

Except that she isn't. Toys might be in Robinson's, certainly. Floss, without doubt, available in Cold Storage. But Francesca Panikkar, if she was ever anywhere near Kampung Ulu, was there in handcuffs and under protest and thirty years ago.

I switch the torch off and sit there in the dark. I must have stared too long, because now I'm seeing colours and starbursts and rings of light. Shapes, faces. Francesca in her handcuffs. And then, out of the past, Mad Ahmad. I remember his drooping eyelids and loose red lips; I remember the burn scars on his neck. He was the only one rescued when the San caught fire. A miraculous survivor, the *Straits Times* said. They even took his photograph.

I take a deep breath. Francesca's an old story, I tell myself. Her picture's in the prayer-room shrine. She was my Amma-friend. We kept her things in a biscuit tin. All that makes sense, in a sad and twisted way. But this list doesn't. Dead people – even burnt-up mothers, even drowned housewives and Pahang's take-your-pick medley of ghosts – don't brush their teeth. They don't eat sweets or wear clothes, and if there are any nightmares going round, they'll be the ones who give 'em.

Which means this list – brand new, written *now*, not thirty years ago – is for someone else. Some other child, some other children Mother Agnes would beg, borrow and steal for. Children she'd lie about even in her sacred red exercise book, if that's what it took to get Ammuma's interest and her money. Because charity – she's always said – begins at home.

The left-behinds.

I pick the book up again and start to turn through the pages, angrily ripping the edges and glad about it. But there's nothing else in here except Mother Agnes's health worries and her money troubles that I've no sympathy for, not any more. There's a chill rage inside me, the sort that'll build until it lights me up like a firework. Ammuma *hates* the left-behinds. She wouldn't give them the time of day, let alone some socks and dental floss. She'd have to be tricked into it; she'd have to be cheated and lied to and begged-from borrowed-from stolen-from, because charity – she's always said – begins at home.

I wonder just when Mother Agnes decided to do it. Did she see a left-behind girl – like Siti, with her dolls and sanitary pads and all-too-alive *needs* – that she couldn't afford to help? Mother Agnes can't say no to the left-behinds, but perhaps she reached a point where she couldn't afford to say yes. Did she think that someone else *could*, if only that someone would take her eyes off her own dead daughter?

I wonder how long it took to convince Ammuma, who's half-way to believing in ghosts without being given any encouragement at all. *A second chance, Mary,* Agnes would have written. *That left-behind girl is your daughter, your grown-up-and-dead daughter resurrected; brought back to life with a tomboy grin and dirty knees. It's Francesca before her hair was cut off; before the Japanese walked in and common-sense and common decency walked out. Before she got herself pregnant and everything went wrong.* Francesca in Kampung Ulu, of course, because ghosts in Pahang stay where they died. And charity begins at home.

And Another Princess is Born (A Tale)

You can't lie in mathematics. A lie gets you nowhere; tangles you up in your own proof and dumps you out again at the beginning. In mathematics, lies are pointless. In stories, of course, it's different. Lies are practically required.

But mathematics and stories need the same things, when you come down to it. A premise, to get you started on your way. An inference or two, to keep you on your toes. And a conclusion, a suck-it-and-see, to tell just how badly you all went wrong.

So, let's take a story that Ammuma's told me again and again. 'How You Were Born, Durga': a sweet little tale of beginnings. Let's stand it up in the light of facts – facts about left-behinds, for example, facts about handcuffs – and see just how well this tale really hangs together.

Ammuma's Tale: The Premise

You can't argue with premises. They're not amenable to interpretation; they're factual and feet-on-the-ground. You can look them up in reference books, you can cite them without fear of contradiction. They won't get you far, premises, but perhaps that's no bad thing.

By the time the war ends in 1945, Malaya's overrun by competing factions. There are Japanese soldiers stubbornly holding out; there are Malay Wataniah resistance fighters and vindictive British pen-pushers; there are hooligans and rebels and collaborators. And then, of course, there are the Bintang Tiga. Depending on who you ask, they're Communists, or Malayan independence fighters bent on overthrowing British rule. They're merciful, they're terrorists, some of them are your neighbour or your best friend, even though you'd never know it. They're the jungle guerrillas whose war begins where the road ends.

The British, of course, don't agree with Malayan independence. They just got the place back, after all, and they're damned if they're handing it over now to a bunch of natives. And so they act, spiriting away the Sultan of Pahang to keep him safe in case any rebel fighters have assassination on their minds. But things don't stop there. There are still pockets of Japanese soldiers here and there, and when Tokyo learns the Sultan's gone, it panics. The Sultan's safety, after all, was in Japanese hands, and if he's been lost somewhere, then who knows what the victorious British will do in revenge. Tokyo concludes the Sultan must have been captured by those rebel fighters – because where else could he have gone? – and send out a retaliatory force that kills nineteen kampong villagers and Cecelia's mother, Yoke Yee, before anyone can sort it out.

It's a difficult time for everyone, the ten years from 1948 to 1958. Malaya's only just put down its weapons to celebrate the end of one war and now it's picking them up again to fight for independence. 'The Emergency', this fight will later be called. For ten years there are food shortages, gunfights and curfews. On the street corners where Japanese soldiers used to stand there are now British officials, demanding travel passes and respect. If you blinked, you might have thought nothing had changed.

By 1954, though, things are slowly becoming calmer. The worst of the Emergency is over, and in just three years' time Malaya will win independence. It'll transform into Malaysia, with as many birth pangs as you might expect.

Ammuma's Tale: The Inference

Inferences are trickier; there's nothing to stop you leaving logic and common-sense behind. 'We leave this as an inference for the reader,' a mathematician will happily write. Too trustful, these mathematicians. Too trustful by half.

Ammuma always insisted 1954 was a peaceful time. By then she'd closed off most of the rooms in the house and the dung-plastered compound yard had been given over to vegetables. A peaceful time, a time of growing and taking stock.

Mary and Francesca are *managing* in 1954: they're making do, they're raising guinea fowl and growing yams. Francesca is sixteen and nearly grown-up when she delivers her momentous news. She's sitting on the verandah in her school uniform and scraping the shells from a bowl of hard-boiled eggs.

'What did you say!'

'George and I are going to have a baby, Amma.'

George is her classmate. Only fifteen, from a St Thomas Christian family and nervous enough to come out in a rash during mathematics tests. He's not the kind of boy you remember, and Mary has a hard time even picturing his face. Francesca keeps right on shelling the eggs. She's a pragmatic child.

'But your – your training course. And his university plans – and what about –'

Mary drops her spade and treads through the vegetable beds to look up at the verandah with her hands on her hips. She has a right to be aghast, after all she's done. She's kept a tight hold on Francesca all through the Emergency, only permitting boyfriends with the most impeccable credentials and no Communist leanings. Boys with shining teeth and Brilliantined hair, with sky-high ambitions and life-size finances. And now, with the Emergency nearly over, Mary's treasured daughter has only gone and got herself pregnant.

'We'll have the baby first,' Francesca tells her calmly, and puts a clean egg into her overflowing basket. She's certainly one for metaphors, this girlish mother of mine. 'Then George will go to technical college in Ipoh, and I'll do secretarial training. In KL.'

Another shock for Mary. KL is a long way from this bungalow in Pahang, with all her daughter's toys only put away yesterday and those shut-up spare rooms that would be perfect for a nursery. All her hopes, wrapped up in this one girl-chick who might just fly away. She pulls herself together.

'I expect you'll be wanting me to organize the wedding,' she grumbles. 'And at a moment's notice, too.'

She's shocked enough, but not wholly so. There's a part of her that likes the sound of another wedding; thinks back fondly to her own red-gold sari and the pre-war extravagance of snake charmers. She'll open up the old annexes to hold the sangeet in, she thinks. Invite friends. Invite relatives, such as they are. No parents, sadly enough. No Anil (and here's a tangent, here's a thorny, thickset path: how *did* he die? Best not inquire; Mary stitches up a new version every time she tells the story and in Pahang, at least, people understand why).

'We aren't engaged, Amma. George hasn't asked me.' Francesca gives a doleful sniff that shoves her heavy breasts together under her outgrown bodice.

Mary's jaws snap together. Her fingers curl and her eyes turn to tiny chips of light. She might have learnt patience, but she's certainly not practising it. Her hiss carries on the wind; the grit of her teeth drowns out the kampong's evening call to prayer and her flare of anger turns the rice in cooking pots for a mile around to charcoal. It's no wonder that, within a day, Francesca's boyfriend George finds himself climbing up those verandah steps in response to Mary's summons. Poor George; a burnt dinner is only the beginning of his problems.

'November,' is how Mary greets him. 'After Diwali. That's when you'll marry.'

It's an auspicious time. It's also a cheap time, snake charmers typically vanishing in the rainy months to coax their charges out of baskets somewhere drier. Mary's hard-headed; she's counting her pennies and counting her blessings and counting on George's proven cowardice.

And, indeed, after a few pre-matrimonial scuffles, Mary prevails. George is still in school himself, he's young enough to be quixotic and old enough to be romantic and he doesn't stand a chance against Mary when she's made up her mind. An engagement is announced and a house is bought, just on the outskirts of Kampung Ulu. There is, in time, a measured amount of rejoicing. Henna is painted, auspicious dates are forecast and there's a certain pleasurable bickering over the fit of Francesca's wedding sari. Mary's in her element and she has things under control, right up to the point Francesca gives birth three months earlier than she'd foretold, and ruins the fit of her wedding sari for good and all.

Ammuma's Tale: The Conclusion

Conclusions, now – conclusions are where the real difficulties start. You don't like where you've finished up, you don't like how it's all been left. And who are you going to blame? The storyteller, that's who. The mathematician. The monster.

Ammuma always finished this story with a single phrase: 'You can't count your chickens without breaking eggs.' And the way she told it, something does break inside Francesca. Francesca dies three days after the birth, almost peacefully. Ammuma says there's even a smile on her face, which is wildly unlikely. Ammuma's story concludes that I'm a gift. A mistaken gift – the kind of present you'd never have asked for – but one that was somehow welcome all along. No wonder Ammuma steers clear of logic, she's worried I'll disappear in a puff of it.

*

So that's Ammuma's story, and she'll stick to it for as long as it's convenient. But let's postulate – let's hypothesize – that there might be another story. One that fits the facts better – one that has Francesca ending up in the San in handcuffs, for a start. This story won't have the same shine, because I don't have Ammuma's imagination. I don't have her ability to add two and two and come up with five or seven or something else entirely. All I have is logic, and a photograph I'm beginning to wish I'd never seen.

Durga's Tale: The Premise

In this other story, perhaps it would all begin badly, right from the start. Mary and Francesca would be at loggerheads, and Mary ironed flat with grief. In this story Anil would have died in prison, his body dumped at the house by an indifferent official. Francesca would have nightmares for weeks, the sort of nightmares that mean she inevitably ends up in her mother's bed, or a friend's bed, or any bed at all.

Durga's Tale: The Inference

'You're so old-fashioned!'

Mary and Francesca are snappish with each other these days. It's hard for them both, as Francesca's breasts have swollen and Mary's flattened, as Francesca's dreamt of love and Mary's drunk strong coffee to keep away any dreams at all.

'That's enough out of you, young lady,' Mary retorts. Francesca's sitting at the dining table eating hard-boiled eggs and dropping the shells for the kitchen cats. Mary's tired these days, sagging under her own sparse flesh. She should feel liberated – like the younger ones do – but as far as Mary's concerned, the Emergency's nothing but another war.

She has a point. Malaya's barely looked around from celebrating the end of the Occupation before another load of would-be soldiers have plunged them into trouble. The MPAJA – the Malayan Peoples' Anti-Japanese Army – who coordinated those fluid raids against the Japanese occupiers, stabbing with venomous fangs before gliding back into their jungle camps: well, they're still here.

They're the Malayan Peoples' Anti-British Army now, they're the three-star Bintang Tiga, they're a liberation army and a Communist militia; they're bandits and folk heroes and, according to Mary, a bloody nuisance.

And now the British have begun to uproot whole kampongs and march the villagers away to resettlement areas. These areas are barbed-wire swamps of mud and tree roots, where families labour to build houses only to find next morning they're six foot deep in floodwater. The resettled villagers are caged in by wire and sentries and searched each morning to stop them smuggling out a single grain of rice for the Communist jungle fighters. When the villagers arrive at their rubber-tapping and farming work empty handed, those same Communist jungle fighters aren't happy. The British are hanging everyone who smuggles food, goes the saying, and the Communists are shooting everyone who doesn't.

'That's enough out of you,' Mary repeats. Francesca doesn't answer and Mary stamps away to the kitchen. She opens the cupboard by the chapatti oven, pulls out her pans, and only then notices that the sack of rice that lives behind them is missing.

'Francesca?' she calls. Francesca's left the table in a litter of discarded eggshells and gone out to the verandah to do her calculus homework. Francesca's sixteen, she's smooth as butter in her starched school blouse and blue pinafore, her temper says she's trouble and her brassiness confirms it. She's Mary all over again, and it's no wonder things aren't going well.

'What's happened to the rice?' Mary asks, folding her arms by the doorway. Francesca pauses, licks the point of an impeccably sharp pencil and begins to write. *Proof*, she sets down, and then looks up.

'I gave it to the People Inside. The Communists – the fighters. They came here yesterday looking for supplies.'

Theorem, she writes delicately, a slice of pink tongue sticking out of the corner of her mouth.

'Francesca! How could you!' Mary's aghast. The jungle around the house isn't hospitable enough for a Communist camp, being full of vicious rattan spines and slippery, unexpected holes where Stephen dug his many abortive wells. But once Francesca starts giving the fighters food, Mary knows they'll never leave.

'Like mice,' she snorts. 'Like rats,' and Francesca slams down her pencil.

'What do you know?' she bursts out. 'You've never fought, you don't care about independence or anything, but they do! They're brave, and strong and kind, and . . .'

They is rapidly slipping into *he*. The women in my family are like that, full of murky female proclivities. They're swayed more by the turn of a man's jaw than the turn of his mind. Mary remembers her own youth, and feels a pang of sympathy for her daughter.

'Is there a boy, then?' she asks gently. 'One of the bandits?'

Francesca sniffs, crunching the wet end of her regrown plait between her teeth, and refuses to answer. If there is a boy – a Communist rebel with wild black eyes and a body like copper wire – then she's certainly not going to tell her mother. In this version of the story Francesca isn't tractable; she'll have nothing to do with those nervous and rashy Georges in her class. She's on her guard against traps, this Francesca, she's not going to be snared with weddings and babies. *Counter-argument*, she inscribes neatly into her calculus book.

And it's rather a shame she wasn't on her guard against anything else, because a few months later – after many gifts of rice and other, less quantifiable things – Francesca is still on the verandah doing calculus homework. But now the problems are harder, the proofs don't come out so easily and she can barely see her pencil over the bulge in her tight-waisted blue pinafore.

Beside her Mary shells the hard-boiled eggs for dinner, her lips tight and her fingers tearing off those protective cocoons. The smell turns Francesca's stomach and sets up a queasy, rushing feeling inside her belly. Her own baby is being unshelled, beginning a long journey to an apartment in KL and a thousand regrets, and there's nothing Francesca can do about it.

Durga's Tale: The Conclusion

A few weeks before the birth Francesca will go into hiding in the jungle, since a squalling scrap of an infant is incontrovertible proof of consorting with *someone*. The British soldiers, by then, will have become frantic. They're seizing hearts and minds, they tell each other, and they keep right on incarcerating the bodies that hold them. Francesca, at risk of being hanged for fraternizing with rebels, will retreat into the rattan spines. She'll lurk there with her copper wire of a Communist boyfriend and the half-drowned women he's dragged along to cook and clean. She'll follow him, her three-star lover, into the jungle near Kampung Ulu. She'll learn to set off bombs and fire guns and then one day she'll be captured by the British and imprisoned in the San with all the other fallen girls. She'll give birth in a room that stinks of blood and piss, and then she'll catch childbed fever and die in her sleep, leaving Mary with nothing but an ungrateful baby and a basket of eggs for shelling. (*QED, Mary. QED.*)

*

There are alternatives, of course, other stories that would work just as well. In one, Francesca consorts with a British soldier, old enough and pale enough to be her own grandfather. In another the only clue is the oily footprint of an orang minyak jungle spirit outside Francesca's bedroom and the hallucinations that send her to the San. Stories on stories, and my mother walks through them with a smile and a blue school pinafore. She sheds her virtue at every dainty step. Here she is, creeping into the attic to make love or get herself raped. There she is, strolling amongst half-starved guinea fowl who swallow sand and lay eggs that are nothing but shell.

We don't do well across generations, the women in my family. Someone's feelings are always being hurt, toes are being stepped on and home truths are being told. There's enough pity in those truths to go around too, which doesn't mean it always will.

25.   Wednesday, 1 a.m.

It's late by the time I get back. Midnight's slipped past, with its witching-hour devilment and without me even noticing. My legs itch from pitul seeds and the autograph book bumps against my thigh. When I reach the verandah steps, I stop. There's a sound I can't place. A harsh, sawing kind of noise that stops, then starts again and builds up to a cut-off rasp.

'Ammuma?'

She's still in her chair where I left her, but she's tilted. Lopsided, as though she climbed out and couldn't resettle herself. One of the hurricane lamps has been lit, with the wick turned low. Was she looking for me? Her skin's washed jaundice-yellow in the lamplight, but I can see a blue tinge to her lips. She coughs, and a thread of blood dribbles down her whiskered chin.

'Ammuma!'

I shake her. She doesn't move, even when I shout into her face. She crumples again as I tug her upright. There's a feeble trickle of air from her mask. I shove my fingers under the rim, but it's blocked again. Blood coats the inside of the rubber, slimy and stinking. She's champing steadily, chewing on the inside of her mouth, shredding her cheeks and I'm panicking. Pulling at the mask. Slapping the oxygen tank. My fingers are shaking, trying to unravel the tubing.

'Durga. Gone already, isn't it?' The words strain through a sieve of tissue and used-up breath. 'Woke up. You were gone.'

The tubing won't unblock. The mask's half-torn and slippery with clots. I shouldn't ever have left her. She's going to drown in her own blood, and all because I left her.

'We have to go. Ammuma, come on. We're going to the hospital.'

For once, she doesn't protest. Her face is all rims and shadows, white around her nostrils. I heave her from the chair and her legs give way. I catch her, but the oxygen tank slams into the concrete. I jam my hands into her armpits and haul. She chokes, leaning over with her palms on her knees, then summons some air from nowhere.

'Careless, Durga. Always making – some – fuss.'

If she had more breath she'd elaborate: other granddaughters would manage the whole thing better. They'd have fixed their cars, for a start, so we don't waste a few minutes waiting for the engine to catch. Their palms wouldn't sweat as they babbled on and on about whether the road to Lipis was even open or whether it was flooded shut. They wouldn't swear as they stamp on the accelerator, as they wrench the steering wheel to avoid a raw mud-slide near the palm-oil plantations. They'd have come back earlier, they'd never have left in the first place, they'd have thought things through. She conveys all this in the hump of her shoulders, in a huff that uses up the air she doesn't have. All things considered, she gets her points across pretty well.

There aren't many cars on the road, not at this time of night. A few motorcycles swarm up from a side track, skinny men with tired eyes and jackets draped back-to-front on their chests. The Gua Musang road must still be blocked. Nothing's going to get through tonight and whatever our problems – hypoxic grand-mothers, inattentive granddaughters, ghostly mothers – we'll have to deal with them ourselves.

Ammuma starts coughing again just outside Lipis. There's more blood this time, and foamy spit. She dribbles, sucks her cheeks in and then begins to choke.

'Ammuma, hold on. Hold on.'

Her fists are clenched tight and her legs stuck out straight. I grabbed mismatched shoes from the pile, and one of Karthika's cracked plastic sandals drops from her toes. She spasms, chokes again and then gets her breath.

'Holding already, lah. You drive only, get us there . . . safe – instead of – playing tomfoolery.'

The engine starts to whine as we go round the huge roundabout just outside Lipis. Ahead I can see the curve that'll take us to the hospital and the fish-shaped fountain by the railway bridge. It's garish in my headlights.

'Come on, come on. It's OK, Ammuma. You breathe, it's going to be OK . . .'

I change down a gear. We're passing rows and rows of motorcycles now. The roads around the hospital are jammed like a termite nest: ambulances and medi-vans and blood wagons that don't know anything about the darkening hours. Delivery motorcycles slew together, parked in a tangle of wheels that stretches all the way up to the narrow Pahang Club road. A few men stand protectively over them and turn to watch us pass. One of them laughs.

The car park's almost empty, with only a few cleaning staff squatting by the phone booths. Their cigarettes are tiny swerving dabs of light. A match flickers to show the gold outline of a chin, the rim of an eye, a flaring nostril.

'Ammuma, stay here. I'm getting them to come, OK? Just stay here.'

She coughs again, waving one bony hand at me. I push the car door, letting it swing and bounce with a protesting creak, and then I'm running across the car park. My shoes squelch at every step, and my heart slams into my ribs.

'I've brought . . . please come –' I jerk the double doors open. It's busy and bright inside, full of patients on stretchers and wide-awake children running through the lobby. The curved reception desk's covered with stacks of admission papers and plastic-wrapped syringes. A nurse sits there, licking her finger and paging through forms.

'Yes, can I help?' She looks up with a professional smile.

'My grandmother's outside. She's Dr Rao's patient, she can't breathe. She was in here before, just a few days ago. But the oxygen tank isn't working and –'

She cuts me off, holding up one hand and reaching for the beige phone that sits on her desk. She gabbles instructions down the line – *porterage needed* and *triage free*. I find myself staring at her hair. It's dry and frizzled, spreading like a broken umbrella around her head. A tiny fleck of dust clings to one strand.

'The porters will be here directly.' She makes a note in one corner of a form. 'They'll bring your grandmother in.'

'She can't *breathe*,' I say again. Everything's slowed down, like the air's too thick to be pushed aside. The nurse is glass-clear against a blur of sound and light. There's a line of pimples just at the neckline of her dress, and every time she raises her head the fabric scrapes slowly across them. She's all raw skin and bleached-dry hair and she doesn't have time for this.

'Don't worry. They're on their way.'

Her fingertips stray up to that scatter of acne. She dabs at it gently, experimentally, and rubs her fingers together. A minute stretches out like sugar-syrup and then two men come jostling out of a side door. They're carrying a stretcher, and bursting with greasy, side-swiped laughter.

'Haziq, Ibrahim, we need porterage for an incoming hypoxia.'

The men stop laughing. Her neck flushes red under their stare and she puts her pen down. Spins round in her chair, with her knees neatly pressed together and waves them over to me. Haziq smiles at me, a burly middle-aged man with a belly held in check by exercise and will.

'Come on, come on,' I tell him. 'It's this way. Come on, quickly. Please.'

He folds the stretcher down on its wheels, turning to give the nurse a wink. She looks down – blushing, like a teenager – and scribbles something on her notes.

'Calm, slowly now,' he says to me. 'We take her to the doctors.'

They wheel the stretcher close behind as I hurry to the car. Ammuma's got herself out of her seat and stands peering across the darkened car park. Her hands are on her hips and her chest heaves like porridge on the boil.

'Ammuma, they've come, they'll help you.'

'Plenty time . . . I've been waiting,' she snaps. 'Enough only – to mend – this tank.'

The words come out in between breaths. Whispery, tinged blue by effort. When Haziq takes her arm to help her onto the stretcher she nearly collapses. Haziq straightens her legs and drapes her sari back over her swollen knees. They carry her past the cleaners: men in sarongs picking at a shared bowl of rice with their knees up like flamingos. To them, Ammuma's only another patient, one more in an infinite series. They watch her go past, indifferently, detached as mathematicians.

'Wait here, please.'

Haziq pushes the stretcher through the double doors. He turns to me and points at a row of metal chairs. Ammuma looks so small, flat on her back under these harsh lights. She turns her head away from me to stare out into the night. She can't be doing with this fuss, that head-turn says. With Dr Rao and his impolite stethoscope, with nurses and their questions. *Does it hurt when I press here? How about here? When did you last –? What first happened when –?* 'Questions again,' she'd say. As though the answers ever did anyone any good.

I watch her wheeled away through heavy swing doors and slump into a chair. My eyes feel scrubbed with exhaustion. The chair digs into my hips, where my skirt pulls tight and lumped from everything stuffed in the pockets. Car keys, a few coins I snatched up from the hall table. The autograph book on one side. The photograph of Francesca on the other.

I pat the pockets again, then plunge my fingers deeper. The metal arm of the chair jabs against my elbow, but I barely notice it. I can't find my mother's plait of hair. It must have fallen out somewhere: in Mother Agnes's house, in the jungle, even out in the car park. I stand up, digging my hands into both pockets and shaking out my skirt. Brushing myself down, checking pockets and waistbands and everywhere it couldn't possibly be. I turn round and peer under the metal seats, but the plait isn't there.

The nurse looks over at me and dabs at her acne again. Don't touch it, I want to tell her. Don't pick at it; you'll only make it worse. She looks like the sort of woman to appreciate a metaphor.

★

The rest of the night passes slowly. I doze in the chair, waking to the flail and scurry of tiny emergencies. A child with measles, a man with stomach pains. People collect on the chairs, becalmed and waiting, and then disperse in flurries of alarm or relief. At one point I wake to hear the noise of metal shutters, and see the hospital café opening. A Sikh man lays out bowls of rice and pieces of wrinkled fruit, but nobody moves. An hour later I open my eyes again, and this time there's a queue of men in vests and sarongs. Their toenails are sharp against their bare feet and they stink of cleaning fluids.

'Durga?'

And then I'm awake. Properly this time, cold-water awake. Tom's crouching in front of me. A stethoscope swings from his neck and he wears an unbuttoned white coat with green scrubs beneath.

'Durga, wake up. I've just been in with Mary-Auntie.'

'But . . .' I'd been expecting Dr Rao, with his heron-limbs and apologetic face. I rub at my eyes, drag my hands over my cheeks.

'Is she all right?'

He nods, then looks away. He's uneasy, shifting his weight between his thighs. Europeans can't squat – they hover, all stretched tendons and creaking muscles – and Tom looks uncomfortable in his too-tight scrubs.

'I'll take you in to see her, but . . . look, we should talk first. We'll have a coffee.'

He tucks his hands behind his back as we walk to the café. His shoulders are set tight, chilled with disapproval and dignity. He doesn't ask me how I take my coffee, just orders for us both – yes, sir; nice to see you again, sir – and picks up the cups without a smile. The Sikh café owner shrugs, watching as we scrape into aluminium chairs.

'How did it happen, Durga?' Tom asks, when we're sitting down. 'The equipment shouldn't have broken like that.'

'She bit it,' I say. 'It was . . . no, actually, it *wasn't*. It wasn't an accident. She did it on purpose.'

'She bit it? What do you mean she bit it? How long ago?'

'Oh . . . I – I don't know. It's been – I mean, I had to go out this evening.'

He nods. 'So she did it while you were out?'

I look down at my hands. 'No,' I say quietly. 'I went out afterwards. I thought she was OK.'

'You did what?' He looks disbelieving. 'When she'd already started having breathing difficulties? You should never leave somebody in that condition, Durga. *Never*. Surely Rao told you that?'

I don't say anything. Tom pushes a hand over his forehead. He's tired, spots are breaking out under his jawline and he looks pasty and exhausted.

'What are you still doing here anyway?' he asks, sounding distracted. 'I thought you were going back to KL yesterday.'

'I was, but the road was blocked.' That flooded road seems a year ago by now. Sitting in the car, turning to go to Tom's house, and everything since is disintegration.

His reflection in the polished chrome table top looks smug and self-satisfied, his mouth still square from telling me how I should have managed better with Ammuma. I stare back at him. It's been the longest night I can ever remember. And now Tom's sitting there with the calm and cow-like expression of someone who'd never be careless. *Who'd never leave anyone to run out of oxygen*, Peony adds with a shrug of her thin shoulders. He's a mirror image, flipped Tom; the opposite of anything real, and I want him to take his fair share of blame.

I met Alice, I could tell him. *I met your wife. With her lacy English name I've never heard you say once. Not even by accident; not even how you say Peony's.*

And he'd try to explain – no, even worse, he'd bluster and

bluff – and I'd be sarcastic, and then he'd say it didn't matter anyway. And I'd ask what the hell he thought he meant by that, but I'd know. He'd mean Alice doesn't matter, and I don't and even Karthika and her baby don't. We're not fifteen any more, we're not bright-eyed and tangle-haired and burnished up by Tom's unreliable mind. We're grown-up now and turning into our own grandmothers. We're washed-up and ended-up, and none of us is Peony.

'I'm sorry,' I say instead. 'I shouldn't have left Ammuma.'

He leans closer and puts an arm around my shoulder. He feels very hot and there's a stickiness to his hands, as though he hasn't rinsed the soap off. He's had those hands in people's bodies, I think, pulling out organs and stitching their hides back together again. A wave of dizziness passes and I taste coffee sugar mixed with bile.

'Come on, Durga, we'll go up and see her. She'll be on the ward by now.'

He pushes his chair back and takes me through the swinging double-doors and up the metal staircase behind. On the third floor a blue sign reads 'Short Term and Emergency'. There's a corridor leading off it, with more chairs and a few nurses chatting. Tom pushes the first door open and stands there with a practised-in-the-mirror smile, just like a doctor should.

'Mary-Auntie,' he says. 'Mrs Selva.'

There are only two beds in here. Ammuma's nearest, with pale blue curtains drawn half-round. Mrs Selva must be the woman by the window. She's propped on wedge-shaped pillows and attached to machines by a tangle of tubes. Rows of faded Christmas cards stand on her bedside table, some so old I can barely make out the design. She stares at me, her eyes newly hatched and tender, then looks away.

'Ammuma?'

Ammuma's in a white hospital gown again, and the fabric smothers her. She still looks so much smaller than her size. She looks like a patient, or an invalid. She looks like Mrs Selva.

'Ar, Durga.' She sounds weak and breathy. 'Wait already for hours for you.'

There's a rap at the open door and a nurse puts her head round. 'Dr Harcourt, you're wanted on Ward Nine.'

Ammuma narrows her eyes. 'Aiyoh, no privacy in here.' She doesn't think much of Ward Nine, or their wantings either. 'People walking in-out, cannot be sitting with my granddaughter without fuss.'

The nurse flushes and Tom gives her a quick, apologetic glance. I don't care. I'd take every single nurse flouncing away in disgust, if that'd mean Ammuma was back to her old self.

'I'll just be outside,' he says. 'Call me – either of you – if anything happens.'

When he's gone I sit down heavily on the bed. The dawn light filters through the window, giving everything a cigarette-ash haze. Ammuma watches me in a companionable silence.

'Ammuma . . .' and then I burst out – 'I lost Amma's plait.'

I don't know where that came from. There are a hundred other things I'd meant to say – practical, logical things – but here in this milky morning light I've forgotten them all.

'I went to Mother Agnes's house and I dropped it there or in the car park, or . . .'

I'm shaking, and I can't stop the words spilling out. Why now, I don't know: now when she's safely in hospital and the worst is surely over. *Don't be stupid*, Dr Panikkar would say. *Pull yourself together*, she'd add, as if that was all it took.

'You went to Agnes's house?' Ammuma asks. She doesn't sound angry, just curious. Her arm snakes out from under the heap of her too-large hospital gown and she takes my hand.

'I wanted to ask about Francesca and the San. I didn't know you were choking. I thought . . .'

She clucks her tongue. 'Oh, Durga,' she says. 'All this mathematics, isn't it? Always wanting for it to be right, instead of true.'

She sits there quietly then, breathing slowly. There's a hum from the machines hooked up to Mrs Selva. The three of us are silent, listening to that hum and the squeak of sturdy shoes in the corridor outside. It's enough, in a way.

After a second Ammuma stretches up, and I feel her stroking my hair. She combs her nails through it, tugging the knots as carefully as she did when I was small. I close my eyes and feel her palm run like water down the length of it. The air's cool on my scalp as she divides the hair into three sections.

'And when the sun came up,' she says in a low, soothing voice, 'they knew that they were safe.'

'You used to tell me that story, didn't you? Almost every bedtime.'

I remember the smell of Nivea, the sound of Flit and the shutters being closed, the dim hallway light blurring through my mosquito net. I twist round to see her, but she puts her palm flat on my shoulder and gently pushes me straight again. She's known that story for sixty years, her little push says – long before Nivea and Flit and hallway lights – long before she was anybody's Ammuma at all. Back when she was Mary. Plain Mary, thirty-two years old, with a nine-year-old daughter and not much else to show for it.

'And when the sun came up, they knew they were safe.'

Mary finishes with a flourish and a sigh of relief. These days she has to do the best she can with the tiger-prince's growls, snorting them from the back of her throat. With half her teeth gone she doesn't have much of a choice.

'No! No!' Francesca screams.

Mary doesn't mind her daughter's temper; after two years in a Kempetai prison she never even expected to find Francesca again. Mary was one of the last to be released, weeks after the Japanese surrendered. She fought, she wore her fingernails down in scraping at her cell wall and her tongue down in screaming. And that got her nowhere at all, so she cultivated patience and politeness instead. She told herself they'd be fair. (Oh, Mary. Why start believing in fairness now, of all times?)

So, with one thing and another, Mary stayed locked in her makeshift Kempetai cell until the end of 1945. She'd hoped to find that Anil had already been released, but there was no trace of him. All she got for her pains was a chilly, official letter from the government, agreeing to make inquiries into his whereabouts. Didn't she realize – the letter sneered through its mistyped address and ill-glued stamps – that there'd been a war on? Other people were missing, said the creased envelope. Mary would just have to wait, and the official stamp confirming this sloped halfway off the page.

In any case, Mary had no choice. She'd contracted TB in prison, her skin and lungs damp from stagnant water. She was released on a stretcher and taken to hospital, where it took her three months to talk and another three to stop screaming. And then she was handed her bus fare and a packet of nasi lemak wrapped in a banana leaf. And she came back to Pahang.

The house, when she arrived, was swarming with monkeys. They'd pulled down her father's ramshackle rooms and moved into the cellars. They'd uncovered the wells, they'd made cubby-holes behind the doors and tucked themselves into the rotting beds. Mary flung them out in furry armfuls and kept right on looking for Anil and Francesca.

She searched for two years, knocking on doors and questioning street-beggars. Francesca? Four years old when . . . do you remember her? Did you see her? Did you help her? She got nowhere. Mrs Varghese had fed Francesca for a week until her rice supplies ran out and her own children chased the girl back into the jungle. Agnes would have taken her in, of course, but Agnes was in a prison camp herself in Kedah. Yoke Yee wouldn't have helped, Noor Abi might have but didn't, and everyone else in the village was mired deep in their own bad endings. Mary ripped that government letter to shreds, set her teeth, and refused to conduct a funeral for her husband or her daughter. Rajan could manage that for himself, she declared, and Francesca – well, Francesca wasn't dead.

And so on, until an ordinary day in 1947. Mary was in the garden, hacking with a changkol at the tapioca plants. She wasn't even thinking about Francesca when she heard the voice.

'No!'

There was a figure standing at the edge of the compound, where the walls had crumbled. A naked figure, stick thin and scarred by ringworm; hair tumbled into a bird's nest and a distended belly caked in dirt. Mary will never be able to explain how she knew it was her daughter straight away, how every molecule in her blood leapt nearly out of her veins, how she found herself on her knees in the mud with her arms around her daughter and the tapioca plants gone to glory.

*

It only took a week at home before Francesca made her preferences clear. Pencils instead of dolls. Dal instead of tapioca. A bedtime story she wanted again and again.

'And when the sun came up,' Mary repeats obligingly, 'they knew that they were safe.'

'No!' Francesca says again, squirming off her mother's lap. She squats in the dirt at Mary's feet, poking at ants with her finger and repeating, 'No!'

Francesca doesn't say much else, but that's hardly surprising. She's nine years old, and four of those have been spent hiding in the jungle. She's seen war from a thicket of rattan spines and peace from a vine-fringed ditch. She's seen her mother taken away and come back to find her bony and utterly, utterly changed. *No!* is the only word life needs, so far as Francesca is concerned right now.

Mary picks Francesca up and takes her to the shower room. It's only been in the last few days she could bring herself to let her daughter out of her arms long enough to bathe her. And she repays the effort. *She's beautiful*, Mary thinks. *She's the most gorgeous little girl there's ever been.* There'd be no hiding her now, no passing her off as Joseph-the-boy, should it be needed. But it isn't needed, Mary knows, it *isn't*, and she could nearly explode with the sheer, fizzing joy of that.

'No,' Francesca observes, splashing the water in the shower-bucket. She squirms against Mary's knees as Mary trickles palmfuls of water over her. Mary rubs her daughter with a piece of old serge, then braids and plaits her hair. One-two-three, twist, with Francesca protesting all the time. Tonight Mary will tuck her daughter up under the only mosquito net, which by now has holes large enough for a civet-cat to get through. Not that it matters; those years in the jungle have toughened Francesca's skin until any mosquito would break its nose on her carapace. Francesca will lie there, batting placidly at huge, soft moths. And Mary will tuck her dupatta over her head and finish the story of the tiger-prince and the princess, the one which ends with the sun coming up and everyone safe.

'No,' Francesca will say. 'No.'

★

('But Ammuma,' I interrupt. Because I can. Because this is, after all, a story. Liable to interruptions, to corrections, to obfuscations and lies and tiny changes. 'You said you got out of prison quickly. You said it was only –'

'Didn't say, Durga. Always with assumptions.' She gabbles this out triumphantly, sounding uncannily like me. *Score one*, I think, *to Ammuma*.

'And Dr Rao. You said you'd never had TB. He asked –'

'Yes, and now telling, isn't it?'

'But they could have treated you. It was important. You should have *said*.'

'Secrets, isn't it.' She looks stubborn and mulish. 'No need for telling secrets.'

Hypocritical, when she can't hold anyone else's long enough to melt on her tongue. She pats my hand and settles back against the hospital pillow. One big breath and then she gives a deep, rattling cough. A consumptive cough, weak in the lungs and strong in the throat.)

*

'I'm perfectly well. Never been better.' Mary coughs again, and Agnes flinches slightly.

Of course you are, she prints diplomatically.

By 1954, Agnes isn't living in the convent any more. The building's fallen to ruins, mossed with butterflies and wild frangipani. A damn good thing, Mary says, and Agnes is diplomatic about that, too.

She's sitting with Mary on the verandah, both sipping glasses of well-water and listening to the evening. It's so still that sounds can be heard from a mile away: children playing with kites in the padang, Mrs Varghese slapping out her chapatti dough and the slippery noise of Arif-the-postman relieving himself on the trunk of a handy teak. In 1947 this peace would have seemed impossible, but since then the Emergency has come and – largely – gone.

A handful of deaths in the valley; a handful of resettlements behind the barbed wire of the New Villages. Registration for most, deportation for some and food shortages for all. But life's nearly back to normal now. A few black areas still bristle with roadblocks and heave with Communists, but none in this valley. There's room for the smaller things in life here, room for chapattis and poor hygiene.

Why don't you go and see the doctor anyway? Agnes persists. She doesn't like the sound of Mary's cough, or the way her friend has to squint into the fading light. TB can take your eyesight, Agnes knows, but Mary sets her jaw and shakes her head firmly at the suggestion of a doctor.

Or a bomoh . . . But at that Mary stands and claps her hands sharply together.

'Francesca!' she calls. 'Go to the kitchen. Now!'

'No,' floats back an answer from the corner of the compound. Francesca's huddled against the wall and digging her way along the side path. Tunnelling out, or in, depending on how you look at it.

Francesca's a large girl, now. She's sixteen years old and heavy-limbed with it. Every night Mary cleans her daughter's teeth and tucks her in under the mosquito net, buttoned into a fresh pink nightgown with her hair plaited. And every morning Mary wakes to the sound of digging as Francesca – naked, her hair filled with mud and twigs – tries to scrabble under the compound walls and get back to her jungle home. Francesca's determined to get away and Mary's determined to keep her here, whatever the cost in pink cotton nightgowns.

'Don't talk about bomohs in front of her,' Mary snaps.

Because Francesca's already seen a bomoh. Of course she has. What else would you do with a girl who can't even read, a sixteen-year-old who spends all her time drawing or digging? She's no interest in books or boys or even the lipstick Mary had hoped to forbid her from wearing. Francesca thinks like a child; she likes pencils and toys and satin ribbons; she likes party frocks and sweets that make her almost too large to fit in them. Mary only got her to the bomoh by bribing her with laddoo and sugary bur-phi. The bomoh was underwhelming: a gentle man in spectacles and a link-detached house. He greeted them with courtesy and a mild insistence that Mary put Francesca into an institution. 'No!' Mary told him, and he raised his eyebrows as though he'd realized where Francesca got it from.

So Mary's had quite enough of bomohs and doctors, one way or another. But something's upsetting her tonight, more than usual. Perhaps it's the strangled quality of Francesca's grunts, or the way the shadow of a sapling durian tree nudges her daughter's feet. Perhaps it's the tricky evening light, the sound of Arif's bicycle; perhaps it's nothing at all but hindsight when she tells this story forty years later, but Mary suddenly stiffens.

'Agnes,' she says quietly, bolt upright in her rattan chair. 'Some-one's coming.'

Both women freeze; the Emergency isn't so far gone. Footsteps come down the drive. Strange, dragging footsteps, from feet without any toes. From club-feet, the nails long since pulled off – and the fingers, too, and the lips and tongue that he barely used anyway, and –

'Anil!'

Standing on the drive is a figure that Agnes wouldn't have recog-nized. He's dressed well, in a suit too large and too thick for his frame. It could conceal a lot of things, a suit like that. Wasted limbs, ulcerous skin, muscles that don't work and nerves that work only too well.

Mary flies off the verandah to Anil, wrapping him in a hug. He's so thin that her arms go around him twice, and she has a sudden ugly panic that when she takes them away he won't be there at all.

'Where have you been? What's *happened*?' Mary's hands flutter over him, registering his changed shape. A bulge here, an unaccountable hollow there. Behind her, on the verandah, Mother Agnes knows only too well. She writes a single word on her paper and stands up – tea and handbag tipping to the floor, her armpits moist and her lacquered nails catching the last of the sunset – and she holds up her page.

Leprosy.

Because of course Agnes knows, given the peculiar circumstances of her own birth. She's delivered her message at last; twenty years too late she's come out with a prophecy that's enough to knock the very breath from Mary's lungs. Leprosy. It means something worse than death, it means shame and isolation and loneliness for ever. It means Mary can't expect any more visitors, ever, not even Arif-the-postman, who'll start leaving the letters on a tree stump where the mites and silverfish will get to them before Mary does. No more visits to the night market, no more sharp words with the butcher over his propensity to stretch out the chicken with year-old mutton. No, Agnes thinks, Mary's life will be changed for ever, and the best thing Anil could have done for his sister is to have stayed away and drowned himself quietly in the Jelai.

'Don't be horrible.' Mary can see all this in the single flicker of Agnes's calligraphic eyebrows. 'He's going to live here and that's that. You don't know everything, you and your . . . your convent-ery!'

Shades of her failed Junior Cambridge exam, perhaps; even at forty she still blurs the odd word or two. She puts an arm protectively around Anil's shoulders, and feels something crackle under his shirt. She takes a deep breath and plunges her hand in, next to his skin. Eyes shut, of course, my canny young grandmother knows better than to look. She pulls out an envelope, limp and sodden with oil from his body.

Sungai Buloh Leprosarium, it reads. *Anil Panikkar, discharged to the streets. Non-infectious.*

And there's a great, glorious government stamp to attest to the truth of the words. This stamp doesn't slope off the page, it doesn't ruck itself up in creases or fade where the ink runs out. This stamp has its hands on its hips and it's proclaiming with all the breath in its lungs that the Panikkar son and heir has finally come home.

★

It's an evening of rejoicing after that, an evening of eating and drinking and making merry. A rather silent evening, certainly. Perhaps not so much eating and drinking as would be expected either. So, an evening of the eyes instead.

Mary sits on the top step of the verandah, her gaze fixed intently on her brother. She's produced a bottle of cod-liver oil for him, to build up his condition, and every few minutes she raises a finger to remind him to take another gulp. The hurricane lamps can flicker and smoke, the kueh can congeal on their plates and the tea go cold; the ghosts of drowned women can clamber out of the wells and stamp their feet till they bring down every durian in Pahang, but nothing will make Mary take her eyes off Anil.

And a pity it is, too. Because as she sits there, eyes on her brother and slapping automatically at mosquito bites, Mary misses rather a lot.

The way Anil looks at Francesca, for a start. When he left he had a boisterous, skinned-knee split-lip thug of a toddler nephew. Now he's being faced with a blossoming teenage girl, her hair plaited and her body hinting at all kinds of things under a clean pink nightgown. Anil, whose body hints at all kinds of things too, doesn't know what to make of her. Nephews don't turn into nieces — Josephs don't turn into Francescas — and that simplifies things. This girl, then, can't be anything other than a beautiful stranger. He doesn't, of course, say a word to her but as the evening express train whistles a drawn-out note in the distance, Anil tumbles head over ulcerated heels in love.

And Francesca herself? Mary strokes her daughter's hair in the lamplight, feels the flicker and shine of it under her fingertips. Francesca's watching Anil too, her head turned to him like a fern after rain. The whole time Anil's been here, Francesca hasn't said *No!* once.

Agnes is watching everyone else. She always is: Agnes has grown up quiet, overlooking and overlooked. She sees the love in Mary's steady gaze, she sees the twining glances of Anil and

Francesca and she does her desperate best to keep up her Christian cheer. Agnes will for ever reproach herself for having said nothing that night. She'll wear herself out with new ways to do penance; she'll work her fingers to the bone for charity and sacrifice every dollar she makes. But she'll never make amends – Ammuma tells me now, snapping an elastic band around my plait – for holding that non-existent tongue of hers.

*

Ammuma brushes the end of my plait against my cheek. 'That Agnes, ar,' she says.

She coughs again, and a trail of blood and spittle clings to her chin. Her eyes are dreamy and filmed over. The sun beats in through the windows, and our shadows lie tar-black on the sheets. The whole room seems to quiver with heat, with the low, strong pulse of machines keeping Mrs Selva alive. Ammuma looks desiccated against the pillows, a grinning skeleton held together with oxygen tubing and bad intentions.

'The war was over for ten years, when Anil-Uncle came back,' she says. 'So Francesca was . . .'

'Sixteen years, Ammuma,' I remind her gently and she gives me a black look.

'Ar, very clever.' She flicks a finger at my blouse. 'You think I need to go to some Canada university to wear tight tops and learn to count, is it?'

'So. Sixteen years. Aiyoh, too old for bothering Anil-Uncle like that. Not a moment for him to drink his tea.'

*

In fact, Anil has all the time in the world, and more tea than he knows what to do with. Francesca stations herself by the stove, dousing it each morning with enough kerosene to choke it. As soon as Anil's had his tea, she lets the fire go out. The rest of them, so far as Francesca's concerned, can subsist on old-food-cold-food-no-food, but Anil must have his hot drinks.

She's in love with him, drowned in desire until she almost forgets to breathe. She fixes him with her eyes – weeping with kerosene and love – and refuses even to blink. She doesn't say *No!* any more and hasn't for weeks. With Anil's scent in her nostrils strong enough to slice, there's nothing she wants to deny.

And Mary is completely oblivious.

'Anil, the child's bothering you? You send her away.'

Anil blinks at his sister. They're sitting together in the back of the compound, squashed together on a garden seat by the cool draught of the bathroom window. Mary coughs, covering her mouth. Blood spatters her palm, and she wipes it casually on her skirt.

'Anil? Is Francesca bothering you?'

'Fran-cesc-ca', Anil says carefully. It's the first time he's said anyone's name but hers, and Mary's delighted. She leans close and gives him a fierce hug. The movement makes her cough, again, and Anil covers her mouth with a gentle hand.

'No!' Francesca's been crouched in the annexe near the back wall, drawing some of her beautiful, intricate pictures. These pictures are how she talks, these days, people and animals and fantastic landscapes springing out from her pen. She comes striding out angrily as soon as she sees Anil touch her mother. She's magnificent in the afternoon light, her hair tidy for once and cobwebs clinging about her sturdy knees where she's been crouched on the ground.

'All right, all right,' Mary laughs, holding up her hands, and gets up to make room for her daughter. Her cough's been worrying her lately, and if Anil truly doesn't mind this puppy-love of Francesca's then she's quite happy to leave them to it.

She walks into the kitchen, cool and dim after the brightness of the garden. She coughs again, chokes, then picks up the bottle of cod-liver oil kept on the kitchen almirah for Anil. She takes a cautious gulp. Disgusting, that taste, but it's done wonders to cure

Anil. Already his eyes are so bright and his skin so clear that you'd hardly know he'd had leprosy at all. Perhaps, Mary thinks, it'll do the same for her cough.

What Mary doesn't know, not yet, is that she's the one they should be worried about. Anil's doctor in Sungai Buloh was conscientious through and through, a Chinese collaborator who poured his heart and his bank account into making amends. There's no doubt: Anil's perfectly safe to be around. But Mary, though, Mary's a different matter. She's leaving a slime of TB bacilli wherever she goes – when she wipes blood from her fingers or coughs on Anil, when she gulps from his cod-liver oil bottle or offers him a morsel of meat from her own plate.

In a few months Anil will begin to cough, too. His veins – already weakened from leprosy and unsafe doses of cod-liver oil – will strain and begin to leak. He'll bleed under his skin and from his lungs, coughing up fluid until his tongue starts to swell and his fingers curl. He'll die within a few weeks of falling ill, on a quiet afternoon with the breeze rustling the durian trees and the chickens pecking up dirt. By then he'll be so frail that Mary, holding his head on her lap on that cramped garden seat, won't even notice he's gone. Not until she hears Francesca wail. *No*, Francesca will scream from her hiding-place in the annexe where she's been watching the whole thing. *No*.

But it's yes. It's a yes that will tinge the rest of their lives with regret and if-only. It's a yes that'll bury itself and come out years after in the stories they tell and the lies they hold under their tongues. It's a yes, quite frankly, that Francesca and her mother have no say in at all.

27.   Wednesday, 10 a.m.

'I thought Anil-Uncle died in the war,' I say. Ammuma's been plaiting and replaiting my hair all this time, and my eyes feel tight with headache. Mrs Selva watches us from her bed. She's rippling her fingers like waterweed, imitating Ammuma as she combs.

'*Because* of, ar.' Ammuma snaps the hair-tie around the end of my plait and lets it fall against my back. 'Because of the war.'

It's true that she's always been vague about Anil. She sometimes says he died from wounds, or shock, or old age and even – when she's not in the mood for questions – that he never died at all.

'So what happened after he died?' I'm humouring her just a little. I can't quite bring myself to believe in that TB. 'To you, I mean, you and Francesca?'

'Difficult,' she says promptly. 'So much fuss, forms to sign, got certificates and letters.'

'But what did you do?'

'Agnes some help, but flighty only. Cannot focus, not so clever for a schoolteacher.'

'Ammuma –'

'So much fuss also from her, wrong colour of book it is for her to write, wrong pen. No thinking –'

'Did you put Francesca in the San?' I interrupt.

Ammuma stops mid-sentence. She turns away with a heart-breaking, offended dignity.

'Ammuma?'

She scrutinizes the wall clock, refusing to look at me. Out of the corner of my eye I see Mrs Selva turn over too. Her arms are weighted down with tubes and needles, but her hands still tug away at nothing. Plaiting invisible hair. Soothing invisible ghosts.

After a few minutes Ammuma's voice comes quiet, cracked as a split cashew nut. Everything inside spilling out, whether you want it or not.

'Had to, ar. Even my own daughter. So sick, after Anil died. Not her body, Durga. Her insides, her being. She wasn't safe –'

'She'd have been a lot less safe in the San!'

Ammuma shakes her head. She doesn't even scold me for interrupting.

'She wasn't safe,' she says again slowly, 'to be near.'

She's facing away from me, limp under the heap of her stiff cotton gown. She turns, with effort, and pushes the gown sleeves up above her elbows. Her burn scar is there, keloided and rope-like, puckering the skin beneath.

'Always lighting fires. Lighting the stove, making coffee. Trying to bring back Anil-Uncle.' She rubs at her scar reflectively.

'When that didn't work, lighting more fires. Kitchen. Bathroom. Bedrooms. Like you, Durga, last week,' she adds with a trace of her old sharpness. 'Always to burn down the house. Get it from your mother.'

I can't quite catch my breath. 'Did she – is that how you got that scar?'

Dr Rao asked me about that scar when I brought Ammuma in the first time. Wondering whether I'd done it, though he didn't ask straight out. *No*, I should have said. *No. You've got the wrong generation in your sights.*

'Not so bad, Durga, when she lit fires only in the house. But she ran away. Eight months pregnant, and setting fires in the jungle. Maybe hurting someone, getting hurt.'

Ammuma stops talking then. There's a hum and clatter from outside as a stretcher wheels past the door. A nurse's rubber-soled shoes, squeaking with efficiency and the smell of overcooked breakfast from somewhere down the corridor.

'Agnes drove us to the San,' Ammuma says very softly. 'I sat in the back, with Francesca. Told stories.'

She closes her eyes, then says under her breath, 'And when the sun came up, she knew that she was safe.'

Mrs Selva closes her eyes too, and breaks wind defiantly. Like Ammuma, she's matter-of-fact about her body. Blood, pains, cramps, the empty-balloon breasts revealed by her hospital gown. She's seen worse, and most of it's been right here.

'So. Enough of questions, Durga.' Ammuma crosses her arms. She's had enough of me, of Mrs Selva, of the stink of break-fast congee from the corridor. She's all in favour of smells and stubbornness, but they've got to be her own. She shuts her eyes defiantly. Daylight reveals all the scuffs on the skirting board and the darns at the bottom of the bed-curtains.

I can't let it go, though. 'I thought you sent her there just to have me. Because she wasn't married . . .'

Ammuma snorts. 'Couldn't know who to marry, is it? Some George-boy, Anil-Uncle, Arif-the-postman. Eenie-meenie, it is, like on the playground.'

Anil-Uncle? She gives me a cunning, sideways glance. *See, Durga*, she's saying. *A woman who seduces her own uncle, well, who knows where she'll end up? Fallen. Ruined. Scarlet, and wicked and witchy as snakes. Locked up in the San for her own good, and for everyone else's too; when we dragged her out she was fucking the postman.*

'But you told me my father was a boy, from her school . . .'

Ammuma gives me a loving smile that doesn't quite come off. Too much gleam to it, too much fang and impatience.

'And now I tell different,' she says. Which is Ammuma through and through. She tells stories; she tells drowned women and Malay housewives and tiger-princes, and she's told me all along that she's not to be trusted.

'More than one way to be right, isn't it, Durga? Your math-ematics, hanh?'

'But this isn't . . . I mean, it's facts, Ammuma. It's not math-ematics, it's –'

It's real life, I'm about to say, and she gives me a triumphant look over her bedsheets.

'In love, they were,' she goes on calmly. 'Your mother and Anil-Uncle. Your mother and anyone.'

'But . . .'

'And then he died. Romantic, all this kissing-mooning, but not right for her. She needs safer. Needs locks on the gates and windows.'

Locks on the gates. I can feel Ammuma wince as she says it, and I squeeze her hand tight. 'So Francesca died in there when it burnt down? Oh, Ammuma, I'm so sorry, I'm –'

'No, Durga!'

As Ammuma says *No!* there's a sound from Mrs Selva's bed. A bubble of foul air forces its way from the tissues of her chest and her ribs begin to cave. There's a sound like air being blown into a crumpled paper bag, and an alarm goes off on one of her machines. She coughs, making a noise like chickens squabbling, all snapping beaks and wings clapped together. Another alarm starts, blaring in the corridor outside. There's a thud of feet on the vinyl floor. Ammuma turns to me quickly, her eyes bright and urgent.

'Still see her,' she whispers in my ear, a hot gush of words under the howling alarm. 'My baby one, every month. In Kampung Ulu.'

She gives me a grin – a shocking, toothy flash – and pushes her legs down to the end of the bed. Her lips are closed firmly over her teeth and she's sitting back now, watching the show.

The machine gives another shriek and Mrs Selva yelps. She's woken in a flurry, her hair on end and no breath to complain about it with. I jump as the door's flung open and Tom hurries in with his white coat flapping. He runs to Mrs Selva's bedside and pushes a code into the machine's front panel.

The alarm ratchets down a notch, then starts to rise again. Tom turns a dial, adjusting a bag that's pumping fluid into her withered arm. After a few seconds the alarm cuts out. It leaves the room ringing with silence and the scrape of breath. Mrs Selva's Christmas cards flutter in the breeze and Tom reaches out to set them straight.

'Don't worry,' Tom says. He sounds professional, all-under-control, but his forehead's furrowed with tension. 'All OK, Mrs Selva, Mary-Auntie.'

Neither of them looks convinced. The noise of the alarm seems to have hammered them down, left them flattened with unease. If bodies can fail even here, in the lights and disinfectant of a hospital bed, then how can they be trusted at all?

Ammuma shoves her teeth out with a clack. They drop into the palm of her hand, glistening with spit, and she puts them on the bedside table. She's done with talking, she's done with being questioned, and she's certainly done with explanations. Mrs Selva, with no teeth to make her own statement with, looks mutely envious.

A few nurses come bustling into the room, their white coats stiff with authority and starch.

'Thank you, Dr Harcourt,' one of them says. 'We'll take over now.'

She gives him a toothpaste-commercial smile of her own, and holds the door open for us. Tom ushers me out in front of him, but he looks less sure of himself suddenly. He's been dismissed. He's not wanted; he's been replaced by shining hair and lipsticked smiles and competency in skirts.

'Sorry about all that,' he says when we're in the corridor. 'We're a bit stretched, you see. Mary-Auntie wouldn't normally be in with Mrs Selva.'

I don't see why not. Someone worse off than herself is exactly what Ammuma needs to pep herself up.

'Hopefully she'll be out in an hour or so. We're waiting on the last scan results, but as long as they're fine she's good to go.'

'Sorry?' I don't understand. 'You're sending her home?'

He nods. 'We'll sort out a nurse to help you. Perhaps one of the girls from here, just for a month or so . . .'

Tom goes on talking, stringing out a future with me knotted firmly in it, but I barely hear him. Back here in Pahang, kicking my feet uselessly and never getting out again. Nursing Ammuma. Having Tom and his wife round for coffee; having Peony around for ever. Having nothing else but a copy of my resignation letter and some maths textbooks I won't understand any more.

'I'm not staying,' I interrupt. 'I still have to go to KL.'

He blinks. 'You're still going back?'

Yes, I tell him, I'm going back to my *life*, to category theory and proofs and things that stay where they're put. To Anwar, to Sangeeta, to Deepak with his middle-of-the-night calls and his angry wife. Even if all I end up with is a lifetime of evening classes and quarrelsome silences down the phone line, at least I'll have come out ahead.

'Oh.' He sounds – disappointed. Perhaps Tom was hoping I'd rescue him too, somehow. Run away with him, like Bonnie and Clyde, while Peony and Alice shake their fists in a rear-view mirror. A nurse walks past at the end of the corridor with bobbed hair and strong, bony ankles in white stockings. She takes down something from an alcove and the air fills with splash and the clinking of spoons in medicine bottles.

'Well,' Tom gives himself a shake, like a dog after rain. 'Of course, of course.' He doesn't say of course *what*. 'We'll still get her a nurse. And Karthika's there. Of course . . .'

Of course, again. At least Karthika can be relied upon, he implies, as if any woman wants that. He stares gloomily down the corridor, with his hands in his pockets like every doctor on TV. It looks false, it looks like he's playing dress-up in a white coat and a middle-aged body.

'You can't send her home,' I say. 'She needs to see someone. A psychiatrist, or a psychologist or something . . .'

'You don't want her to be discharged?' He looks incredulous.

'No! Look, it's not that – oh, forget it.' I take a deep breath. 'Listen, you've been taking her to Kampung Ulu, right?'

Tom looks guilty at that. Jumpy. 'Who told you –' he starts, but I interrupt.

'Well, she thinks she's seeing Francesca there. My mother. My *dead* mother, remember? Ammuma thinks Francesca's in Kampung Ulu.'

Tom stares at me. 'Durga,' he says, slowly. 'Listen. I take her there every month, so she can drop off donations for the left-behinds.

Toys and things. Mother Agnes says there's a whole crowd of kids up in those mountain villages.'

'Ammuma thinks one of those girls is Francesca,' I insist. 'Her baby one, she said. Reincarnated, or a ghost or – or – I don't know. Agnes told her some pack of lies and now Ammuma really believes it.'

He gives me a look. 'She's just going outstation to help a few left-behind kids. It's nice. It's normal.'

'She doesn't do normal,' I snap. She doesn't do nice either. 'Look, she *told* me. Just now, she said it was Francesca out there. She said it was her baby one –'

'And would she tell a psychiatrist?'

There's a silence.

'No,' I admit. Ammuma might be losing her mind, but she's doing it in a way that's thoroughly Ammuma. She'll be practical about it, when she finally does succumb. Demanding. A hands-off, keep-your-distance madness, that's what she'll go in for.

'So,' Tom says, 'you're the only one who says it. You've no proof at all.'

'I don't *need* proof. She's Ammuma; I know her.'

We face each other for a second, squabbling over Ammuma like two cats with a bone. A pair of nurses brush past, rubbing their eyes. Tangled hair, clutching cups of coffee and smelling of a sleepless night.

'So what do you want me to do?' Tom asks brusquely. 'You think she's hallucinating, so we should just lock her up in here? Like Mrs Selva?'

He rubs a hand through his hair, leaving it bristling with static. 'No friends, no visitors – because you won't come, will you, you haven't for ten years – nothing but a card from some charity every Christmas? "All on Ward Three, Lipis Hospital", that's what Mrs Selva's cards say.'

His words snag on a memory, like fish spiked by a river hook. *All on Ward Three, Lipis Hospital, Pahang, Malaysia, THE WORLD.*

'Wait . . . Tom, hold on – stop *talking*, shut up, OK – let me show you. Ammuma wrote Francesca's name. In the autograph book, the one from your fireworks bag. Here . . .'

Tom raises his eyebrows. He folds his arms, watching me as I tug the autograph book out of my pocket. It's wedged into a seam, and the fabric twists above my thighs. Tom looks down – a sizzle of a glance – and I feel cold air on my skin. The book looks more battered than before, and the paper's gluey. It clings to my fingers with a jackfruit stickiness.

'What . . .' Tom stares at it, then frowns in recognition. 'Where did you find that?'

'In your bag, the fireworks bag. You were bringing it to her.'

'Mary-Auntie took that book to Kampung Ulu a few months ago,' he says, each word careful and clear. 'It must have fallen out in the car on the way there. I found it last week, under the back seat, when I was with – when I was with a friend.'

With a friend. Strong-legged Alice, no doubt, or Karthika with her sleeves rolled high, or even the bobbed-haired nurse mixing up her innocent medicines. I shove the thought out of my mind.

'Ammuma wrote Francesca's name in the book,' I say again. 'This wasn't for a left-behind. It was for my mother.'

I lean over him to point at the inside cover. I can feel his warmth against me, heating as durian in this frigid air.

He barely even looks down. 'So she scribbled a few pictures in a book. That doesn't mean anything.'

I stop, my fingers spidering over the pages. 'What pictures?'

'In the book.' He taps it impatiently. 'I ripped the pages by accident and found the drawings. She must have stuck the thing together with fish glue. God knows how I didn't smell it on the trip out.'

He thumbs the corner of the last page. After a few seconds the edge curls, then suddenly springs apart. It's two pages there, thin as rice-paper and glued together. Tom works his finger between them carefully and rips upwards.

'Here. Careful, in case it sticks back together again.' He turns the book to show me.

There's a procession of tiny figures spilling over those hidden pages. All in pencil and all beautifully drawn. There's a prince, with a mouthful of teeth like knives and tiger stripes running down his sides. A princess, leaping past him with a sword clutched between two of her many arms. Tom moves his thumb then and there's a city, all houses and windows and froggish monsters springing from the sagging spine. Of course there is, because this is my bedtime story – this is Ammuma's story – and what you see is never all you get.

*

'It's only pictures, Durga. Mary-Auntie must have drawn them before she took it out there.' His voice sounds concerned. Warmer than it was before, as though I'm Durga again and not just a problem on two legs. Or on no legs at all; I've sat down heavily on one of the padded green chairs in the corridor and I can't stand up. My bones feel chilled, hips and knees weak as fractured glass.

Tom brings me a cup of water from the nurses' station, a chilled pointy cone of paper that starts dripping straight away. The bobbed-haired nurse avoids my eyes. They're used to devastation in these corridors. They're used to bad news and worse outlooks, and paper cups of water being handed round.

'But why? She used to tell *me* this story, when I was small. She used to tell it to my mother, too. Why would she glue it . . . ?'

He shrugs. I don't blame him. To anyone else, it's just a story. It's a fairy tale, a fable with its own happy ending and not even a whiff of what-happens-next. But that's wrong, because there's always a what-happens-next, and a what-happened-before. The what-happened-before is Anil and Francesca, alive and dead and something in between. What-happened-before is a left-behind girl or a vanished best friend. It's tiger-princes and monsters. What-happened-before spreads like leprosy, with Ammuma as patient zero.

'Look.' Tom's taking the cup from my hands. He drops it in a bin and grips my shoulders.

'Look, I know you're exhausted. I know you're tired. But it's just a story,' he says patiently. 'Maybe she was telling it to one of the left-behinds.'

'Let me ask her,' I say stubbornly. 'I want to know what's going on. I want to *know*.'

He doesn't stop me as I stand up. He lets me go, slumped on the chair with a few inches of tired sock showing. I wrench the door to Ammuma's room open.

'Ammuma?'

One of the nurses gives me a look. She pulls Mrs Selva's curtains around with a quick tug, so all I can make out are shapes moving behind the material, backlit by the window.

Ammuma's lying flat on her pillows with her arms by her sides. I put the book down gently on her flattened chest and her gaze sharpens. She tenses. There's a creak of bedsprings and secrets in the air.

'Ammuma? Did you draw these?'

She turns the pages over, propped up on her elbows. No sign she recognizes anything, from the inscription to the pastel angels. And then she sees the pictures.

She stops. For a heartbeat, nothing else moves. Somewhere a long way away Mrs Selva's coughing. The nurses are twittering, graceful as birds and Tom's in the corridor and the bobbed-haired girl is pouring a dosage into a measured cup and wishing her shift was over. Everyone, everywhere else, getting on with their lives.

And then Ammuma swallows.

'How did you find this?' Her voice is quiet, and she gobbles slightly. Her words are stripped down, all the ornaments of Malay and Tamil withered into cut-glass vowels.

'Tom found the book in his car. He said you dropped it there,' I say.

'No.' Ammuma doesn't even look up. 'I left it in Kampung Ulu,' she says. Simple. Certain as two multiply five and five multiply two. Certain as a proof. She'd swear to it, with all the bad language she can summon up.

'But you drew the pictures? The tiger-prince and the princess, like you used to tell me?'

Ammuma looks up then, her eyes limpid and alert as though everything's just fallen into place. She doesn't look old any more. She doesn't look like a patient, or an invalid or anyone but herself.

'No,' she says. 'Francesca did.'

Francesca did. It's taken Mary seventy years of listening to finally get her say, and now she's going to clear things up. Speak for herself, for once.

'Taking liberties,' she mutters to herself as the car bounces over a pothole. 'Everyone prying into things these days.'

She pushes her teeth out with a clack. Tom looks up from the driver's seat next to her.

'What's wrong, Mary-Auntie?'

'Nothing, nothing. You watch the road, ar. No point getting us crashed already.'

Tom slows down obediently. *She's looking forward to seeing the left-behinds*, he thinks. It's a wholesome, tolerant thought and it's wrong, as wholesome thoughts often are. He drops a gear, waits as a lorry trundles across the road between two palm plantations. He hates this drive to Kampung Ulu – always has done, he thinks, forgetting it was once a treat. He can smell smoke from one of the new processing plants, and burning rubber from deep in the plantation. In fact, Tom thinks, the whole place reeks of a lack of soap and a lack of civilization.

Mary rolls her eyes. She's a shameless eavesdropper, listening at doors and listening to hearts. Tom's thoughts are as clear to her as pebbles in shallow water, and she doesn't think much of them. 'Civilization,' she mutters. So much for this sweat-haired boy in his doctor-lawyer suit. She's no time for his civilization.

And so they drive on, each with their own thoughts. Past the Lipis trunk road, past a few deserted roadblocks made from barrels and planks, past the first faint, sludgy signs of the Kampung Ulu swamp. Tom keeps up a tactful silence and Mary a quarrelsome commentary.

'So sharp, ar, braking. Trying to push my head off its shoulders, is it? No, far enough already. Here, stop here.'

They've circumnavigated the swamp and they're on the far side where the San once was. This whole area was evacuated during the Emergency, with villagers snatched up and loaded onto trucks without time to put on so much as a pair of shoes. Since then it's been deserted, except for the San, of course. The odd itinerant family sets up house here and there, but they don't stay long. They can smell the blood.

A crumbling wall runs a few metres along the road, all that's left of the San's compound yard. Ferns sprout from the edges of the tarmac and the ground's claggy and drenched. The remains of the San loom over the swamp, chilly and shadowed. Tom feels a vague, cloudy guilt every time he thinks of the games they used to play. 'Locks on the gates,' they used to sing, but now he imagines all those poor patients burnt alive in their beds. He's learnt sympathy in his middle age.

'Mary-Auntie . . . hold on, let me get your door.'

He scrambles out of the car but Mary's already gone, stumping her way down the track with her carrier bag over one shoulder. From here Tom can see mud caking the bottom of her sari and dragging it down stiff as a weighted curtain. He sighs. He's neglecting a lot of work in order to stand here on the edge of a swamp and watch Mary-Auntie walk away without so much as a thank-you-for-bringing-me. Back in the hospital three little Varghese children have come down with dengue fever simultaneously, writhing in hospital cots with their arms spasming. Tom doesn't know it, but in just over a week the smallest boy will die and Tom himself will be moved off the surgical team – he should have noticed the first signs during pre-surgical checks, he'll be told – and onto the wards to look after old ladies and their Christmas cards. No wonder he feels put upon.

And it isn't an easy trip, either. Mary-Auntie likes him to park right near the swamp, and although he does his best not to look up, he's always aware of the banyan tree across the water. And the smell, of course. That rot-and-water smell hooks right into his guts and pulls them out through his toes. It brings *her* back to him.

He approaches the edge of the water with a sideways, crabbish stride. He needs to get at it sideways, he needs to pretend it isn't there. He sits down to wait, pulling his knees up to his chest and watching the surface of the water, broken only by banyan roots. He thinks of Karthika and the feel of her high, swollen breasts; thinks of Alice too – lovely, legitimate Alice – and pretty nurses who won't and never will and just might some day. But it's no good. Wherever he turns he can see somebody's smile flickering under the water. Somebody's fingers clutching beneath the surface.

You don't go away, do you, Peony, he thinks. *You mix yourself up in everything, like a drop of dye in water. You stain everything with yourself.*

*

Not half a mile away, Mary snorts. *Not much count,* she thinks, *that boy. Getting that Peony-girl drowned, then strutting back as though nothing happened. He shouldn't be allowed to get over things so easily. Not when other people* – and here Mary switches her thoughts onto a different track, thinking of daughters and granddaughters – *don't ever manage it.*

She's out of sight of the car now, right down amongst the trees. The San looms black and squat in front of her. The gates are closed, but the walls have long since fallen in, and Mary steps carefully over the rusty barbed wire and the scattered blocks of stone.

'Locks on the gates,' she mutters to herself, and for a second she could swear she hears a giggle. She steps inside the lobby of the San, through the doors that are jammed open, and looks around. It's a maze in here, all dead-end corridors and walls that have tumbled down. She passes closed doors and others overrun with crawling vines. A sink drips in the corner, and a flake of rust breaks off as she turns into the largest room. There are a few bed-frames left in here, coated in mud or rusted right through. You can barely see where the handcuffs were.

Mary sits herself down on one of these beds. There's a heap of rubbish by one wall. Old cooking pots tip over onto plastic sandals, and layers of mouldy cloth melt into each other in a shirt-socks-sarong jumble. Left-behind families don't look after themselves too well, and every time a new group moves in they scavenge from what's left.

Mary clacks her teeth in disapproval, and starts to pull gift-wrapped parcels noisily out of her striped carrier bag. Usually there'd be a grubby rag-tag of left-behinds by now, snatching at the toys as though they think they deserve 'em. She doesn't want her daughter to pick up those sorts of manners, though. Not when she's old enough to know better.

She takes the toothbrush out first, then a packet of sweets and a pair of beautiful drawing pencils. And then, finally, a doll. Nothing special, just an off-the-shelf rubber girl-doll from Robinson's, but Mary's carefully chosen it nonetheless. It's an Indian doll – the ones she brings always are – and they're always in satin saris. Durga, she's written on the inside of its blouse collar. Francesca shouldn't be allowed to forget her own daughter.

'Fran?' she calls. Nobody answers. There's a giggling and a rustle of tiny, jostling bodies peeping from behind the far wall.

'Let me see!'

'Don't *push*, Divya!'

The giggling gets louder. There's a knot of children huddling behind that wall: all of them unwanted, all of them more trouble than they're worth. If Mary looked closely she'd see several pairs of bright little eyes peeking through holes. Sharp noses, pushing themselves round corners; scrabbly little monkey-hands climbing up to get a look at her. Not that Mary does look closely. She's never had time for the left-behinds.

But then she hears the whisper. She can't ignore this; it's real as a cold-water shower.

'She's a loony.'

'Hush. She'll *come after you*!'

'Locks on the gates! Locks on the gates!'

The children tumble away, running back into the jungle, and Mary winces. It's a sore spot, that game. Bad enough when Durga and her friends played it, but these left-behind brats haven't got anything right. And now they've run off and left silence behind them, full of weighted and waiting expectancy. Outside, a tap drips onto the concrete floor with a horrible, plinking exactitude.

And then she hears it. The sound of cloth sliding on stone, as though someone's leaned a sizeable rump against the corridor wall and sunk cross-legged to the floor. If Mary looked right now, she might see the flicker of a shadow out there. And if she listened, she might hear a dull noise: water dripping on skin instead of stone. Heavy skin, sagging a little from the years and the lack of a good coconut-oil bath. That's no wispy ghost out there – as if she'd trail all the way out here for ghosts, when they're ten a penny in her house – but a skin-bones-teeth-and-fat daughter.

Mary smiles. 'Fran.'

'No . . .'

It's a familiar word, rolling off a muscly tongue. It's a word in Mary's head, or in the world or perhaps even in that liminal no-woman's-land between the two. But wherever it is, that's the *no* of a woman accustomed to using it a lot. A woman who's had a lot to deny in her life, one way or the other. *If only the locks on the gates had worked*, thinks Mary, *if only locks could keep a daughter right where she was put.* She looks at the burnt-out walls. She's nearly given up guilt these days, but not for this. Never for this.

Because that's Fran out there, in the corridor. That's no left-behind four-year-old, that's a daughter Mary knows in her blood and in her bones. That's Fran, who must be fifty years old by now but who will always be Mary's baby one. Fran who loves strangers and drawing pencils, who loves digging tunnels and setting fires.

'The fire was an accident,' Mary recites quietly. She does this every time she comes here, in the hope that one day both she and her daughter might believe it. 'It was an accident.'

Francesca, one way or the other, has always been an accident.

She's been an escape artist, she's been an arsonist. She's been a loony; she's been a story; she's been a bad girl and she'll always be the best daughter Mary's got.

Mary lines her gift-wrapped packages up more neatly. They're a tempting row at the foot of the bed, but still that shadow in the corridor doesn't move. She takes the doll onto her lap, dandling it.

'You remember Durga, don't you?' She holds the doll up. 'Your own little girl – here, like this doll.'

The bed's uncomfortable, with the springs digging into Mary's hips. She arranges her sari modestly over her bony ankles. 'You'd be pleased. So like you, she is. Coming to see me next month for Diwali.'

It's an effort to contort her tongue back to English grammar. Mary's slipped into rubber-estate talk, as she calls it, over the past few years. Too much time alone, with nobody but the servant-girl to care. But she tries to speak differently when she's here, to set a good example. A mother's work, after all, is never done.

'At the university still, putting these numbers together faster than you can count.' Mary hesitates, revises. 'Faster than I can count.'

She takes another breath, peers into the shadowy corridor. It's cool out there, dank and wet, with drinking-tanks dripping from every crack. There's a figure there, she's almost sure of it; a glint of grey at its head and a swaddle of fat around its waist. These days, Fran's too old to escape from a locked hospital room; to slip out of her handcuffs and set fire to whatever she left behind.

'Are you writing in the autograph book?' she asks into the silence. 'The Little Twin Stars book? I brought it last month for you.'

No answer, and Mary's starting to get impatient. 'You should write in it. So ridiculous, your age and can't write. Can't even write a note to say hello to your little girl.'

This time the silence has teeth. A touchy subject indeed, and Mary sighs. *Write a note to your little girl*: a sentimental, useless thing to have said. Not like her, really. She must be getting old.

'Sorry,' she says. She can hear a noise out in the corridor, as though someone's moving away. Footsteps, followed by a fainter rustle from the lobby, and the barely audible tramp-tramp-tramp of someone walking back up towards the swamp.

'Fran?' Mary says, but all she hears is the stirring of leaves against the walls. Francesca's gone, then, she's decided she's had enough. Mary tightens her lips. She has to expect these disappointments, as a mother, and especially as the mother of a disappointment herself.

It's almost time to go by now. The sun will go down soon, and there's still an hour's drive back to Lipis. Thick shadows have crept out from the corners of the room, and mosquitoes have gathered around Mary's ankles. She slaps them off as she bends to retrieve her slippers. A gecko stares up at her with great, green eyes and through a hole in the roof she can see a few oily stars winking already in the heavy sky.

'Will come again,' she says. 'Soon, don't you worry. You'll stay here?'

It's her secret worry, that Fran will up and leave one day. She has form, after all. She moves on, leaving destruction in her wake.

And then there's a noise. Perhaps it's real, perhaps it's all in Mary's head. Hard to say, and Mary never will. It's the sound of a car door slamming, back near the swamp. It's the sound of a fifty-fat-and-fragile woman crawling into the back seat of a car left abandoned by a doctor who's breaking his irrelevant heart just twenty metres away. It's a pencil scratching on paper covered in pastel angels; a picture when writing words is out of the question. It's Francesca, saying hello to her little girl.

'You're a good girl, Fran,' Mary says into the warm, listening silence. And then – because old habits die hard, and here in Pahang nothing really dies at all – she squats back down on the bed, and pulls her dupatta over her head. Ready or not, living or dead, your daughter's your daughter all your life.

'Listen, my baby one,' she says. 'There was once a tiger-prince. And a warrior princess, who challenged him to a duel . . .'

Mary's good at bedtime stories; spins them out of nothing but leprosy and logic, till they grow big enough to swallow themselves. Those stories have minds of their own, running in the family like a splash of kerosene. Her own mother told them. Karthika still does. Anil would have told them if he'd only had the words, and Francesca might still find a way. She's resourceful, Fran, with her autograph books and pencils. *Cleverer than her daughter*, thinks Mary. Mary loves her granddaughter, but she got the measure of Durga years ago. Swap out numbers for words, put in a few categories and count on your fingers; Durga's no better than the rest of them.

After this, everyone takes Ammuma more seriously. Tom, in fact, takes her so seriously that he calls up Dr Rao and dumps the whole problem in his heron-like lap.

'This confusion, it could be very serious,' we hear him explain out in the corridor, sounding professional to the very ends of his teeth. And then, 'She's like family to me.'

Ammuma rolls her eyes. It might have taken her seventy years to figure it out, but she knows her family.

'Fran drew them for *you*, Durga,' she insists in a dry, rasping voice. 'Your bedtime story.'

Ammuma and I are sitting tight-together in her bed. Over the past few hours she's been taken away and then brought back, stuck all over with words and labels that don't seem to have anything to do with her. She's had a bleed on the brain, Dr Rao explained after one of these tests. A trickle, a lovely and poisonous flood of red exactly where it shouldn't be. Who would have thought the old woman had so much blood in her?

She's still Ammuma, despite it all. Tetchy, unforgiving. Calling her brain bleed a 'burst heart' and refusing to hear a word of contradiction. 'Same same,' she said when Dr Rao corrected her, but different. To Ammuma, her heart and her mind have always been identical.

She's been talking constantly about Francesca, too. Each time she says her daughter's name she forgets a little more detail, sending memories spinning with glorious sky-high tosses. There's a kind of relief shining through her, budding and blooming where the X-rays can't reach. She's letting go, and glad of an end to it all.

'You find Francesca,' she tells me in a sliding, vague voice, and I agree. I hold her hand and agree with everything she says while

Dr Rao mutters at the foot of her bed. He draws up some clear liquid into a drip bag. Ammuma talks urgently while he slides a thin, flexing needle into her arm. She tells me to go to Kampung Ulu. She tells me to search for ghosts and girls and real-and-fleshy women. Her body shakes as the drip pumps its liquid in, and then she tells me to feed the kitchen cats and post her letters before it gets dark. *Are you listening, Durga?* she says at first. And then her eyelids are drooping, and my name's starting to slip away. *Are you there, Fran?* 'Yes,' I'm saying. 'Yes, I'm here.' *Anil?* she's asking. *Cecelia? Rajan? Amma?* and I'm holding her hand and I'm answering yes.

★

Later, Dr Rao takes me down to the hospital lobby. My eyes feel scratched and exhausted and my skin's raw from the air-conditioning. My hair still smells faintly of Ammuma's Nivea cream.

The hospital lobby looks different in daylight. No more quiet desperation; people stalk right up to the reception desk and rap on it impatiently. We don't meet each other's eyes, we daylight survivors in our suits and our get-it-done frames of mind.

'She must have had high blood pressure for years, Dr Panikkar.' Dr Rao ushers me into a little closed-off room with a glass door. It's hot in here, smelling of day-old sweat and baked-in worry. 'When she choked on the oxygen tube it was the last straw. She burst a blood vessel on the surface of her brain.'

He has a plan of attack, he explains. This medication, that therapy. Fall-back options and alternatives and last resorts. He has so many last resorts. Ammuma's confusion isn't the worst he's seen after a brain haemorrhage, he tells me. He talks about patients who thought they could fly, who thought their bed was a coffin, who lost their language and thought nothing at all. He tells me all these things – which are all worse, which are all much worse – and none of them make it any better.

'We'll put her in long-term care here,' he says. 'If you're going back to KL?'

I just manage to nod. I don't meet his eyes. I can't explain the sheer impossibility of staying, the emptiness of it all. Ammuma not being Ammuma, Ammuma not being anything but a jumble of wrong names and missed memories, of sponge-baths and stains on the mattress and the hiss of water in the toilet pan at 3 a.m. while I wait outside the door.

Even though I don't say anything, he still listens. We sit there in silence, and my breath is loud and shaking, and he watches me across the chipboard table. He's seen a hundred Ammumas – a thousand Mrs Selvas – and he's heard it all before. Promises to visit, to ring; tiny, niggling betrayals and efforts destined to fall short. He's heard everything, here in this glassy room.

After a few minutes he gets up and puts an arm round my shoulders. He feels like a coat-hanger, as though there's nothing under his white coat but bones and simplicity. He stays there a moment, and then the pager on his belt buzzes. He takes it up, looks at it and then sucks in his breath.

'Wait here a second. I need to –' And he's gone, out of the door fast as a thrown stick.

I'm alone in the room, with the air billowing about me. I get up and close the door, leaning my forehead against it as it latches. I'll come back and see Ammuma every weekend, I resolve. I've got the car. I can get back here from KL in just a few hours, even on a weekday evening. The road's good, I chatter to myself, it's really really good; it's so quick to get back here, I mean anyone can do it in just a few hours; it isn't really like being gone at all. And then I look up through the glass door and meet the gaze of the dry-haired receptionist. She gives me a sympathetic smile.

I don't know how long I wait in there. I want to go up and see Ammuma, but I don't know where to find her and I'm scared of leaving this room. Inside here, all I have to deal with are four plain walls and the gentle hum of the air-conditioner. These white-gloss walls won't tell me bad news and that chipboard meeting table won't blame me. We're getting along, this furniture and I.

'Dr Panikkar?'

But now there's someone on the other side of the door. A gentle knocking vibrates against my forehead, where I'm still leaning against the wood. I pull the door open slowly and look straight into Dr Rao's eyes.

'Durga.' He takes my hand, edging past me into the room. 'Please sit down.'

He's shutting the door, taking a long time about it and carefully clicking the latch into position. He doesn't want to turn round, I think, he doesn't want to say what's in his mouth. And then I know what it is.

'I'm so sorry to have to tell you. Your grandmother just passed away.'

*

It's an hour later. I'm sitting on a more comfortable chair in a quiet green room. There's a box of tissues on the low table in front of me, and pictures of waterlilies on the wall. Dr Rao's led me away from my chipboard table and into this room on the fourth floor. It's the room for grief, I suppose. Room for grief, which is something Ammuma never had.

Tom's sitting opposite me. He's found a blue plastic chair from somewhere, but it's child-sized and makes him look gigantic and cumbersome. He *is* grieving, he really is; his eyes are reddened with exhaustion and his lips are tight. He's brim-full, heavy and slow with sadness. She's meant something to him; they've watched out for each other in those fragile silences I wasn't here for. He's the grandchild she wished she had, if only she hadn't.

'Do you want to see her now?' he asks.

I don't answer. Behind my eyes there's an image of a woman, but it isn't Ammuma. It's an old woman, propped up on a wedged pillow. *Mrs Selva*, I think vaguely. Her lungs failed her once too, she's trying to tell me; *her* family did the same. She knew what was coming, that doughty little woman in her tangle of tubes.

I look across at Tom. I don't know why I'm not crying.

Ammuma's gone, but my mind won't hold on to it. Instead, I find myself thinking that Karthika never did sweep those outside drains clean. I'll have to remind her before they overflow again. Ammuma does so hate a mess.

Tom pushes his tiny chair away, coming over to me. He holds my elbow and gets me up tenderly.

'Let's go to her.'

He opens the door and we walk out into one of the hospital's long corridors. Nobody's in sight, and at the end is a stairway. I let him walk me all the way to it, and then I slide my arm away from him. I know where I need to go from here.

'Durga!'

I take a step down, and then another, lowering myself carefully from foot to foot. He scampers after me.

'Stop, she's upstairs. The floor above.'

One more step down, and then another. Tom follows me all the way to the ground floor, where we had our coffee a lifetime ago.

'Durga,' he says again, and this time I do look back. I have to think very carefully what I should say to him, I realize, because this might be the last thing ever. So I choose my words scrupulously, like a mathematician. What matters, after all, is the telling. The telling, and where it all began.

'I used my fireworks at Diwali,' I say. 'Not yours.'

'Sorry?'

'They were my fireworks, the ones that started the fire.'

Tom looks at me, opens his mouth and closes it again. 'But . . .'

And then I leave him there, with all his beginnings, just inside the hospital doors. This is how last resorts happen, I think, they happen in hot milky sunlight under yellow angsana trees. They happen on ordinary days, to ordinary women and mathematicians.

I open the car door and a puff of hot air escapes. There's no other traffic as I back out of the car park and it only takes a few minutes before I'm at the big roundabout outside Lipis. A motorbike idles by the verge, propped up on its stand. The rider's sitting cross-legged on the grass, eating noodles from a Styrofoam container.

I look left. Look right. Check my rear-view mirror and see the hospital. A nasty trick, sneaking up behind me like that. Could give a girl a burst heart.

★

Back on the verge, the motorcyclist looks up in mild surprise. He breaks his journey here every day, and he's never seen a car turn left at that roundabout before. The left-hand road doesn't even go anywhere, just out to a swamp in Kampung Ulu where the black areas used to be. It's not safe for a woman on her own, but by now the car's nearly out of sight. The motorcyclist shakes his head. You can't tell these girls anything.

★

The air gets cooler as I drive. The hills are full of wrung-out mist, and I can see flood damage down in the valleys. Water's bitten away the riverbanks and combed tangled lengths of weed over the rocks. Other rivers flood tidily, retreating with no more than a bathwater ring to show where they've been. Not the Jelai, though. It upends, then drags itself away like a cat that's been sick.

I pass a few plantations, and a police station with skinny caramel-coloured dogs lurking alongside. There are roadside stalls, which I don't remember from ten years ago, selling king durians and mangoes and bunches of rambutans. My left leg starts to ache from the clutch, but I don't stop. This is a journey, after all. A few bruises might be expected.

After half an hour I see a blue sign, faded from wind and rain. Kampung Ulu, it reads. There's an iron lamp-post with a broken bulb, and a bus shelter just beyond. You'd have to wait a long time out here for one to come along. A lifetime, give or take.

I slow down and turn left onto a narrow track. The road feels spongy under my tyres and I start to see slicks of water amongst the trees. The swamp isn't far away now. I've never approached it from this side before, and the top of the burnt-out San gives me a shock when it appears. There's barbed wire everywhere. It's rusted and toothy, hissing *keep out* with every twist and stab.

I can feel sweat springing under my arms as I open the car door. The swamp's waiting for me, just a few scrubby trees away. I wonder if Tom parked here while Ammuma trudged away with her gifts. I wonder if he sat waiting, knees curled to his chest and Peony wedged under his ribs. I smell rotting weeds and muddy water, hear the sound of hot metal as the car cools down.

I walk to the edge and stare across at the banyan tree. Oily star-bursts of mosquitoes rise from the water but nothing else moves. The swamp looks flat, unbothered, as though it could easily wait another fifteen years for me to get to grips with it. *You're wasting your time,* Peony whispers. Being dead, she doesn't bother with manners – and didn't when you were alive, either, Peony. You weren't a *saint,* with your ballpoint tattoos. With your truths and your dares.

My lungs feel slimed, thick and smudged with stink. But I can still breathe, inhale and exhale, and if this is drowning then I can cope with it. I can last another fifteen years, and another fifteen after that. It's only time, Peony. It doesn't last for ever.

My legs are rubbery as I walk slowly away, back towards the San. The ground's wet with rotting leaves and my steps are punctuated with skidding little slips that knock me off balance. It doesn't seem to get closer, and then I'm there, right outside the building. All the windows are smashed and gaping lidlessly at me. There's a froth of rubbish around the edge of the building: old clothes and polystyrene containers and the discarded rattle of aerosol cans. Graffiti covers the walls. *Fuziah 4eva,* it says. *SKINZ. Ali was here.* This last one is in a brilliant, clear blue, all the letters straight as if Ali had lined them up with a ruler. A boy after my own heart.

It feels as though somebody's watching me from the jungle. Mad yellow eyes, peering out of feral hair. A stringy woman, with burn scars and a grudge. A Communist guerrilla, armed to the teeth and beyond. A mother or two.

The main doors stand open, almost rotting away. When I step through, the floor sags in a stinking pulp. A few puddles inside are dimpled like pewter with the dip and suck of insects. Two dark corridors lead off the main lobby. I don't see any rooms, or anything else Ammuma described. I don't see any bedsteads or handcuffs; any dripping tanks or left-behinds or ghosts. I wonder what else Ammuma saw, in the blood-images of her brain?

As I walk up the corridor it widens into a clean-trodden bare patch. It's half-jungle and half-room in here, with jagged brickwork up to the height of my knees. There's a smell – a sound – a movement from the corner of my eye. There was someone here just a second ago. I'm sure of it. I can even smell her: sweat and a between-the-legs stink of old clothes. But she's gone, somehow. The walls bristle with layers of barbed wire, and the only way out is past me. But she's gone.

There's a neat pile of rubbish left by the door. I squat down, raking through it. Scraps and tatters of clothes. Barbie dolls with missing heads. A toy pony, a tin can. A picture book. A grubby doll in a blue satin sari, the kind of toy you find in any sundry store. At the bottom are some pencils and a few scrunched-up bits of paper. They're soaked through with damp and mould, but the pencil-strokes are still visible. The pages are covered with swirling, fragile calligraphy that nearly makes sense. Like letters, if they were drawn by someone who never wrote a word.

No. It's a breath of wind. It's a flicker of movement right at the darkened end of the corridor. Nobody's gone past me, though, I could swear to that. I don't even know whether I really heard it, or whether my mind's beating up fancies like eggs in a cake mix.

Dr Panikkar would know. She always does. She'd stride out down the corridor, hands on hips and face set into a glare. She'd drag out everybody by their ears: ghosts and left-behinds and prison escapees. She'd send the ghosts packing, she'd scrub the left-behinds and set them back down in their places. Dr Panikkar would know the difference between alive and dead and just what's to be done about it. And she'd do it, too.

She wouldn't crouch down, picking up one of those pencils and pulling the autograph book out of her skirt. She wouldn't lick the pencil lead – ugh, *imagine* the germs – or set it down on one of these pastel-angel pages. And if she did, there'd be a reason. She'd write a note. A letter. Instructions. She'd demand the left-behinds obtain birth certificates and the ghosts furnish themselves with autopsy findings. She'd write something dry, something cramped, a story that never got away.

She wouldn't draw a river in full flood. She wouldn't draw a tangle-haired Chinese girl looking over her shoulder, or a handsome boy with a stethoscope watching her from behind. There'd be no durians in her picture, no grandmothers or leprosy, and certainly no handcuffs. She probably wouldn't even draw a tiger-prince, which goes to show how much she knows.

No. The almost-sound comes once more, and then there's silence. I close the book and slide it into the middle of the pile of rubbish. I'm leaving my own mark: leaving a garrulous and girlish ghost who'll answer to Cecelia or Anil or any name that takes her fancy. To Peony. To Mary. To Francesca. To Durga.

I stand up straight and listen, but there's nothing. No more sounds from the end of the corridor, no more flickers in the sunlight. Just a few echoes – *no* – spreading through my head and over Pahang. Past Mrs Selva, grimly reading Christmas cards in her lonely bed. Past Karthika, pinning movie-star cuttings to her bedroom wall. Down Gua Musang those echoes go, past the girls in pink hijabs studying behind durian stalls and the cars blasting Pahang FM. Past the university, where Sangeeta's calls go unanswered and Anwar marks answers incorrect – *no, no, no.* Overhead and out to KL, where they're drowned once and for all by the roar of traffic and the thrum of a thousand other lives.

Acknowledgements

I am most deeply grateful for the support and encouragement of my parents, Dr Alexandra Menon and Dr Nanda Menon. Although the characters and events in this book are fictional, the war and subsequent Malayan Emergency was a turbulent and violent time. I'm immensely grateful both for the memories my parents have shared and for their wisdom. I would also like to thank my brother, Anand Menon, for all his interest and encouragement.

My wonderful agent, Zoë Waldie, has been the best guide I could possibly have had throughout the publication process; I have benefited immensely from her warmth, skill and never-ending patience. I'd also like to thank all the staff at RCW, who have made me feel so welcome.

I couldn't have asked for a more enthusiastic, skilful and tireless editor than Mary Mount. I'm indebted to her for her sensitivity and for her wonderful editorial eye. My thanks must also go to my copy-editor, Trevor Horwood, for his meticulous attention to detail.

My particular and very heartfelt thanks go to all my writing group friends; their feedback, support and generosity have been immensely helpful during the whole process. Particular thanks to Katy Darby for her admirable teaching skills: without her short-story course I would never have begun to write at all.

I am also deeply indebted to all the staff on the City University Creative Writing MA course, particularly Jonathan Myerson and Clare Allan. Jonathan and Clare have read, critiqued and supported this story throughout all its drafts, and I cannot express how much I've learnt from them. And, of course, I'm very grateful to all my classmates on the course for their endless generosity, feedback and support.

My deepest thanks also to Professor Michael Johnson, my PhD supervisor. Michael is an immensely talented teacher, researcher and mathematician, who 'knows all that there is to be knowed' about category theory. Any mathematical mistakes in this book are unquestionably mine alone.

Finally, to my wonderful husband Dr Paul Emberson, who is my bedrock and my Pole Star. Paul, this book – like everything else – would be so many blank pages without you.